DARK NESS

TABITCA COPE

Edited by Corinna Downes
Typeset by Jonathan Downes,
Cover and Layout by SPiderKaT for CFZ Communications
Using Microsoft Word 2000, Microsoft , Publisher 2000, Adobe Photoshop CS.

First published in Great Britain by Fortean Fiction

CFZ Press
Myrtle Cottage
Woolsery
Bideford
North Devon
EX39 5QR

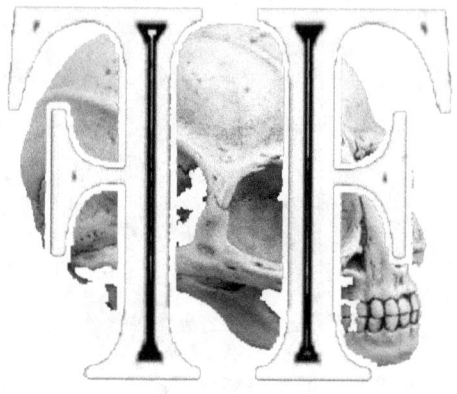

© CFZ MMXII

ISBN: 978-1-905723-84-3

This book is dedicated to cryptozoologists - all those brave souls who seek unknown creatures and often suffering ridicule because of their efforts.

This is a work of fiction, and with the exception of known historical facts, any resemblance of any characters to anyone living or dead is purely coincidental.

My thanks to Naomi Cope-Selby, John Kuchanny, Nick Kiep (Canada), Jonathan Downes, and Nessie hunters past and present

PROLOGUE

In the beginning was the darkness

The Loch was in frenzy; the wind screamed as if all the banshees in limbo were riding upon it. A wave, taller than a man, crashed to the shore as if it was trying to wash away the very beach itself.

In the hamlets around the lochside, the inhabitants shivered and huddled closer together, pulling their woollen blankets tightly around their shoulders. They crossed themselves and prayed, and moved nearer to the fire burning brightly in the hearth. The sky was now so dark that not a finger of light could be seen. From the gloom, a figure appeared by the side of the loch, and almost seemed to evaporate and reappear in the poor light. Gaunt-featured, slim but strong looking, he stood - hands raised to the storm.

The wind whipped his words from his mouth almost as soon as they were spoken.

The wet cloak he wore flapped around his legs as if trying to escape. The chanting went on relentlessly…nothing distracted him from his task.

"Valdea malefactum demonis archea" - ancient words from a time before written language as we know it. Words passed from mouth to mouth of those willing to pay the price for their power. How long he had stood there could not be counted. Time seemed to stand still, as if the storm had stopped the great hourglass mid grain.

At last, as the thunder roared, a great fork of lightening hit the loch and lit up the area and the alchemist was revealed. He held a staff aloft as if conducting the storm. A makeshift altar on the carved stone in front of him held several articles, which strangely did not move in the wind. He seemed to be urging the loch to come to him.

The water in the loch began to boil as if a cauldron from hell had arisen from its depths. The man gasped as a large creature began to emerge from the seething waters and head for the shore on which he stood.

The time AD 506…the place Loch Ness.

CHAPTER 1
A light in the dark

Laura yawned and stretched, brushing her hair from her forehead, even though it was barely long enough to reach her eyes. She liked to keep it short and spiky, she hated the feel of it on her neck. Time to head home she decided. The words on the computer screen were starting to blur and she would fall asleep in the stuffy room if she stayed much longer.

Gathering up her coat and bag, and checking everything was switched off, she headed for the stairs. The security guard was on his way up as she descended and they called good night to each other. How much use he'd be in stopping a burglar though always intrigued her...a puff of wind would have blown the old man over. He had a dog that dragged him all around the campus chasing squirrels and would probably lick an intruder to death. She smiled to herself as she headed out through the main entrance and waved to a group of students who were passing by on their way to the union building.

"Are you coming to the bar Laura?" one shouted.

"Not tonight," she replied. *"I'm bushed. Maybe Wednesday."*

The student signalled that he had understood. She smiled to herself as she walked along to the bus stop. The students made the job worthwhile. She could take or leave (mainly leave) some of the people she worked with, but the students - even those that were trouble - she loved. Their company made her laugh and the things they said, and they challenged her at every turn. It was to her they also came to dry their tears and help them out when things were a problem. *"That's me, everybody's mum,"* she sighed.

The bus was late as usual and as the short walk to the bus stop had cleared her head, she chatted with a teaching technician whilst waiting. The lady was rolling a cigarette and stood downwind of Laura. The smoking ban has isolated smokers from the rest of us, made then lepers, she thought to herself.

Laura never learned to drive. She had tried to learn on more than one occasion, but it appeared her co-ordination was so bad she was a danger. At least the last white-lipped instructor had intimated such, as he slammed on the brakes and the car shuddered to a halt.

She mused on the bus home about what to have for dinner and what she might do with her evening as the bus dawdled through the traffic and then when hitting the clear road to the village shot off to make up time. It was wise to hang onto the seat in front at this point in the journey. She once made the mistake of sitting in a side seat to her detriment; she still felt the embarrassment of having to be helped up from the floor by other passengers. Luckily she usually wore trousers, but she felt the silky knickers she had been wearing underneath hadn't helped much for traction as she slid from the seat sideways to the floor as the bus went around a roundabout going full pelt.

Friday night. A bottle of wine after a shower, then relax with the cats, and maybe watch some TV. She suddenly noticed the bus had reached her village and got ready to ring the bell so she didn't end up in the next one.

The driver wanted to get home too. Stepping off the bus, she had her head down walking along deep in thought. As she walked along the road to the cottage - she thought it always seemed longer when you were tired - one or two other residents called hello. That was the thing she liked about living here, she hadn't been here that long but everyone spoke to you. She loved the village hairdressers; they always included her in conversations as if she knew the people they were talking about: *"You know Laura, our Margaret's cousin. The one with the funny eye."*

At last she saw the gate and as she opened the door the cats' plaintive cries could be heard as they shot out from wherever they had been sleeping. Two tabbies, one elderly and one middle-aged, greeted her and before she did anything else, she put some food in their bowls. Otherwise she wouldn't even be able to go to the bathroom without them shoving open the door to protest at their lack of attention. *"OK guys, anyone would think you were starving,"* she said, laughing at their antics as they jostled around the bowls and her ankles.

She had picked up the post on her way in and as the kettle boiled she examined it. One was a letter from a solicitor. Intrigued she opened it first.

> Dear Ms Loomis,
>
> We have the unfortunate task to inform you of the death of Robert Loomis-Carr, your paternal uncle.
>
> Could you contact this office etc?

Blimey, poor Uncle Bob. She felt guilty that she hadn't contacted him in some time. I'll ring in the morning and see if they are open; some places are open Saturday morning. He probably wants me to see his collections are sent to a university or something. She remembered there were a lot of old, and probably quite valuable, books as well as all sorts of knick knacks.

Sighing, she remembered how much she loved to chat with him and put the world to rights. *"You'll be missed Uncle Bob, by this woman, that's for sure."* She said it out loud which made it feel better somehow. Shaking her head at the sadness of it, she set about preparing something for dinner and then tried to put it from her mind.

The next morning, after the usual cat ablutions and her shower it was already 9.30am, so she rang the solicitors whilst sipping her second cup of coffee. After being passed around some, she was put through to Malcolm Schaeffer, presumably her uncle's solicitor. She was rather shocked to hear that Uncle Bob had left her £25,000, to - as he put it - pursue a year's research without worry.

She stammered her thanks and they asked for details in order to arrange payment, and - she presumed - to check she was the right person. Stunned after she put down the phone, she sat for a while and then jumped as one of the cats dived on the table and nearly spilled her coffee. Scolding him, she went through to the sitting room and considered this chance she had been offered. Uncle Bob knew about her interests, and how she always wanted to spend time researching, but how finances got in the way. Instead, she worked all hours in an attempt to keep her rent paid and the cats fed.

She looked at herself in the mirror, a plump 50-something widow. Widowed at a young age, she'd had her moments, especially in her younger days. No one seeing her now would believe two famous rock stars had fought over her in the seventies, or that she modelled for Biba. She sighed, she missed those days; the sixties and seventies had been fun. Her only daughter Roz, had left to pursue her own studies and her life was now, after all these years, her own again. She had never re-married, and had brought Roz up alone from being a few months old. Her husband had been killed in an unfortunate accident.

She had taken what *most* people considered risks all her life. Some people stayed in the same job, in the same town all their lives; she on the other hand, with cats and daughter in tow, had travelled and worked all over the place. It stops me getting boring she had often told herself. Now she had a chance to do something she wanted to do. The safe option would be to invest the money or use it as a deposit for a house, but Uncle Bob knew when he left it to her she would use it for something more interesting than that. A lot to think about she said to herself, choices, and options.

After a weekend of pondering the pros and cons, she went in early on Monday morning and announced her intention not to return next academic year, and wrote out her notice. Shocked looks from most staff....you don't just leave a job.

"What about your pension?" one said. *"I am unlikely to ever get chance to claim it, I can't see me living that long,"* Laura laughed, *"Roz will probably benefit from it."* Her boss tried to dissuade her, but she was fed up of carrying half his work load as well as her own, for half his pay. She liked him, but his laziness was legendary in the university. They got on well together and she knew he would miss her not just for the work she did, and she would miss him, but they would keep in touch. He was genuinely interested in what she wanted to study and they

spent some time discussing it, another ploy for him to avoid work.

She rang Roz at lunchtime, knowing she would be out of the lab and in the tea room. Her daughter had not been surprised when she told her about the plans for the money. *"Go for it,"* was her response. *"Mum, you always do stuff for other people, do something for yourself. You can always keep some of the money for later in case you don't get a job straight away."*

It was the response Laura had expected, but you never know with children. Here starts an adventure she laughed to herself as she started to sort out her office and organise her work, in preparation for departing in three months.

CHAPTER 2

The dark arrives

Are you sure what you saw laddie?" The water bailiff looked at the white faced youth beside him. His paleness made the adolescent red spots on his face stand out more prominently. The lad looked awkward and worried.

"Aye as sure as I see you, there was a beastie in the loch."

"You've been watching too much TV."

"Nay it was massive, black and shiny and had big teeth. Should I report it Mr Stewart?"

"Well....., I suppose you'd better tell the laird, he likes to ken what's going about."

The lad shuffled off and Hamish shook his head. There was no doubt the lad had had a fright alright, but a beastie ... in the loch, with big teeth … he chuckled, yes too much TV and tourists' talk. The young gangly lad was a relative by marriage he'd taken on at the request of the lad's mother. He was a hard worker but not very bright.

Hamish carried on coiling the ropes in the boat.

A while later he heard the laird's voice, and looked up to see him approaching with the lad in tow. He nodded, *"Yes sir, what can do for you?"*

"Hamish, I've told the boy we need to keep this quiet. We don't want to be invaded by newspaper people." The laird always reminded him of Christopher Lee, the actor, similar in looks and stature. He had been educated in England and had no trace of a Scottish burr in his voice.

"Aye, no problem there Sir. You'll not hear me speak of it and neither will the lad."

Hamish was in his 50s with the weather beaten look of someone who worked outside. His red hair was thinning, but he held himself erect and was muscular from the work.

"I'll see you and the boy get a bonus in your pay. You've both obviously been working too hard and the boy needs to have a few days holiday. See to it please. You can both have a week off."

With that the laird turned and strode off. Hamish and the boy stared after him.

"Well that were real queer Uncle Hamish."

"How so lad?"

"Well I told Gordon and he fetched the laird straight away. The laird, he was a wee bit agitated when I told him and then came straight down to see you."

"He just doesn't want the news people here lad. Can't blame him for that. Now get yourself home and you needn't come back until next Thursday. A week off with pay. You cannot complain about that laddie, but mind you don't tell anyone you saw a beastie, or you might be on permanent holiday, unpaid. Away with you."

The lad stood for a minute as if wanting to say something and then changed his mind, turned and ran off up the shore, to home.

Hamish stood thoughtfully watching the boy make his way along the shore to the road. The laird had acted a bit queer alright, but maybe he just didn't want the TV people and the like hanging around being a nuisance. He'd never known the laird come down to the loch before. He always summoned Hamish to the big house if he wanted to talk to him or give him orders. Giving them time off and a bonus, sounded like a bribe. Why would he need to do that? If he just said not another word to be spoken about beasties in the loch, no one would have said a word. Hamish shook his head. He decided to go see the ghillie and see if he could get someone to cover his duties for a few days. Even Hamish wouldn't turn down a free week off. He could go fishing and finish some jobs in the house, and stop the wife nagging. Sadie was awful fearsome when she got a bee in her bonnet about something needing doing, and something always needed doing.

In a local hotel that evening, the word was already spreading. *"I tell you I saw it, a great back like a whale, in the water."* The speaker was a thin man in his thirties, with wild hair and a rat-like face."

"And how many had you had Angus, before you set off home?" The barman's words raised a shout of laughter in the bar.

Angus slammed down his empty glass and made to leave. *"You'll see. The newspapers will be interested."* As he reached the door a man in a dark suit stopped him.

"Will you have a drink with me, sir and tell me what you saw?"

The accent was American; Angus knew that from all the tourists he met.

"Are you from the papers?"

The man smiled. *"Something like that."*

Angus readily sat down as the man called to the bar for more drinks and then Angus started to tell his story. The man had piercing blue eyes and thinning black hair. His suit was impeccable and he was obviously wealthy. Angus thought the gold cuff links alone must be worth a pretty penny. Angus began to tell him about how he had been walking along the shore, just as it was getting dark and a noise had alerted him to something in the water. He looked up and saw a huge creature briefly in the water, a large black shape that opened its mouth to show some razor-like teeth. Angus hadn't stayed to see what happened next, he had shot off into the hotel calling for whiskey. The locals had thought it was a con to get free drinks and they smiled when they saw the American buying them for Angus. He'd caught one alright, they whispered to each other. After the third drink, Angus began to feel woozy. He tried to stand and staggered. The man looked concerned, *"Hey fellow you OK?"*

The barman called over. *"Set him off in the direction of the village, and he'll find his own way home, sir."*

The man helped Angus to the door and Angus started to weave his way along the shore.

He couldn't understand why he felt so drunk; he'd only had 2 pints and 3 whiskeys. Normally it would take a lot more than that. He staggered on feeling worse. He'd get home and have a sleep, and he'd be OK. Must have flu or something he muttered to himself. Suddenly someone grabbed his arms, there were two of them, big fellows. He tried to struggle. In the dark and in his inebriated state he couldn't tell who it was. *"Hey get off me. It's no joke you ken. Leave a man be."* He thought it was a couple of the local fishermen having a joke at his expense. Probably going to throw him in the loch. There was a sharp pain in the back of his head, and then darkness.

A man walking his dog found Angus' body early next morning laid on the shingle beach, with the waves lapping over it. He saw the dog making a fuss. *"Here Bonnie, leave that alone."* The dog continued to bark and prance about. Getting closer he saw it was a body. Grabbing the dog by its collar, he leant over the lifeless form. He recognised him instantly and got out his mobile phone whilst putting the lead on the dog, a mongrel with a large wagging tail. Ringing the local station rather than 999 seemed best. *"Poor bloke must have fallen in the loch drunk,"* he told the policeman who answered. *"Shall I pull him out?"*

"No, sir, just stay where you are. We will be with you shortly."

The sergeant sighed and grabbed his bacon sandwich to take with him. He liked living in the police house, but it meant people expected you to be on call all hours. He picked up a constable on the way, after ringing to make sure he was awake and was on duty that day.

They arrived at the shore to find Campbell Fraser holding his dog and standing guard.

"Looks like he bashed his head when he fell," said the dog walker to the sergeant as he leant over the body.

"Well coroner will decide, that but I think you are right. Poor Angus, sad way to go," replied the police sergeant. The police sergeant was English and seen as an outsider but he got along well enough with the local inhabitants. There was a quite large English community living alongside the loch, mainly business people and the odd artist or writer. They were tolerated, but not always included by the locals. Some things the locals kept to themselves.

The sergeant spoke into his radio and summoned the ambulance. *"Someone will have to tell his kin,"* said the dog walker. *"Yes I will go see his sister now"*, replied the sergeant, *"as soon as the body is removed. Don't you say a word to anyone Campbell, until I've seen her. Don't want her to hear from the local gossips."*

"Aye alright." Campbell dragged the dog off the shore. He would go to the bar tonight and regale them all with the gory details.

The constable, a little pale, looked at the body, pointed and said: *"You would think they were teeth marks, those rocks are real sharp."* The young constable hadn't expected to see many bodies when he accepted the job up here and was already starting to regret the decision. He had helped pull the body of a fisherman out of the loch only the week before.

"Yes, damn shame. Poor fellow was harmless. He was in the pub telling them a story about seeing Nessie in the loch. Maybe he wandered in a bit to see if he could see anything and slipped. There would be no one around at night to see him and get help."

He shook his head. *"Well I'll leave you here lad until the ambulance arrives and I'll go see his sister. Sometimes I hate this job,"* and with a loud sigh he walked up the shore leaving the constable shaking his head in sympathy. The constable had brought a plastic sheet from the car and put it over Angus, so he didn't have to look anymore. If anyone asked he was protecting the evidence, he said to himself.

CHAPTER 3

New beginnings, a step towards the darkness

Laura put down the phone and smiled. *"Well this is it cats, all arranged. We are off to Loch Ness for six months, the lease is sorted"*

The cats continued to sleep, one of them opening one eye to see if she was heading for the fridge. When she didn't, he returned to his slumbers. Laura was excited and afraid all at once; a new step on the journey of life.

Laura's daughter came a couple of weeks later, to help sort out what was to be stored and what was going to be binned, and - Laura hoped - leaving only a car full of stuff to go with her. Hiring a large car for her daughter to drive up and then return back to Norwich, where she was living, seemed the best idea.

She liked the cottage she rented, and would miss the garden, but as it wasn't hers it wasn't such a big wrench. The neighbourhood was friendly and she hoped to come back there one day.

The day of their journey north started off quite bright and fine. The car was packed and after a struggle, the cats put in their baskets. It's amazing how they seemed to have six legs when they had to go in the cat basket.

As it would take 6 hours to get there, they would stop every two hours or so to check the cats were fine and use the roadway facilities. Laura had always needed coffee, and loo breaks every couple of hours. They set off with the cats protesting at their incarceration, but they gradually settled down.

"I hope Buzbi isn't sick," commented Roz. He was, in fact, her cat but had always lived with Laura. Mischief was his middle name and his ability to throw up when he was scared or didn't like something earned him the nick name of the bulimic cat.

"He might poop but I have stuff to clean up and change the baskets if needed," laughed Laura.

Aristotle the old cat braced himself against the side of the basket and started to doze. He was just hoping it wasn't the vets they were going to. Laura and Roz had once brought both cats on the train from Aberdeen to Hull and amazingly, apart from an incident when Aristotle had pooped in his basket on the way to the station, they had been fine. There had been a slight incident when some oil rig workers were eating and drinking at the next table and Aristotle had smelt sausages and tried to beg for some. The oil riggers were a bit drunk, but very friendly and Laura had to dissuade them from feeding the old cat, in case he was sick. They were great cats, full of character and good-natured.

It wasn't quite dark when they arrived at the cottage. It stood alone at the end of a row. The lights were on and the landlady came out to greet them. Laura had taken it furnished as it had heavy old-fashioned wooden armed furniture and nothing the cats could damage. The landlady, a Mrs Wilson, was pleased to have it let for the winter from September to March. From Easter onward it would be weekly tourists living there and it made a good profit, but leaving it empty most of the winter meant constantly visiting to check pipes hadn't burst or the cottage been broken into.

Mrs Wilson showed Laura how the oil heating and hot water worked and she had lit the coal fire. Leaving them with a list of instructions, phone numbers and details of where to get what when it ran out, she left them in peace to unpack.

The cat tray and food and water were put out in the kitchen and then the cats let out whilst they unpacked the car. The cats wandered around crying and sniffing but would soon settle. They were used to moving.

Roz would stay overnight and travel back next day, stopping to take a break at a friend's house in York. She was first into the shopping they had bought in Inverness and got the kettle on. *"Ooh sausage rolls, Aristotle, I'll share one with you whilst mum makes dinner."* The old cat trotted obediently after Roz to get his share. Laura laughed and got out a pizza to heat up and some salad. She wasn't keen on pizza but it was easy when they were both tired. A couple of hours later they were both in front of the fire sharing a bottle of wine before going to respective beds.

"Well, here's to your new adventure mum. Hope it is a good 6 months."

"Cheers."

Next morning, both said they had slept like logs, despite the cats' best efforts at keeping them awake by wandering around the house, getting into everything. Buzbi had tried to climb over Roz in the night and push her out of bed, but she was too tired to notice.

Breakfast was scrambled eggs on toast, though it was still early to eat but Roz wanted to make an early start. Laura packed her daughter some sandwiches to take with her and waved her off. *"Don't forget to ring when you get back."*

"Yes mum," said Roz in a long suffering voice that grown-up children adopt when they think a parent is fussing.

Laura went back into the cottage to explore. *"Well cats, this is us for the next few months, better see if the internet works and then unpack and see what shopping we need."*

The cats looked interested and then seeing no treats were forthcoming, wandered off to find the best places to sleep. Buzbi spotted a box and sat in it even though he was too large which caused the sides of the box to bulge alarmingly. Luckily it was empty. Aristotle trotted upstairs to settle on Laura's bed, from where he could see birds in the tree outside the window. This was his idea of a room with a view. He dug up the bed until it was what he considered comfortable and went around and around in a circle several times before deciding it was right to sleep on.

Laura meanwhile was pleased to find the wireless broadband worked. She had checked with the 'phone company and they said it was on, but would be slower than what she was used to. Slow is better than none she said to herself. She looked around and sighed, *"Well this is it girl, your chance to do something you want to do,"* and with that she started to set up the files she would need before checking out the supermarket deliveries. The afternoon could be spent unpacking clothes and books. She hadn't brought a great deal with her as she could buy anything she needed either online or in Inverness.

CHAPTER 4

Dark Waters

The funeral of Angus had long since passed when Laura arrived at the cottage. The verdict had been accidental drowning whilst under the influence of alcohol. Some had their suspicions there was more to it than that, but life goes on and the village returned to its normal way of life.

Out on the loch the hired boat sped along. The spray stung his face but Donald didn't mind. He loved being out in the boat. He was studying at Aberdeen University and when this opportunity came along to study at Loch Ness for a year, he jumped at it. He found Aberdeen a miserable grey place and the people didn't really accept anyone who wasn't Doric born and bred. He preferred Glasgow, with its golden stone buildings. They drank a lot too in Aberdeen and he wasn't a big drinker, so felt left out of his fellow students' social lives. He was what people called a "nice guy" and sometimes he wished he wasn't. A sigh, the girls all seemed to like the bad guys and he spent his time studying or on the internet. Donald wasn't classically handsome but had a pleasant face and was quite strong physically. Wearing his hair very short, he thought made him look a bit tougher, but in fact it emphasised his youthfulness.

He was taking water samples to study the micro-organisms that grew there, as part of a team looking at Arctic char numbers in the loch. He gathered up his test tubes and placed them carefully in the stand provided. It was easy to lose things over the side or for them to spill or get contaminated with spray.

"Don, can you take the wheel a minute whilst I get a brew?" John Draycott, the team leader for their group yelled above the noise of the boat.

"Aye aye skipper," laughed Don. John was well known to be a big coffee drinker and couldn't go half an hour without a mug steaming in his hand.

Don kept the wheel steady and watched the sonar. John re-appeared a few minutes later. *"If you are okay there I'll drink this whilst you drive."* He was a large man, with a thick head of hair that always looked like it needed cutting. Donald always felt small beside him. John was a good sort though and took a real interest in the students whilst they were in his care. He had children himself, now grown, so he felt a paternal duty to the younger ones. Life had changed for him since his wife left him for a mathematician, who stayed home most of the time and wasn't away doing field work every summer. They parted on good terms as the children were grown and the house sale profits were split between them. John planned to buy his own houseboat to live on with the money, and was thinking about where he would moor it, when Donald's voice cut into his thoughts.

"John, what's that?" Donald pointed to the sonar. A large blip was passing under the boat.

"Must be a large shoal of fish. Funny I saw this yesterday as well." John stared at the screen as if he could see right under the water and see what was there.

"Maybe it's Nessie," Donald laughed.

"Don't mock Don, there are some strange things I've seen and heard since I've been on the loch. I am sure most can be explained away, but you never know."

Donald wasn't sure if John was teasing him or not. You could never tell with academics, so he concentrated on steering the boat.

The blip came past again and John tried to estimate its speed. Must be going at 20 knots, so quite speedy, he thought to himself. Maybe a seal is chasing a shoal of fish. He felt uneasy though and decided to come back on his own and see if he could pick up the trace again. He didn't want any of the students chasing it and getting into trouble, as the loch was unpredictable at best.

"It's time we headed back Don. We need to get the samples stored before we stop for the day. It's getting darker on an evening now September is here."

Don nodded and turned the wheel to the shore, heading for the small pier that they used. Suddenly there was a bump. The boat shook and John's mug hit the floor and smashed. *"What the hell?"* shouted John. He grabbed the wheel from Don and struggled to gain control of the boat, which was starting to rock alarmingly. Don looked more startled than scared. Then suddenly all was calm again. *"What was that?"* gasped Don. "Did we hit something?"

"Probably a seismic disturbance blowing up from the loch bed. No damage seems to be done. Are you OK?"

Don nodded and hoped it wasn't something he had done wrong to cause the boat to rear like that. John steered the boat towards the jetty and Donald got ready to jump off and tie it up.

Hamish, the water bailiff - who worked for the local laird - was on the pier, sorting out some netting. He waved when he saw them. The university staff and students were usually good for business locally and the majority were well behaved.

John steered the boat in and as Donald jumped off threw him the ropes. Once Don had been dispatched back to their make shift laboratory with the samples, he called the water bailiff over.

"Hamish. We had a bit of a problem there. Felt like something hit the boat, thought we were going to capsize. There are no divers in the loch are there?"

"No, not today John but it looks like you scraped against something." Hamish pointed to the hull, as it bobbed on the waves. Scars could be seen in the paint.

"I better get it checked out before we go out tomorrow." John looked at Hamish, *"Any ideas?"*

"Aye, probably a tree stump come up from the bottom. Happens all the time, volcanic activity or some such thing. Yon people from the other university can probably tell you." Hamish nodded in the direction of another group of people that John recognised as being from Cambridge.

John noticed Hamish was avoiding his eye though. *"I'll have a word with them. Thanks. I'll get the boat checked over though to be on the safe side."*

John walked over to the other group to be greeted by catcalls and laughs. *"Hey John, how's it hanging?"* His counterpart Daniel Woolf called to him as he approached.

John raised a hand in greeting. Though from different universities, the two groups were looking at different aspects of the loch and the rivalry was on the surface and usually resulted in practical jokes.

"Everything OK man? You look a bit unfab." Daniel still thought he was in the 70s, and often dropped into the phrases of the time.

"Have you recorded any seismic activity in the loch today?"

"Nope not today - been calm below. Why?" Daniel looked quizzically at John.

"Come and see the hull of the boat. Water bailiff reckons a log thrown up from the bottom did it." They both walked across to the small jetty, followed by a couple of curious students.

"Bloody Hell man, you hit a submarine?" Daniel examined the marks. *"It was no tree stump did that."* He called to one of the two students: *"Andy, your opinion?"*

A young stout rugby type came forward and, brushing the hair from his eyes - which was in the current floppy style - peered closely at the scars on the boat's hull.

"It wasn't a tree, there would be wood or mould or algae in the scratches. If I didn't know better I'd say an animal did it."

This produced laughter from the group. *"Yeah Nessie,"* said another student - a pale girl with long thin blond hair.

Daniel looked at John and told the students to finish packing up the gear. *"OK man, what's on your mind?"*

"Do you think there could be something, some large creature in the loch? This isn't the first time we've had things happen this visit. That trouble you had with the 'phones, and I swear to you it wasn't my lot messing about."

Daniel looked thoughtful. The 'phones John referred to were hydrophones they had placed on sites under the water of the loch to record any sounds of the plates moving, but several strange noises had been recorded and sometimes the mikes had been removed when they hauled them back in. Hamish had said seals might be responsible or curious otters.

A whistle escaped Daniel's lips. *"Well that's the biggie, no proof either way. I tend to the negative, but I would dearly love to have proof Nessie existed. Hey man, imagine the headlines!"*

"Nessie ate my boat." Both men laughed.

"Yeah you are right mate, there's probably a simple explanation. I'll get the boat checked tomorrow."

"Take some photos before you go in case you need them for insurance," advised Daniel.

"Good idea and I'll take some samples from the scratches; you never know what it might show up."

With that they parted and John fetched the camera and took some photos and some scrapings before heading back to the cottage that their group was renting. The kettle was on when he got in, and the other three students in their group were all hanging around the kitchen chatting. These three were due to return to Hull University in a week. They had been good fun and a pleasure to work with. Donald will miss them, John thought; there will only be me for company until next term. I should try to get him friendly with Daniel's group so he has some company. After some bantering with the other students, he asked where Donald was, and they pointed him towards the makeshift lab set up in what had been the dining room of the cottage. He went in, carrying two mugs of coffee for himself and Donald, who was putting samples on to slides.

He put the accident with the boat from his mind and concentrated on trying to teach Donald to use the microscope properly. Donald was a bit of a butter fingers with slides.

CHAPTER 5
Meeting in the dark

The laird paced the floor with his hands behind his back in typical autocratic pose.

Why now he muttered to himself. Why now? What did it mean?

The room was furnished in almost medieval style. Its high ceilings and the sweeping drapes made it look like a film set. Suits of armour shone in the firelight from a pile of burning logs in the huge stone hearth, and large wooden settles on either side of the fireplace were covered in throws and cushions.

The laird was not a happy man. He was ill at ease at what might come.

Pictures of ancestors stared down from the walls. Did they know, he wondered catching sight of them? Did they suffer as I have? He knew the answer to that, they had suffered too. No one had an easy life and suffering and death stalked them all.

He decided to take a walk by the loch side. The air might help clear his mind, help him think clearly. Pulling the bell rope, he summoned his butler, Gordon, and instructed him to have the car ready.

Laura was wandering along the beach, breathing in the autumnal air and feeling glad to be alive. She felt free somehow and happy. Suddenly she saw someone she recognised. *"John. John Draycott, is that you?"* she called out. Laura couldn't believe her eyes.

The figure, bending over something in the sand, straightened up and turned. His face lit up. *"Laura Loomis what on earth are you doing here? On holiday?"*

"Not exactly, research for six months, funding myself."

"Someone leave you an inheritance?" He laughed. He knew most academics seemed to live from one pay cheque to the next these days.
"Actually yes, my uncle."

"Oh sorry hope I didn't upset you." He looked so contrite that Laura had to laugh.

"Not so you'd notice," she smiled. *"I just can't get over seeing you here."*

"Well come to the pub for a swift one, it's freezing out here and we can swap information." She looked quizzically at him. *"On me,"* he said. *"No strings, just old friends."*

She linked his arm and they set off to the local hotel further up the beach.

Sitting beside the roaring fire, John with a twelve-year-old Glenlivet whisky and Laura with a red wine, they soon warmed through. John told Laura about his research into the Arctic char in the loch. *"Warmer here than the Arctic to study them,"* she giggled. *"You nearly died of shock when that research funding came through and you thought you would have to go there."* John laughed out loud. He liked Laura's company; she was never boring, she was certainly a character, but she was never boring.

He leaned towards her, *"So let me guess…you are here to look at your Merlin theory."*

"Of course…where better to do it, but in the very place?" She told him about the money, and how she had given herself 6 months so she would have some money left until she got another job.

"I keep finding evidence that Merlin lived in Scotland, and that one of the knights of King Arthur spent his years questing the killing of the Loch Ness beast. This is a chance to search around the area and write up some theories."

John looked at her smiling, *"And what do you hope to find around the loch?"*

She sighed, *"Well some evidence of his having been here. Maybe an inscription or an altar. Who knows until you look?"*

"Maybe I can help you find the Loch Ness beastie."

She laughed, *"Didn't know you believed in it John."*

"I don't, well…" he hesitated, *"at least never thought it could exist, but something attacked my boat. Probably a seal we accidentally hit but it left some damage."*

"REALLY … you will have to let me take a look."

John nodded. They continued to chat for a while about old colleagues and gossip about universities and the problems in the press recently about over-awarding of final marks for degrees. Laura sighed, *"I still remember that exam meeting in 2002 where we said any degree awarded after this year will not be worth it's mark, the old 2:2 had become a 2:1. You know some universities have stopped awarding 3rds and give them all a 2:2?"*

They both shook their heads. *"And now with fees,"* she continued. *"I used to tell everyone they should have a university education, it would change their outlook, teach them to think better, now I would be condemning them to a life of debt, so I don't encourage them so much."*

John nodded in agreement.

"Well much as I would love to sit here and continue this I had better get back to my students. Where are you staying?"

When Laura told him, it turned out they were almost neighbours and so they set off back together. As they walked along the shore, Laura spotted someone.

"Hello who is this heading this way; blimey he looks like Christopher Lee!"

"It's the laird," laughed John. *"Come on, I will introduce you."*

The tall man greeted John with a wave and headed towards them. He knew John from previous visits by the university to the loch. *"John, how are you today?"* The tall man smiled and John turned and said:

"Henry, Laird of Cragneghil Castle and Barony of Dores and Drumnadrochit, let me introduce my good friend and former colleague Laura Loomis."

The laird shook her proffered hand. *"Delighted to meet you my dear. A friend of John's eh?"*

"Yes", Laura replied and laughed. *"He does have a few friends."*

The laird laughed and continued, *"Are you here on holiday or assisting John?"*

"I am here to do my own research."

"Really, more loch biology or something different?"

"More myth than biology. I am researching into the stories of Merlin and King Arthur being in Scotland, and more specifically Merlin being at Loch Ness."

"Then I must insist you must come to dinner at the weekend as I will be fascinated to hear about your research, and there may be some books in the castle library that might be of help."

The laird was obviously not used to his invitations being refused by the way he spoke and John breathed a sigh of relief to himself when Laura replied in the affirmative. Laura was very independent and could be quite bolshie.
"Thank you," she said and the laird smiled.

"Are you staying locally Laura - may I call you Laura?"

"Yes of course. I am staying at the little white cottage down from where John is staying."

"Ah yes, Mrs Wilson will have sorted that out. Splendid. I've invited some of the Cambridge people as well and if you bring your assistant John, that will make the numbers up nicely and make for some lively discussion. One gets few chances to discuss things with like-minded people here as one would like. I have to be aware of my position around the locals."

He gave a sort of grim smile. *"A pleasure to meet you, and I look forward to Saturday evening. I will send Hamish to pick you up in the estate vehicle in case the weather changes."* And with that he doffed his hat and carried on with his walk. They continued on their way to the road and up to the cottages.

"You will enjoy dinner Laura, he is good company and a very intelligent man, and the food isn't bad either." John held open her gate as he spoke.

"This may turn out better than I expected, he could have all sorts of stuff in his library, see you Saturday if not before, John," called Laura as she headed into the cottage.

Henry walked back to the car deep in thought. Could this just be a coincidence? Harris, his driver for the day - one of the estate men - saw him coming and quickly stubbed out his cigarette. The laird however appeared not to have noticed and as Harris opened the door for him, he just said thank you and back to Cragneghil please, and settled in the back seat. Henry remembered reading something about a law of coincidence and sat forward. Paul something, no Paulo. That was it; Paulo's Law of Coincidence went something like: People often note some unlikely conjunction of events and marvel at the coincidence, but the most amazing coincidence of all would be the complete absence of coincidence. It is just coincidence then; he smiled to himself and settled back in the seat.

Chapter 6
Food for dark thought

Saturday turned out to be a pleasant September day. There was a hint of frost in the early morning air as Laura let the cats out for a run. They had settled in, in a couple of days as usual. She could never understand this buttering paws business; she had moved eight times and the cats always settled in a few days and she could let them out.

She had decided that she ought to wear something a bit dressy for tonight so had a floaty tunic top and some smart wide leg trousers hung up to let the creases drop out naturally. Her daughter always said, "Who needs to iron, the creases drop out once you have worn something for a couple of hours." She laughed to herself. She also had bought a shawl on a visit to Drumnadrochit as she thought it might be chilly in the castle-like house, or the 'big house' as the locals called it.

She loved Drumnadrochit; the original Loch Ness monster exhibition, the shop full of stuffed Nessie toys, and the hotel with the tartan room, where her daughter and herself had lunched when her daughter was younger. It always felt nice there, a good atmosphere.

Daughter had loved it too. They had travelled by bus from Inverness and wondered as they boarded the bus why there were seat belts on the ordinary double seats. It wasn't a coach, just a single decker, get-up-and-press bell-type bus, if slightly old and rattled a bit.

They had soon discovered why. The bus, once it left town, set off at a hell of a speed and as they started down the road along the loch, the reasons dawned. On one side of the road, the bank was held up with wire netting and there were 'danger - rock fall' signs; the other side was a sheer drop in places down to the loch. The road was narrow with the odd passing place to pull over and they hung on for grim death as the bus careered along the narrow road. The loch could be glimpsed in places through the trees, but a lot of the loch was shielded from view from the road.

She often found that people didn't expect that and thought that Loch Ness was just a lake with easy access.

They were in giggles by the time the bus turned into Drumnadrochit, from being tossed around and the sheer breathless feel of the journey. The bus driver had been very helpful, however, and advised them where to get the bus back and what times it ran.

They had once visited one of the other Ness exhibitions, run by Hayden Stark, but left unimpressed at its commercialism, and returned to the original. The staff were friendly there and the old photos fun to look at, and they loved the Loch Ness shop, and the hotel menu. She had once worked in a university college for someone called Hayden. He was a hopeless manager, full of himself and thought he could do what he liked, even when the university said no. He said he was thirty-nine but looked older than her. She had always found men called Hayden to be prats. Though that was probably unfair to the fish of (very nearly) the same name, but maybe it is a stupid fish, she laughed to herself.

"Well better get on," she muttered and began some domestic chores before sitting down at her laptop to write. She couldn't manage without a mouse and she knew computer people who also attached a keyboard to their laptops - a bit over-kill she thought but each to their own.

At 6:00pm, she fed the cats and had a shower and changed - bit of make-up, some long ear-rings and a pair of low-heeled shoes and she was ready for the evening. At 7:00pm precisely Hamish knocked at the door and John appeared behind him in an approximation of a suit. *"I've come to fetch you for dinner Mrs Loomis, and the university lot."*

Laura looked at John's suit. Well, there was a jacket, a shirt and tie, but the trousers didn't match the jacket. However, for John he looked quite smart and Laura said so. *"You look pretty darned good yourself dear,"* he grinned. Hamish smiled and said nothing.

Donald appeared in a kilt and Laura duly admired how smart he looked too. He did look quite good in a kilt. Not many did, and most didn't have the legs for it. She suppressed a smile to herself of the thought of John in a kilt.

The estate vehicle turned out to be a vintage Bentley, that gleamed and smelt of old leather. *"Wow this is something,"* said Donald settling in the front next to Hamish, so he could admire the dashboard, leaving Laura to sit with John, in the back. It was too dark to see much but the journey was only short and the car comfortable.

The car swept up a long drive and turned a corner in front of large castle-like house, brightly lit to welcome guests. Laura got an impression of trees on either side of a wide road, whose branches moved as they passed.

The car stopped and Hamish opened the door for her to get out. They faced a large wooden carved door up some wide shallow stone steps. The door opened as they arrived as if by magic and they entered a large hallway. The ceiling was ornate and a huge stone staircase swept off to the side to the floors above. Before they had chance to take all this in, and after their coats had been taken, they were ushered into a sitting room by a butler in a kilt. This made Laura want to giggle again. It must be an English thing to find kilts and evening dress incongruous she decided.

The laird appeared silently before they had chance to admire the room and said, *"Please be seated, Gordon will serve drinks."* The laird was wearing dinner dress but with tartan trousers, though Laura thought he would probably look just as gentlemanly in a kilt. Donald looked more Celtic in his, more barbarian somehow. A round of Sherries, and gin and tonics followed. Gordon then announced, *"Your other guests have arrived milord,"* and two young people appeared at his elbow.

"Daniel sends his apologies, his wife has gone into labour and he has had to dash back to Cambridge," said the young man.

The laird introduced Andy and his companion Emily as Daniel's assistants and, *"Oh dear I hope it all goes well for Mrs Woolf."*

"Daniel said he would let us know when there is any news," piped up Emily, a frail looking girl with pale blue eyes and wispy blond hair. She was pencil thin as if a puff of wind would blow her away.

Andy looked like the rugby player he was, stocky and square headed and had a firm hand-shake besides Emily's rather feeble one.

"Your hands are cold dear," said the laird to Emily. *"Come by the fire. Gordon will bring you a sherry."*

Laura asked Emily and Andy what research they were doing with Daniel. *"We are looking at seismic activity in the loch, there was quite a big earth tremor in 1997 and several smaller ones since,"* replied Emily.

Andy continued, *"Daniel is hoping to find that the plates are unstable under the loch and that measuring it can be used to predict earth tremors not just locally, but anywhere in the world that is along the same fault lines."*

"Worthwhile research I think we will all agree," put in Henry.

"Unlike mine, which is purely for my own curiosity," laughed Laura and she explained her theories about Merlin to the two students.

"Curiosity is a valuable thing, my dear, and don't demean yourself, your research is just as important but in a different way. After all, it is only by studying the past we can understand the present and how we got here and perhaps where we are going in the future," Henry raised his glass in salute to Laura. Before she could answer, the gong sounded and Gordon appeared to announce dinner was to be served.

Henry took Emily's arm and Laura took Donald's. She heard John and Andrew having some facetious argument behind her on who should lead as they took each other's arms and followed. Looking ahead to the open door, she saw into a great hall, hung with pennants and weapons of a more warlike, but chivalrous age. The laird turned and said, *"Yes I apologise gentlemen for the lack of extra female companions but I am sure these two delightful intelligent ladies are better company than four boring ones."*

They all laughed politely.

A huge fire burned in the large stone fireplace and, in the centre of the room stood a table that could hold 30 people. The table was set at one end only and Laura found herself next to the laird, who was at the head of the table and opposite Donald. Emily was next to Donald with John on her right and Andy next to Laura.

The butler poured some dry white wine whilst a maid placed plates of soup or crab cakes in front of them. Laura chose the small crab cakes on a green salad - she had never liked soup. Andy was explaining more about how they conducted the study they were making on seismic activity when the main course arrived. Lamb or trout with roast potatoes, new potatoes, mashed turnip, baby carrots and mange tout. Laura chose fish again; she didn't eat red meat. The conversation changed to John's study of the Arctic char. The butler offered Laura red or white wine, *"I prefer red thanks, at the risk of being a philistine."*

The laird laughed, *"I think the days of white with fish and red with meat no longer apply."*

Donald interjected, *"At the risk of also being a philistine what should we call you sir?"*

"My friends call me Henry and I would like you to do the same, I don't like ceremony."

Laura tasted the wine: *"This is really nice wine."*

John chortled. *"Laura knows her wine, she may not know what it is but she can tell good from bad. I would trust her judgement on wine any day."*

"It's Pinot Noir, which John told me is your favourite," smiled Henry.

"It is really nice, probably better than any I could afford and thank you for serving it," she said.

"You must come and visit the wine cellars here for a tasting, in fact you should all come. We will arrange a date. It will be great fun. Last time I got lost in my own cellar but found a wine I didn't know I had!" They all laughed with Henry.

By the time pudding arrived Laura was telling them about her research. A sweet white wine went well with the raspberry sauce and vanilla cheesecake, and the mature Scottish cheddar and oatcakes that followed.

She was explaining her theory of Merlin being in Scotland and about Sir Pellinore's questing beast being Nessie, and how it was connected.

"You must come and spend some time in my library. I think you will find some manuscripts in there that might help. There's one condition though..." smiled Henry.

"Oh what's that?" asked Laura.

"You let me know if you find anything interesting...like the cellars I am not sure exactly what is in the library."

More laughter. After the men had second helpings of pudding Henry suggested they all withdraw. *"I don't think we should have our cigars and leave the ladies alone. It is, after all, the 21st Century and the Victorians are long gone."*

They went back to the sitting room for coffee, and port or brandy. Laura found herself on Henry's arm this time and Emily didn't have enough arms so Donald walked behind alone. After they were seated with coffees, and John and Henry with brandies, the conversation started up again.

"So have you not lived in the house long Henry?" asked Laura. *"As you don't seem* au fait *with its nooks and crannies."*

"I have not lived here for many years, mostly been in England but returned a few months ago when duty called. The house has been somewhat modernised in my absence, for the better I am sure, and we at least have modern bathroom facilities now and some central heating."

"The locals don't seem to mind you having been away" said John. *"They seem to just accept you."*

"My family have been here for centuries, so I am local," laughed Henry.

"Well you do own the place," continued John. *"Have your family owned it long?"*

"Oh dear, well my direct family have owned it for over 300 years but their relatives owned it before that. My surname is Fraser-Grant and both the Frasers and the Grants have been the lairds around these parts for centuries."

He turned to Laura. *"The castle library has records , maps and books going back hundreds of years , so you may find it helpful."*

Emily stifled a yawn and Laura seeing it said, *"Thank you. I will look forward to having a look but I think we may have to leave soon I'm afraid, we all have early starts tomorrow."* Emily smiled at her gratefully.

"Of course dear lady, forgive me. I should have realised the young need their sleep. When you get older you don't sleep so well."

He pressed a bell in the wall and Gordon appeared, and was instructed to tell Hamish to have the car outside in 10 minutes to take the guests home.

"Tell Hamish to make sure he sees people into their houses, you have to be careful these days as there is a rough element about even here."

They bade their farewells; the men shook hands and the women a peck on the cheek and then collected their outer wear from Gordon. Laura had arranged with Henry to come back on the following weekend to look through the library.

They dropped off Daniel's students first and then set off to the row of cottages. *"Nice man, Henry,"* she said to John after Hamish had dropped them off at the door. *"He's old school isn't he, a real gentleman. Goodnight and sleep well."* John agreed. *"Goodnight Laura, we'll catch up some time in the week,"* and then he turned and headed for the cottage his group were renting, with Donald trailing behind waving to Laura.

CHAPTER 7
Dark moorings

The following day dark clouds scurried across the sky and Laura decided that if she was going to look at John's boat she should go early. She thought she would walk down to the local shop and get a Sunday paper and maybe pick up some odds and ends, and then walk down to the jetty where they moored the boat. There wasn't a jetty in the village but further along the Loch there were several. She knew John said they would be there. The cats had settled once they had been fed and been out. It was too windy and chilly to hang around outside for too long.

At the shop she bought three sausage baps, still hot, to take down with her. She knew they had a coffee machine on the boat so could make bringing them breakfast her excuse. The chill in the air made her glad of her warm coat and gloves. She was a bit breathless with the effects of the wind and was glad when she rounded the bend and saw the boat moored at the jetty. She could see both John and Donald onboard and waved to them as she approached. Donald shouted to John, *"Here's Laura!"* and John appeared on deck. *"Hey come aboard."* Their faces lit up when she shouted, *"I've brought breakfast, so get the coffee on."*

Donald helped her clamber aboard. *"I am not built for boats,"* she grinned.

"Rubbish," came from John in the cabin pouring out mugs of coffee. *"I have seen you climb a mountain. Get on board woman, and put that young man down."*

Laura laughed. *"You don't change much,"* she said winking at Donald. *"Always were too cheeky by half."*

They sat in the cabin out of the wind and the spitting rain, and ate breakfast. *"You are a gem Laura. After this I will show the damage to the hull,"* said John as he bit into the still warm bun.

"And the sonar readout," put in Donald.

"You found something?" Laura looked incredulous.

"Well there was a large blip on the sonar, but could be a shoal of fish."

"Except it was moving too fast," said Donald before John could finish.

Laura examined the read out whilst Donald explained what it showed. *"Blimey,"* she said. *"Here be monsters."* She finished her coffee and then, helped by John - grinning cheekily - clambered back onto to the jetty to have a view of the boat.

She bent down to look at the hull. There were clear marks as claws or teeth might have made, but could also have been done by a branch. *"Hmmm,"* she said. *"It's our old friend inconclusive ... have you taken some samples?"*

"Aye and photographs," said Donald. *"For the insurance mainly."*

"The thing is, it could have been done by a branch, but the water would surely have made the wood soft so it would have broken the branch off, not damaged the boat."

"Not necessarily," replied John. *"The wood could have been petrified and like stone. It does happen."*

"Well the samples you took should show that," Laura continued to examine the hull for a while.

"Actually I think we might have a look at those samples today Donald, as I think it's going to be too rough to go out." John turned to Laura, *"We'll walk back with you, if you like, I've got a small lab set up at the cottage."*

Laura looked at the sky. The rain was starting to sting when it hit her ears - a bad storm was ready to break. *"Better set off now then,"* she laughed. *"Or we might need the boat to get back in."*

Donald offered to carry her shopping for her and John carried the equipment they were taking back. They were all short of breath by the time they got to the road after battling against the wind. It was a relief to be sheltered by the trees, which acted like a windbreak.

"Are you two doing anything this evening?" Laura asked as they reached the cottages, all of them rather damp and cold. Donald handed over her shopping bag.

"Nothing in particular, why?" John looked at Laura, puzzled.

"Well come round for dinner about 6:00, both of you. You can bring something to drink if you want. It's not worth cooking a whole chicken just for me and the cats so it will help me out if you come and eat some."

"With Yorkshire puddings?" John grinned.

"Yes the works, go on," she pushed them both playfully. *"See you at 6:00pm and don't be late. Oh casual dress guys, but make sure your hands are clean."*

"Yes mother," they both chorused as they walked away.

She laughed and went in.

They arrived carrying two bottles of wine at 6:00pm sharp. After removing their coats they both showed her their hands. *"Will they do?"* said John laughing. Laura slapped their hands one after the other and scolded them, for being childish; they just laughed. *"Do you need a hand with anything?"* asked Donald.

"Not at the moment thanks, go sit near the fire and I'll shout you when it's ready."

Laura busied herself putting out dishes on the kitchen table and making sure there were enough implements to serve.

"Come on guys, whilst it's hot, serve yourselves," she called.

They didn't need a second telling and were seated almost before she was.

"Looks great," from John and then the serving plates and gravy bowl started to be passed back and forth. Laura had done her usual Sunday lunch for when daughter or guests were staying, chicken, stuffing, roast potatoes, two types of vegetables - today carrots and broccoli - Yorkshire puddings and gravy. It always went down well, but then food always did when someone else cooked it, she found, especially if they were, like herself, a reasonable cook. She roasted the potatoes in a mixture of sunflower and olive oil, not like the old days, she laughed to herself, when lard was predominant, or the fat from the meat.

"The cats are quiet," John said between mouthfuls.

"It's the chicken they have eaten, it always makes them sleepy. Don't know why, must be something in it."

"Well people always want to sleep after a big meal so maybe that is it," Donald put in, once he swallowed. He didn't want to blot his copybook by showing bad manners, after Laura had been so kind.

Dessert was apple pie and cream. A Scottish staple, or seemed to be to Laura, but it went down well with them all.

"We'll clear the table Laura, and I will make the coffee if you want."

"Thanks John."

Laura went into the sitting room and stoked up the fire. The estate ghillie had brought some logs, and left them at the back door. Probably Henry's doing she thought, so she put one on, sending up a shower of sparks. John joined her, bringing coffee with him on a tray Laura had left set up for the purpose.

Feeling rather over-full, John - sipping a coffee in front of the fire - said: *"I forgot to tell you, we found something strange in the samples we took from the damage to the boat."*

Laura, who was starting to feel dozy in the warmth of the fire after the intake of food, woke up and said, *"Well go on then what did you find, don't keep me in suspenders."*

"Oh now you have ruined my train of thought with the talk of suspenders."

Laura hit him with a cushion. Donald who had been washing up came through to the sitting room holding a mug of coffee and sat down. *"Oh dear is it the war of the sexes?"* he laughed.

"No, John just being silly, so what did you find?"

Donald put in: *"There was organic matter in the scratches."*

"Oi," John threw the cushion at him. *"I was going to lead up to it."*

They all laughed and then Laura spoke, *"So what does it mean ... it was a branch that pronged you?"*

"No it was animal matter, but not seal. Not sure what it was."

"A monster," shouted Donald. *"We found Nessie."*

"Who knows, maybe you did hit something large in the loch. There have been enough sightings over the years ...since about 560 AD, I think." Laura had been researching the loch as part of her quest to link Merlin to Scotland.

"Maybe we should tell someone, in case something large is in the loch," Donald looked at the other two.

"Well it depends on whether you want to be called nuts or not," John retorted.

"No, he's right. Well if there is a large fish or something, it could overturn a small rowing boat, looking at what it did to your boat. I am going to have a look around the laird's library at the weekend. I'll tell him about it and he can report it, if he thinks there is a need."

The men both nodded. *"Sounds like a plan to me,"* John said. *"I will send some samples back to the University, for them to see if they can identify anything."* The evening ended in a discussion on myths and legends and the possibility of some truth in some of them. Laura was convinced that some stories passed on had some truth in the original, but like Chinese whispers they got distorted over time.

"Where are you going to start looking for your evidence of Merlin?" asked John.

"Well I am going to look at the local graveyards and parish records, see how far they go back and also look at any ancient stone circles or altars hereabouts that could be old enough to have been used in Merlin's time. I'll search any local historical archives. Henry's library looks like it might be a good place to start."

"Sounds like a plan," said Donald, and Laura laughed. The conversation moved on to ancient churches around the area that John thought Laura might take a look at. When it got to 11:00pm John said, *"We better go Laura, or Donald won't get up in the morning."*

"You mean you won't," retorted Donald.

Laura laughed. *"You don't change, John".* She got up and saw them to the door. As the door closed she could hear them still bickering as they walked to their cottage. Laughing to herself she went to check on the cats, put up the fireguard, and lock the back door before going to bed.

CHAPTER 8

Dark Books

The week passed uneventfully, but as Laura set off to Cragneghil Castle on the Saturday morning she was surprised to see a crowd at the lochside. Hamish strode past her with a grim look on his face. *"Hamish,"* she called. *"Is something wrong?"*

"Aye very wrong. You know the lad that works for me, young Campbell? He's been found floating in the loch."

"Oh no Hamish. That is terrible. He was only a teenager wasn't he? His poor family."

Laura looked at Hamish as she spoke and saw the pain on his face. The villagers, the locals, were very close and some were related. Hamish may be a relative of the boy, no wonder he looked so grief stricken. *"Aye, 17,"* he answered. *"No age at all. I have to go inform the laird. He will want to do what's right for the family."*

"I was going up to the library at the house. Should I stay away, I wouldn't want to intrude?"

"Don't worry lassie. Come on I'll give you a lift. This isn't your concern and the laird will be expecting you."

A stocky man in an impeccable suit stopped them as they approached the road. *"Has something happened down there?"* He was American; Laura recognised the accent straight away. *"A boating accident,"* Laura said. *"A local person."*

"Oh, I am sorry to hear that. I will be on my way, they won't want strangers hanging around." He went to a hire car and got in next to the driver, and it drove off, a bit faster than was warranted on the steep road.

Laura climbed up into the Landrover with some difficulty. She wasn't built to ride in farm vehicles these days she observed to herself ruefully.

The drive up to the house was silent. Gordon appeared at the door and after a brief word with Hamish, showed Laura to the library and went to fetch Henry.

The library was just as she imagined it. It smelt of old leather and old paper and had floor to ceiling shelves crammed with books. There were steps and a ladder on wheels to reach to the top shelves. She put down her bags and just looked around .She felt like a child left to run free in a sweet shop, and didn't know where to start. There was a large old wooden desk at each end of the room and big leather armchairs at various points set at angles to the shelves, with small tables next to them. It must be 30 feet long this room, she said to herself.

She looked at how the books were placed. They seemed to be in alphabetical order in groups of similar subject, so that made it easier. She started with 'M' for Merlin and then intended to go on to 'L' for Loch Ness, and then the Knights of the Round Table.

An hour later she had about 20 books spread out on the desk and was sitting with her notebook and pen going through them ready to take notes. A knock at the door and Gordon entered holding a tray. *"The laird thought you might like some coffee. He would be obliged if you could join him for lunch at 1:00pm if you are free."*

"I would like that, yes and thank you to both."

"If you need anything please just ring the bell by the fireplace. The laird doesn't want you climbing up to get books and risking a fall."

"Thank you, Gordon, I will if I can't manage."

The butler departed and Laura attacked the coffee, gratefully. There was also a selection of biscuits. She settled herself down with the coffee in a large armchair resting the coffee on a small side table and began to skim read the books.

She was so engrossed it took her a while to realise she could hear voices. They were outside the window and she strained to hear out of curiosity.

"That poor wee boy, they say he was all eaten about."

"Aye it's the beastie, no doubt about it. That's why the laird is back. Been summoned I expect."

"My mother can remember, as a wee girl, a fisherman been injured. That's why they'll not go out on the loch at night."

"Ladies what are you doing here?" Laura recognised Gordon's voice.

"If you have finished your duties go back to the village. You will be needed there to help the poor boy's mother."

"Oh aye, he will need to be laid out properly. Annie would want us to do it."

"Do you think it's the beastie, Mr Gordon? Back again?"

"I don't have time for gossip and neither do you. That poor boy's mother will need your support."

"Aye you are right there. See you later Mr Gordon," and with that the two women must have departed. A knock on the door was Gordon coming to collect the tray. Laura pretended she had been absorbed in the books and looked up slightly startled.

"Do you require anything else madam?"

"No thank you, Gordon, I am fine."

"There is water and soft drinks on the side table there if you need them. I will come to summon you when lunch is ready."

Laura smiled at Gordon and nodded as he departed.

She went straight to the books she found on the Loch Ness monster and searched through them until she found one by a former laird of the area. It was more of a pamphlet, but it had sightings by locals and it indeed said that local fishermen would not venture out on the loch in darkness.

> "The waters of the loch are dark, the particles of peat in the runoff from the hills make it so. The monster is dark by necessity to survive in the cold waters and cannot therefore be seen as clearly as in daylight. No man wants to hook it in a net or on a line in the night; truly this is a Dark Ness. The Loch is deeper than the sea and rarely gives up its dead. They must sink to the unfathomable black depths to be consumed by whatever lurks there."

For some reason she shivered.

"Someone walking over my grave," she thought and laughed to herself. She returned to the books about Merlin to alleviate the gloomy feeling that had descended over her.

There were lots of claims that Merlin had been in Scotland and also he seemed to have been more than one person and lived for over a hundred years. Though living to over a hundred is possible and more common these days, she wasn't sure it was such a possibility in 500 or 600 AD. She had filled half dozen pages with notes and references by the time Gordon came back to fetch her for lunch.

Lunch was chicken salad with new potatoes, followed by coffee cake and cheese and biscuits.

Henry was a good host as usual. He offered wine but Laura declined, choosing water. *"Otherwise I will be nodding off over the books this afternoon,"* she laughed.

The discussion turned to some of the information she had uncovered and her plans for the further research, and then she remembered: *"I nearly forgot to mention. John said the boat hit something when they were out a few days ago. It left some damage to the hull. They took samples to test and photos of the damage. He said it was animal in origin or fish and he said to warn you because it was probably strong enough to overturn a rowing boat. He thought it was a large fish or eel of some kind."*

"There has been talk for years of large sturgeon in the loch so perhaps it's true. But thank you for telling me, I'll let the water bailiff know." Laura thought Henry looked perturbed and then he continued, *"Now you must excuse me, business to attend to, but I will get in touch with you about the wine tasting and cellar tour. Feel free to come and work in the library any time. It's rarely used these days and you won't disturb anyone."*

"Thank you, and thank you for lunch. Until we meet again then," Laura proffered her hand and then Henry was gone.

Gordon appeared *"Would you like your coffee served in the library madam?"*

"Oh yes, thank you." I could get used to this, she thought to herself as she settled down again among the books. She had always wanted a library of her own, like this, with the leather chairs and the walls filled from top to bottom with books - old books - and the lovely old desks. Some of the books were bound with old bindings and leathers. She loved the smell of them, but had been careful not to drop them in case they fell apart.

She'd left a huge pot of vegetarian chilli in the slow cooker as she was expecting John, Donald and Daniel's two students over for an impromptu dinner. Therefore, she was hoping Henry didn't ask her to dinner because she would have had to decline.

She also had a huge, cheap fresh cream gateaux defrosting in the fridge, not up to big house standards she laughed to herself, but the students and John would wolf it down. She made sure the fridge door was shut properly, as it was not unknown for Buzbi to get the door open and try a taste of the contents.

It was starting to get dark in the library and she thought she had better start heading back to the cottage. She rang the bell and when Gordon appeared told him she was leaving. She asked him to pass a note to Henry she had written thanking him for his hospitality and listing a couple of books she had found, and a book she had borrowed. She also told Gordon about John's boat and their concerns. *"There may be a large fish or eel in the loch. It had long been reported. The laird will see something is done about it."* Gordon helped her on with her coat, *"Are you sure you wouldn't like me to get one of the men to drive you back ma'am?"*

"No thank you Gordon, the walk will do me good" she smiled and set off down the drive in the darkening gloom. It was with relief after twenty minutes that she saw the lights of the village come into view around the bend. Forgotten your torch you stupid woman she said to herself, you've been here before; you know there is very little street lighting.

The cottage was warm when she entered, the heating had come on and the cats were waiting. She laughed when she saw them, *"Couldn't take you two to the big house, you'd be up on the table."*

She gave them a treat, and let them out for a run and then checked their tray and topped up the feeding bowls and water. She weighed out lots of rice for later in the evening and checked on the chilli. Everything looked fine so she went for a shower and to get changed to something warmer and more comfortable for the evening. Jeans and a long sleeved tunic top I think, she said to herself when she viewed her wardrobe.

About 7.00pm the first knock at the door heralded Andy and Emily, shortly followed by Donald and John and an extra guest. *"Henry was walking by the loch, so we brought him too,"* said John in such a way as to let her know there was a reason.

"If you don't mind the lack of butler service and my cooking, you are very welcome, Henry," said Laura trying not to look as if she was put out or surprised.

She left them all by the fire whilst John dispensed wine he had brought and then Emily appeared, *"Can I do anything? Henry arriving was a surprise."*

"You could put the plates on the table as I serve up, that would be great thanks. I hope Henry doesn't mind roughing it a bit." Laura had made extra rice and baked a couple of ready frozen garlic breads to help stretch the chilli to six people. There was some left so she put it in bowls so people could help themselves to more. *"Dinner is served,"* Emily called. The four men trooped into the kitchen.

"Sit anywhere," smiled Laura. *"Hope everyone likes vegetarian chilli, it's made with vegetarian mince,"* she explained to Henry, who nodded. *"I am sure it will be delicious."*

Henry seemed unsure of where to sit so John steered him to the head of the table. The others sat randomly, but left a space for Laura at the other end of the table.

John poured out more red wine and they all started to eat. *"This is jolly good,"* said Henry, after a couple of mouthfuls. *"I must get the recipe for our cook. She's very good but not overly adventurous."*

The boys soon divided up the second helpings between them and Laura went to fetch plates and the gateaux.

"It's a very unadventurous black forest gateaux I'm afraid, but knowing I was feeding academics and students, I got the largest I could find."

Everyone laughed and Emily passed out plates of cake. Henry seemed to be enjoying himself immensely, and was smiling at everyone. Laura started to clear away plates and told them all to go in to the sitting room for coffee.

They all sat by the fire with their coffee and more wine was imbibed. The students sat on the floor with the cats, who were enjoying the attention - from Emily particularly as she cooed over them.

"Donald washing up again?" said John. *"He's such a tidy chap."*

He ruffled the old cat's ears as he spoke and it purred and stretched out a paw and dug its claws into his leg. *"Ow"*. The others laughed and Donald came in to join them. *"We should hire you out for parties Don, to clean up afterwards,"* Emily grinned. A sound like *"Humph"* came from Donald as he sat down.

"Is there any news from Daniel?" asked Laura.

"Not yet," replied Emily.

"We are at a bit of a loose end until he comes back. Can't start anything new, so if you need a hand with anything, either you or John?" Andy chimed up.

"You might regret that," said John grinning.

"Everything OK Henry?" said Laura as she was rather concerned that Henry was quiet.

"I am fine Laura. Enjoying the company. So did you find anything interesting in the library?" Henry leaned forward as he spoke.

"You have some quite valuable books and some interesting ones. I borrowed one. I hope you didn't mind."

"Not at all, take what you like," Henry smiled.

"Well from what I have found so far, it backs up my theory that if Merlin did exist, he was in Scotland and that he could have been responsible for discovering the Loch Ness monster. Sir Pellinore spent a large part of his life questing for a beast. I have come to the conclusion that Merlin sent him to kill the beast because it was a threat of some sort. I am not sure of the whys and wherefores yet. The other strange thing is if Geoffrey of Monmouth is telling, or should I say writing, the truth, Merlin changed his name more than once and was over 100 years old. Now today a few people live to that age so it's not impossible, but not likely in those days," Laura finished her spiel and looked at the assembled faces.

"Sounds feasible to me," said Andy. *"I had an uncle lived to 102. He outlived some of the family who were waiting to inherit. My mother said he did it deliberately to spite the family."* Everyone laughed.

"Well I must say I am fascinated," Henry put in. *"You must keep me informed."*

"Did you get the message about our boat?" John said, changing the subject. He did it rather abruptly Laura thought.

"Yes indeed. I have had a word with Hamish. He is going to make some enquiries to see if anyone else has had any incidents and then we will discuss what action to take."

"I am glad you took it seriously. I was a bit worried you would think we were a bit odd," laughed John.

Henry smiled. *"No John. One thing I have learnt from living near the loch is always expect the unexpected. The loch is a strange body of water and no one knows all its secrets, not even my family who have lived here for generations."*

Henry's phone rang to announce the arrival of a text message.

"Excuse me, this may be important." He looked at it and said: *"I must really be going, and I have to say I have thoroughly enjoyed myself. Would you all be free for the wine tasting next Friday?"*

A chorus of "yes's" followed and Henry rose to leave. He kissed Laura's hand in an old-fashioned gesture at the door. *"Thank you again dear lady."*

"It's little to repay your hospitality Henry. Thank you for joining us," and with that Laura watched Henry from the doorway for a few minutes and until he turned and waved his torch to let her know he had negotiated the path safely. A car was waiting to pick him up.

When she came back in the others were arguing over the age old problem of whether the loch could support a large beast, or many beasts for that matter.

"It depends if you listen to Hayden Stark and his group or not," said Donald. *"The man has no academic qualifications and goes around pretending to be an expert. I'd trust Rines and Mackal over him any day,"* John replied.

"Well despite what is said, we still don't know how big the fish stocks really are and there are also the spawning salmon to consider as food, when they are here, and seals and water birds if it is a carnivore, so it is a logical possibility that a family of creatures could sustain themselves," Andy put in.

"Well all I know is that Dan Scott Taylor, may he rest in peace, said something turned his 5000lb sub around. Dan was an honest, qualified, and experienced man," Laura joined in as she sat down.

"Do you think it really exists?" from a wide eyed Emily.

"Well I think there is something in the loch, especially after what I've been reading. But what

it is I don't know, probably a family of giant eels."

"Well you could be right Laura, something tried to chew my boat," laughed John.

"It doesn't make me feel any easier, going out on the loch," Emily shivered.

"There has never been a record of it eating anyone," this from Andy. Laura kept quiet about the conversation she had overheard, but resolved to tell John before he went out in the boat again.

"That's right," from Donald. *"It's always been said to be harmless."*

A short while later and everyone started to get ready to depart. Laura stopped John as he was leaving. *"Have you got time to pop by in the morning before you go out. I have something I want to ask you about and it's important."*

"OK, no probs." John looked puzzled and waved as he left.

"Will you two be alright walking back?" she said to Andy and Emily.

"Yes we'll be fine. We have torches." Andy pulled the torch from his pocket as he spoke. They thanked Laura as they left. She put the things away in the kitchen that Donald had washed and went to bed followed by the cats, who would make themselves comfortable on the end of the bed.

Laura slept fitfully that night. She kept dreaming of dark shapes in the water and all she could keep thinking was Dark Ness indeed.

CHAPTER 9

Dark Ponderings

It was barely 6:00am when she rose, but after sorting out the cats, she showered and dressed and put on some fresh coffee. She put down her restless night to too much wine and the chilli being a bit spicy, having been cooking so long. About 8 o'clock she saw John walking up the path. *"You smelt the coffee, didn't you?"* she laughed and continued with: *"Would you like a bagel with it, I was just toasting one for myself."*

John smiled broadly. *"You know the way to my heart."*

"Plain, or cinnamon and raisin, or one of each?"

"If you can spare one of each I can eat them."

"You always could eat one more potato than a pig John Draycott, and worst of all you don't get any fatter." John just grinned. He liked Laura's little phrases. She was North Yorkshire born and bred and despite living all over the world and losing most of her accent, she still came out with the funny little sayings.

As they sat at the table, Laura started to tell him about the conversation she heard and the boy's death. *"Well, they have kept that quiet,"* said John. *"Henry never mentioned it, and no one said a word in the shop or hotel."*

"I know, that's what worries me. I wanted to tell you before you went out again in the boat and I didn't want to scare the others."

"I think I will send the samples we took off for further analysis at the uni. I was going to do it and then it slipped my mind. We could be on the verge of finding a giant eel or something. I would imagine they would attack a human if they were hungry and the human was swimming. They say killer whales mistake surfers for seals sometimes."

Laura nodded. *"I think it would be a good idea. Take the cake left from last night for you and Donald to have for elevenses. It will be your excuse for calling. It has to be eaten today. And take care when you are out there, next time it might be your boat it sinks."*

"I don't need an excuse to call. We are old colleagues and old friends," he smiled. *"But yes, we both will appreciate the cake. I think our boat is a bit big to be sunk by an eel, but I will make sure to keep my wits about me and avoid anything odd or large. The women could have just been exaggerating, how people do when they gossip, but it is still worth bearing it in mind."*

John bade her farewell and thanked her again for the cake she handed him in a plastic container. He was thoughtful as he made his way to the boat, moored further down the loch. Donald was on board. *"Laura sent the rest of last night's cake for our coffee break."*

"Cool. She's a nice woman, Laura. Have you known her a long time?"

"We used to work for the same university years ago. One of her jobs was teaching people how to teach and that's how I met her when she came to our department."

Donald smiled and nodded, and got on with preparing to leave. John seemed a bit withdrawn, and he wondered if there was something once between him and Laura and maybe that's why he had been to see her this morning. People are funny, he shook his head to himself. I wonder why Laura is on her own. She's a nice woman, she can cook and OK she is plump, but she is what they would call a 'handsome woman' where he came from. Maybe she has a boyfriend somewhere, and has told John she is otherwise engaged. Hmm, he thought. That *could* be it. Satisfied in his own mind now at John's taciturn behaviour, he got on with the job.

The loch was calmer today and the boat slid out smoothly. John headed for the deepest bit of the loch near Urquhart Castle. They set about lowering the cameras down to as near to where in the loch they thought they could photograph the Arctic char. If it turned out there was indeed a larger population than thought, it could explain the continued presence of a family of giant eels. They stopped at eleven for coffee and cake, and watched the sonar to see if they could see any large shoals of fish they could follow.

"There's that large blip again," Donald pointed at the screen.

"I think we should bring up the cameras in case it is something that might take a bite out of them."

"You are not serious," Donald started to grin but seeing John's face decided to do as he was told. He started to reel in the equipment. When he got to the third one, it came up so far and stopped. John saw Donald hesitate. *"Something wrong Donald?"*

"I think its stuck." Donald continued to pull. Suddenly the line flung back depositing Donald on his backside. John laughed, *"Well, it's free now."*

Then he saw Donald's face staring at the end of the wire. Something had sheared the thick cable with its optic fibres, right through.

"I think we should head back to shore for repairs to the cable before we lose any more," said John quietly.

Donald nodded and started to coil up the lines. John started the engine and headed for the jetty. He was a worried man. What the hell could have a bite that strong to sever the cable completely, he said to himself? Donald was also thinking, I wonder if Nessie really *does* exist and maybe we might find her.

Back at the cottage, Laura was working on a time line for Merlin. According to Geoffrey Monmouth, Merlin appeared some years after the Roman Empire collapsed about 410 AD, so about 450 AD I think, she said to herself.

>→**450 AD** first mention of Merlin as a teenage boy born without a father brought to help Vortigern with the problem of the sinking castle foundations

>→**530/50 AD** or thereabouts Merlin is mentioned again also known as Myrddin, Lailoken and Ambrosius, which Geoffrey of Monmouth says are all the same person, Merlin. Elsi Gruffudd claims Merlin was re-incarnated.

"I wonder who else you could have been?" thought Laura.

The first sighting of the Loch Ness beastie was 565 I think…will have to look that up. She made a note to herself…St Columba was supposed to have sent it away. So Merlin or some-one with his name would have been around then.

>→Morienus lived in **600AD** ,a hermit and alchemist

>→Suidas **800AD** another alchemist

>→St Dunstan **909-988AD**

There doesn't seem a century where there hasn't been a Merlin-type figure, she said to herself.

>→Artephius (check sp) claimed in **1160AD** to have lived for a 1000 years..

"blimey" she muttered.

>→Albertus Magnus **1193-1280 AD**

>→Flamel **1330 AD** – no body was ever found , and he was said have been seen in 1770…

What is this? I thought this book was about Merlin?

She looked again at the book. It was *The Many Lives of Merlin* by Fulcanelli.

She shook her head. This is going to take some research. I wonder if I can get some help. The number Andy had left her was next to the 'phone so she decided to give the students a ring. Emily answered, and after a whispered discussion on the other end Laura heard her say they would be delighted to come up to the library with her tomorrow to look stuff up. *"I'll treat you both to lunch at the hotel as payment."*

"There's no need", Emily said. *"But we accept."*

Laura got a notebook out and started to make a list of things to look for tomorrow. There was a knock at the door about thirty minutes later. She looked out and saw John on the doorstep. She waved through the window, *"John, come in, its open. What's wrong?"*

John looked grim. *"Look at this cable, Laura."* He showed her a piece of cable he had cut off before sending Donald to Inverness to order a replacement cable and camera.

"What happened?"

"I think something in the loch happened. Something with bloody sharp teeth. I didn't say anything to Donald. Said it must have snagged on something."

"It must be strong to chew through that." Laura knew the cable was quite heavy because it had to endure changes of pressure and buffering by waves.

"It must be a sturgeon or a big eel, surely?" But as she looked at John, she could see he wasn't so sure.

"The sonar shows something large, like last time, when the boat got damaged, but it's no dinosaur."

"Well that was always a nice theory but impossible, the loch was only formed 10,000 years ago."

"Well, whatever it is, it's eating my bloody equipment, and people for all we know, after that conversation you overheard."

"John, I think you should go have a word with Henry and the water bailiff, Hamish. It may be it has to be reported somewhere, to the Fisheries Board or something. Stay and have a coffee first and calm down."

Laura put the coffee maker on and tried to think logically about the Loch Ness monster. It can't be real, it must be a big fish or something. Maybe a mutant pike - they have big teeth. Just like there will be a rational explanation for Merlin having nine lives she laughed to herself. I must be going bonkers. It must be the air here. It's so clean that the high oxygen content is making us all doolally.

She sat with John at the kitchen table and offered chocolate biscuits and strong coffee. *"I thought it best to get Donald out of the way to give me time to think and he'll enjoy a trip to Inverness and do some shopping whilst he's there."*

"You did the right thing. Now finish your coffee, go and find Hamish and go see Henry. You'll feel better once you've discussed it with someone who knows the loch and what it could be. There will be a rational explanation."

"Yes Stark probably released that big eel he was supposed to be fattening up in his swimming pool or something. Internet conspiracy theory number 97." He laughed. *"I'll go see if Henry is available now whilst I still feel strongly about it."*

"Let me know what happens."

"I will, maybe a trip to the pub tonight?"

"Yes that would be good, see you later." Laura waved him off and went to see what the cats were doing. She could hear noises in the kitchen so she guessed they wanted their lunch.

Buzbi, a very large tabby, was sitting on the table when she went in looking hopeful. *"It was you wasn't it Buzbi, swimming in the loch chasing fish? You are so big everyone thought you were Nessie."* she giggled, whilst Buzbi looked pointedly at the fridge. In front of the fridge sat Aristotle, the other cat, waiting patiently. *"Lunch it is then, chaps,"* she said.

John found Hamish talking to some fishermen on the jetty. Hamish was telling them where to fish, what to look out for, and to wear their life jackets. He excused himself, on seeing John's serious face, and came to see what John wanted. John told him and showed him the cable. *"Aye, there must be something in the loch causing damage; might just be debris though. We'll go and see the laird. The Landrover is just up the road. Just let me sort out these fishermen."* The two men set off after Hamish had seen the fishermen were sorted and organised.

Gordon answered the door as usual and said he would see if the laird was available. He returned and took them through to the sitting room *"He will be about 10 minutes, if you care to wait in here."*

"Thanks Gordon," John sat down as he spoke but Hamish stayed on his feet. He didn't normally enter the sitting room and felt uncomfortable.

Henry appeared and offered them refreshments, but they declined and then John showed him the cable and told him about the boat. Hamish stood silently, looking at the floor.

"I am sorry John. I shall have to investigate and see what is causing this before someone gets hurt. I will reimburse the university if need be."

"There is no need Henry, we are insured. However, I understand someone has been hurt. The

boy that works with Hamish was killed was he not?"

Henry's face didn't change. *"We kept it quiet from visitors, but yes the boy drowned. His boat must have overturned and he must have knocked his head on a rock. The coroner could think of no other reason than that at the time. But possibly he hit the same thing you did."*

"Or possible something hit him." said John grimly. *"It's no debris, it's a living thing. The damage to my boat proves that. There were animal traces like fish oils in the gouges."*

"Surely you are not saying it's the Loch Ness Monster?" Henry gave a wry smile.

Hamish still didn't move.

"No but it's something. A large predatory fish or giant eel and it is dangerous Henry. It should be reported to someone official."

"They will think we are mad, John. I will tell you what we will do. Hamish and I will organise a sweep of this end of the loch and see if it can't be netted, if it is a large eel or fish of some description." Turning to the still silent Hamish, *"Can you get enough men to do that from the locals?"*

"Aye no problem. They will be glad to help."

"I will pay the going rate tell them."

"You'll have more than enough volunteers then."

"I'd like to come," said John quickly before Henry could dissuade him.

"You will be very welcome and may be able to help identify anything we find." With that, Henry said he must get back to what he was doing and left Hamish with instructions and the order to include John in whatever took place. John and Hamish left together.

On the drive back John asked Hamish what he thought. *"Well there have always been stories about the loch and local people believe there is some truth in it. But nothing has ever attacked boats before, certainly not large boats. I'm inclined myself to think it's something new in the loch."*

"Hmm I have wondered about that story that Hayden Stark was breeding a large eel or fish in his back garden pool to release. Maybe he has done and because it's not native it's causing problems. The ecosystem of the loch could be at risk, if we don't catch it."

"Aye he's a rum chap alright. Wouldn't surprise me in the least, him doing something daft like that," Hamish nodded as he spoke.

John thanked Hamish for the lift and went into the cottage to look up any possibilities for the creature in the loch.

He sent Donald down to knock on Laura's door at 7.30pm to tell her they were going to the bar for a drink. "I'll be ready in 5 minutes Donald," she shouted from the kitchen.

"I've invited Andy and Emily as well. I told them about your incident with the cable. They were very interested."

"I am not sure about the whole thing," Donald replied. *"It could just be debris and stuff is getting tangled in it or it could be some large creature."*

Donald fussed the old cat as he waited and true to her word Laura was five minutes. They set off, John following a few minutes behind.

They found Andy and Emily already ensconced by the fire and, after giving Donald some money and sending him to the bar, Laura joined them. By the time John arrived, his pint was waiting. "What a service," he grinned.

"Come on then, tell us what happened when you went to see the laird. We are dying to know," Emily looked at John with huge eyes all excited.

"Not a lot to tell. He agreed something has caused the damage and we are sweeping the loch tomorrow with some local men. Donald and I will be part of the sweep."

"Cool, Donald you lucky bugger," said Andy. *"If they find anything, you will be there."*

"Talking of finding," Laura cut in. *"Tomorrow I will meet you at the castle entrance at 9am. So far the research makes it looks as if Merlin has lived for thousands of years or had nine lives, so we need to get to the bottom of it."*

She went on to explain to them all about her time line and there seemed to be no dates of deaths and some names like Flamel were said to have been seen 400 years after they supposedly died, but an empty coffin was found at the supposed time of his death.

"Wow this is turning out a much better time than we expected. Hunting monsters and alchemists. Our friends will be jealous when they hear about it. They said we would be bored silly," Andy was full of enthusiasm.

They spent the next two hours discussing various theories about Nessie and about reincarnation, and as the trips to the bar got more numerous the theories got sillier. Eventually John, his eyes full of tears of laughter at the last suggestion that Merlin was an alien who hid his pointed head under the pointed wizard's hat, and Nessie was Laura's fat cat fishing whilst doing the back stroke, called a halt and said: *"We ought to go, we have to be up early and will need our wits about us."*

They all groaned, but drained their glasses and gathered up coats and set off back to their various lodgings, shouting farewells and see you tomorrows as they went. Laura linked her arms through John on one side and Donald on the other as they walked along, and felt happy to be with such nice people, and to be doing something she wanted to do for a change. When they reached her cottage, she bade them both goodnight and gave them each a peck on the cheek, making Donald blush, and went in to sort out the cats before bed.

CHAPTER 10
Dark Fishing

The sweep of the east end of the loch was arranged for the next day at 8am, so it would be light enough to see. A flotilla of 20 boats with nets, plus some with sonar, were ready to set off up the loch hopefully staying in line. It was chilly, but not bitter cold and not raining, so John thought it would be a good search.

Donald was excited to be part of it. *"What if we find something?"* his face spilt from ear to ear with a big grin. *"We'll be famous."*

"Don't build your hopes up, it's liable to be debris or a large sturgeon," said John.

The radio crackled *"Are you there John? We are ready to go, over."* It was Hamish.

John answered the affirmative and they set off trying to keep in line with the slower smaller boats. As they got further away from the jetty, no one noticed the man in the suit with his high-powered binoculars watching their progress. Donald was busy watching the sonar to see if anything appeared, and John was concentrating on staying in-line, as were the others.

The boats straggled across the loch slowly inching forward. The fishermen looking bemused but they were getting paid, so seemed to be going along with things. It was going to be a long morning one or two thought to themselves with nothing to show for it, but it would keep the laird happy and stop the university people fussing.

After about two hours and Donald was starting to think John was right; that nothing would be found. He was starting to get numb in his extremities and wanted to be back in the warm cottage. Suddenly a blip appeared on the sonar, letting out a beep. *"John!"* he yelled, causing John to jump. "There is something heading towards us." John glanced at the sonar screen and got on the radio. *"Hamish come in."*

"Aye we see it John. We'll try to net it" Hamish replied.

There was yelling from the boat to their right. They had caught something but it was too strong for them to hold it. Other fishing boats came alongside to help. They started to haul the nets up. Donald was beside himself with excitement. The decision was made to haul it to shore in case it capsized the boat. Everyone was waiting to see what was in the net. Donald got out the sampling kit and the camera ready for the testing to see what it was.

A small crowd had gathered on the jetty. Donald jumped over on to the jetty and tied up the boat quickly so he could be first there.

The net was hauled onto the jetty and opened, the men falling over each other to see. *"It's a bloody big eel!"* shouted one. *"Never seen the like,"* from another. *"It's dead,"* said the third, poking it with his foot. On the jetty lay an eel nearly 10 feet long but Donald and John looked at each other. The eel had been dead before they netted it, that was obvious. Something, however, had taken a large chunk out of it.

"Well I think when you hit it with the boat, John you must have killed it," said the laird who appeared from nowhere. *"However if there is one, there must be more."*

"I'd like to take samples Henry, before it putrefies. I think it will need disposing of before the smell gets worse," John turned to Donald. *"Have you got the kit and the camera?"*

"All ready," grinned Donald but his look turned to disgust when he got a whiff of the dead eel.

"Hamish, see that it is disposed of once John has documented the find and taken his samples please. Tell the estate manager who to pay and tell the landlord at the Dores Inn*, the first round of drinks are on me,"* and with that Henry turned and strode off.

"Donald," whispered John. *"Take a measurement of that bite if you can without being seen."*

"No probs. I will need to measure it anyway."

"The man who killed the Loch Ness monster eh?" an American voice said beside John. *"Clayton Blome-Grant."* He offered John his hand. John shook it, *"Draycott, John Draycott."*

John was too concerned with organising Donald and taking samples to take too much notice. He presumed the man to be a tourist or journalist, and therefore best not to get engaged in conversation. Donald was doing a good job of covering up his measurements so no-one would suspect. A journalist from the *Inverness Courier* appeared so John decided it was time to leave, and left Hamish to deal with him. He and Donald headed back to the cottage to look at their findings. John pulled Donald along swiftly so that no one would stop them and ask questions. Donald, who was cold and looking forward to getting warm back at the cottage, didn't protest but trotted along to keep up.

Laura found the two students waiting at the entrance to Cragneghil Castle when she got there. Though it was called a castle, it was painted pink and cream and had turrets more like a fairytale castle than a building built for defence. A lot of old Scottish houses where like this. The local inhabitants would have flocked to it to make a stand before an enemy, but at heart it was someone's home.

"Hi," she said. *"Ready for some digging through dusty old books?"*

"Better than doing nothing," from Andy.

They were greeted by Gordon at the door and as he took their coats he offered them coffee, to which they readily agreed. Laura had rung ahead to make sure the library was free for them to use. She didn't want to impose on Henry's hospitality. They went into the library and stood holding out their hands to the blaze. Gordon appeared with a tray and a coffee pot, which they all greeted enthusiastically. Once they had warmed up and got themselves into a frame of mind to start working Laura took charge.

"Right. Emily I want you to look at alchemists from 500AD to present day. Any that don't have dates of birth or death, or like the Flamels, an empty coffin found, make a note of and take down a reference and we can use it to make a time line. Andy, you can go monster hunting. References to when the monster first appeared and up until 1933 when the main sightings started, again make a note of times and references. I shall be among Arthur and the Knights of the Round Table as a starting point to see what references to Merlin there are. And no playing on the wheelie steps, they are a bit wobbly."

They laughed, grabbed a proffered notebook and pen each and started searching through books.

"I'll start this side Emily and then we won't be tripping over each other," Andy took the left side of the library first.

An hour later and a pile of books were growing beside each of them. *"OK I suggest we mark where we have got to in searching the shelves, and start reading and then swap over again in an hour, then we won't get bored,"* Laura said seating herself on the window seat with her pile of dusty tomes. All that was heard for a while were pages turning and pens scribbling. At 11.00am Gordon came in and brought more coffee and biscuits. *"The laird has asked cook to provide you with a sandwich lunch if that is acceptable as he is out today."*

"Oh thank you, Gordon. Yes, that will be lovely. We weren't expecting lunch," Laura grinned at the other two.

After Gordon left, Emily - helping herself to chocolate biscuits – said, *"He's a nice man Henry, isn't he? Very considerate."*

"That's because he is old school. Good manners mean guests are honoured and treated with respect, and their needs catered for. Manners and good grace are sadly lacking these days," Laura sighed as she spoke. It was one of her bugbears, especially among university staff, that

so few knew how to behave with good manners these days.

Andy said with a mouthful of biscuits, *"Manners maketh the man"* which made them laugh, as crumbs sprayed everywhere.

"Right back to it my Scooby Gang, back to shelve searching for an hour and then we will get an hours reading in before lunch."

The piles began to get bigger again and then the page turning started again. Gordon appeared discreetly at 12.20 with lunch. Two large trays where placed on the library desks, one of assorted sandwiches and one with tea, coffee, fruit juice and small cakes.

After Gordon left the room, Emily examined the sandwiches. *"Oh smoked salmon and cream cheese, cheese and onion, egg and cress and beef ...and I think mustard, no horseradish."*

"Yum," said Andy.

"That's your share, what about the rest of us," giggled Emily. *"You get the side salad and the crisps,"* retorted Andy.

"We can eat all the cakes," laughed Laura, as Andy pretended to look put out. *"OK break for lunch I think. We won't be able to work with them staring at us, begging to be eaten."*

Half an hour later, the trays much diminished, they got back to work. Gordon came in at 2.30pm and removed the trays, and left more tea and coffee plus some biscuits.

They continued until 4pm when Laura called a halt and they arranged to meet up at her cottage the next day after she had stood them dinner at the pub tonight. They spent the next half hour returning books and making a note of where they were up to in case they had to come back. Laura left a note with Gordon thanking the laird for his hospitality , *"Henry is not the only one well brought up,"* whispered Emily to Andy. *"She's a bit of an enigma Laura, isn't she?"* He whispered back. *"Too right. Acts like she is a working class person, but little things point to her being brought up much better."*

She left the students at the gateway to the castle. They were going to get on the local bus, and she walked towards the village.

Laura rang John when she got back to see if he and Donald wanted to come for dinner at the hotel later with the students. They were busy in the make shift lab they had set up in the spare room, but said they would gladly join them, and they could all exchange news.

CHAPTER 11
Dark Discussions

At the lochside, Clayton Blone-Grant stood looking out across the waves. Two large men who were almost identical joined him. *"Well boys, it will have to be soon, it's starting to cause attention, and that ploy of yours won't hold them for long."*

"Have you decided on a day?" the gruff voice was also American.

"The oracle will let me know soon. The guys are working on it Joey boy, they are working on it."

The other man looked identical to his brother apart from a scar down the left side of his face.

"I'll be glad to get it done and get back home. The food here is crap."

"Oh Ed, you are a philistine," laughed Clayton. It was not a nice sound, more like a rasping.

"You did a good job on the boy though, no-one suspects anything."

"It didn't seem right treating a dead body like that, but the cause is more important." Ed had a more refined voice than his brother, but he looked mean around the eyes, whereas Joey merely looked slightly vacant.

"Well boys, we may be able to contribute the greatest gift to the cause since the discovery of heavy water. The master will be pleased." Clayton smiled a creepy sort of smile on that face.

"Let's go and eat out in Inverness tonight, we should be able to find something to your taste," he gestured to the two men to follow him and headed back to the road.

As they got back into the car, *"What about the scientists Clayton, are we going to do anything about them?"* Ed looked at his Boss.

"Na, as long as they don't get in our way, they aren't important. Come on Joey wagons ho!" The large dark car set off along the road.

Watching from the shadows Henry shook his head. What was he going to do about them? He swore many years ago not to take a life even to protect himself. Though he may not be able to prevent what would happen, he doubted they had the power to control what they wanted to unleash. It was his job to protect the local people and he would do that, at cost to himself. It would mean starting again; he sighed, and turned and headed back to the car so he would be back at the house in time for dinner. Cook could get huffy if he was late. Sometimes he wondered who employed whom.

Meanwhile at the hotel, there was a lively discussion going on at the bar when the colleagues arrived. Everyone was discussing the large eel found in the loch and speculation was rife as to how it got there; it was no native species, the local fisherman knew that. Laura had rung and booked them a table in the dining area and they were ushered through when they arrived. After ordering drinks and their food, the conversation started.

John told them about the eel and then said, *"It wasn't a fresh water eel. It was dead because someone had put a sea eel, a large conger, into the fresh water of the loch and something had taken a huge bite out of it."*

"So it can't have been that eel that damaged the boat and chewed the cable. It wouldn't have lived that long surely?"

"It could well have chewed the cable but I think someone put it in there, but for what reason?" John spread his hands in a gesture of exasperation at someone's stupidity.

"It wasn't Hayden Stark was it?" from Andy.

"So you heard about the rumours too," Laura laughed.

"It was on the internet," Andy looked embarrassed. Their food arrived and talk stopped as everyone got themselves organised with cutlery and condiments.

"It still doesn't answer the question as to what did the damage though, and I am now known as the killer of Nessie." This raised laughter and John grinned.

"Well we have all had a productive day, and tomorrow we may come up with some answers!" Laura raised her glass, *"Cheers everyone."*

"Cheers," chorused back, and everyone set to eating their food. The conversation after that was mainly light-hearted banter, much of it aimed at John and Donald's expense as monster killers. The meal ended well and they started off on their various journeys home. They didn't want to stay at the hotel too long as the media had arrived in the shape of local television people, the BBC and several journalists and it was very busy. Their table would be needed. Plus, as John said, they would hound them, if they knew he and Donald had been on the boats when the eel was caught.

Later as they walked back, Laura spoke to John, *"Are you worried about what might be in the loch or is the fact that someone tried to hoodwink everyone?"*

"Both really. I am not sure if there is something in there someone is trying to hide, and let's face it, it may have killed Hamish's assistant, or if my imagination is getting the better of me, being here."

"Your imagination didn't chew through a fibre optic cable and I feel sometimes that there is something not right here. I have spent time up here before over the years, but it's always had a good atmosphere. I feel like everyone in the village is tense at the moment, though it may just be because of the boy's death." She looked at John.

"He wasn't the first Laura. Just before you arrived a local was drowned in the loch. They say he was drunk and banged his head on a rock but no one was ever too sure about it."

"Blimey, the body count is rising! It's like we are in some murder programme on TV, The Loch Ness Killings."

This made John laugh. *"Trust you to think of something silly."*

He gave Laura a playful hug and left her at her door. Donald had already gone on ahead.

"Well cats," she said as they appeared at the sound of the door opening. *"What have we got ourselves into?"* She gave them a treat each, and went to bed, still smiling to herself.

Down at the jetty a torch flickered as a dark shadow made its way around John's boat. It spoke into a blue tooth set, *"Nothing here, no photos and no samples."*

A voice replied, *"Leave it then. If they are any complications we can dispose of them later."*

"People might get suspicious."

Reply came back, *"Not of a boating accident. Happens all the time."*

The shadow grinned and set off back to the road.

CHAPTER 12

Dark Images

Next morning was murky, with a chill in the air and a constant drizzle of rain; the sort that never gets you more than damp, but seems to soak through to your bones. Autumn was advancing, and soon it would be winter.

John decided they would do a sonar sweep of the loch, as if looking for shoals of char, but in reality to look for something else, even if only to confirm for himself it wasn't there. He spoke to Donald who was quite happy to go along with this. He wanted to know too if something was in the loch.

Donald and he called in the shop and bought a supply of sandwiches, biscuits and milk to keep them going. They also got bacon butties to set them up for the day, though as Donald said they were not as good as the ones they got in Durham on a rest stop, on their journey up to Loch Ness. Donald continued to say they were the best he had ever tasted, and they carried on an argument about it all the way to the boat. To anyone watching all was as normal.

As they cast off John noticed a man watching them, with binoculars from the road. He thought no more about it; tourists seemed to be here no matter what the time of year. He decided to start at the east end of the loch and work his way around the loch in circles that decreased each time. It wasn't ideal but it was the best he could do. The loch is fairly narrow in places and two passes would probably be enough.

They spent their time debating what the creature, if it was there, could be. They decided on four possibilities, a very large sturgeon, a very large eel, a giant catfish (not unknown in the world), or a new or previously thought-to-be-extinct species.

"There were giant catfish found in a lake in the USA and another in China. They are carnivorous so it could be our monster," John looked at Donald as he spoke. He didn't want Donald to be spooked by what John thought might really be in the loch. A creature that size, as they had seen on the sonar blip, had to be something new and unknown, or a throwback that had evolved. He didn't think some sort of dinosaur, as they had long since been extinct, before the loch was formed, but it could be some giant hybrid of a sturgeon, or a pinniped (the seal and

---

sealion family). It seemed unlikely but you never know. Men were said to have mated with apes and Neanderthals in the past. He had long thought that if Bigfoot existed, it would turn out to be the result of some prehistoric mating of ape and man, a missing link that had evolved secretly in hidden, hard to access, places such as high mountains and forests.

"We would be famous if we found it," grinned Donald breaking into his thoughts.

"Who wants to be famous? Only people who star in so-called reality TV programmes. Reality TV. That's a laugh, it's in an artificial environment set up from the start, they probably decide from the beginning who will be what and do what. No, Donald, fame by those means, and not for your achievements, is for those who know they will never achieve anything any other way because they are too lazy or too dim."

"That's a bit harsh isn't it?"

"You've seen the so called celebrities, footballers with more balls than brains, women famous for being thin with artificial breasts. They would be nonentities in a world where invention and innovation is celebrated. I once read a Christopher Fowler book in which one of his characters said something about the dull ordinary people of the world try to curtail and disenfranchise the innovators in the world. How right he is. He went onto say something about to be accepted you have to be average."

Donald knew John was on his soap box again. He chuckled to himself. *"Academics. You get them on a subject and they won't shut up."* He remembered someone saying you can always tell an academic because they never look when they cross the road and expect everyone to get out of their way. Laura did that all the time! He'd seen her and the cars going around her in Inverness, whilst she just wandered across the road.

He carried on watching the screen lost in his own thoughts and getting bored.

On the second sweep of the loch, just as they were thinking about stopping for lunch, something appeared on the sonar. *"It's there again,"* shouted Donald stabbing at the screen with his finger. *"Get a printout,"* yelled John. *"Let's see if we can follow it."*

He spun the boat around causing a wave to smack against the shore and saw a group of people staring and pointing at the water. In front of them, a dark shape was just under the surface of the water. *"It must be 15 or 20 metres long,"* gasped Donald and then it vanished under the wave it created. *"It must be diving,"* John was astonished. *"I can't believe what my eyes have just seen."*

"Well unless they put something in the bacon butties I saw it too," Donald looked as if he wished he hadn't eaten the bacon butties; he was ever so slightly green around the gills.

"I think we should head back to shore Donald, in case it reappears, if it is big enough to capsize us and if it has teeth to match its size ...." John trailed off and turned the boat.

Donald just nodded but kept an eye on the screen just in case.

Back at the jetty, they took a look at the sonar print out whilst they ate a sandwich. *"It's definitely a living thing, not just debris coming to the surface, you can see by the movement it makes. Debris wouldn't move like that."* Donald nodded his agreement his mouth full of cheese and pickle. He thought he might feel better if he ate something.

"The question is what do we do now? Who do we tell? Who would believe us?"

"I think we should tell Laura and the others so they are careful around the loch, and the laird should be told," said Donald swallowing his mouthful with a gulp of coffee. *"Henry can alert the locals and decide what to do. Do you remember when we caught the eel he said something about if there is one there will be others. And there were those tourists at the loch side, they saw something, they will be telling everyone."*

"Well you wanted to be famous Donald; we might have no choice in the matter if this gets out. Our academic credibility will be gone if we can't prove anything."

"I remember that bloke at the natural history museum got the sack because he supported a case for Nessie. We should avoid anyone knowing it was us, apart from Henry."

"I agree, the tourists will just be seen as the silly season because of the eel being caught and we can just stay quiet until we know more. All we saw was a shadow in the water and sonar read out of something large which could be a shoal of fish."

They finished lunch, and set off to see if Henry was available. They knew the others were all at Laura's cottage today so they wouldn't be out on the loch, and could be warned later.

CHAPTER 13

Dark Discoveries

They were all seated around the kitchen table in Laura's rented cottage with mugs of coffee and a plate of biscuits. *"OK, Emily do you want to start with your notes and what you found,"* Laura got out her voice recorder in case she missed anything.

"Well," Emily looked at the other two. *"How long do you think it's possible for someone to live? Because so far I have alchemists that claim to have lived 4,000 years, some that seem to have been sighted 400 years after their deaths, and a lot of enigmas."*

She passed around her list. Her writing was neat and tidy, just as you would expect, grinned Laura to herself. Laura's writing was a scrawl at best.

- **450AD** Merlin mentioned as a teenager
- **460-490 AD** King Arthur lead Celtic warriors against Saxons, with Merlin in two. One of his knights Sir Pellinore had a quest to kill a beast, possibly Nessie
- **500AD** St Surf said to have killed a dragon in Perthshire (is this Sir Pellinore?[8])
- **550AD** Merlin called Myrrdin. Geoffrey of Monmouth said this is the same Merlin also known as Ambrosius. There is some mention of him or someone like him, being buried by the River Tweed but this was years before so both stories can't be true.
- **565 AD** St Columba said to have a run in with Nessie
- **600s** Marienus Hermit and alchemist. His book printed in 1144 (how come so long after his supposed death?)
- **800s** Suidas monk, encyclopaedist and writer on alchemy
- **900s** St Dustan abbot of Glastonbury and an alchemist... note the Glastonbury connection with Arthur and Merlin
- **1160AD** Arthephius claimed to have lived a 1000 years in his books

---

* Sir Pellinore is also known as King Pellinore - the king of Listenoise or of "the Isles" (possibly Anglesey, or perhaps the medieval kingdom of the same name), according to the Arthurian legend.

- **1193-1280** Albertus Magnus discovered potassium, another alchemist difficult to trace actual death
- **1214-1292** Roger Bacon - reputation as a sorcerer
- **1330-1417** Nicholas Flamel - but coffin found to be empty. Published his book 596 years later. He was supposedly seen in the1700s. Said to have discovered the philosopher's stone which made him immortal or at least live a long time
- **1370s** John Dastyn left a fortune when he died - supposed to have transmuted it i.e. lead into gold
- **1437** Jubertus supposedly killed children and made them into a powder which was then made into imitation children for demons to inhabit. He looks like he lived in Scotland at the time so a warlock probably.
- **1452-1519** Leonardo da Vinci famous inventor and possibly alchemist
- **1560s-1600s?** Paracelsus - his influence found well into 17thC and Paracelsians, his followers, are still around today
- **1642-1727** Sir Isaac Newton - again reputed to be a magician
- **1784** Comte de St Germaine was apparently 124 but claimed he had lived 4000 years
- **1833** Gregor Mcgregor alias Willox the warlock found dead in the Loch Ness area . In his possession a strange bridle of yellow metal said to be for riding the water kelpie (Nessie)
- **1920s** Fulcanelli thought to be Flamel - still alive in 1978 in Florence according to rumour. Someone told a story of how he was living there according to locals. Was 70 in 1920s
- **1899-1982** Eugene Canseliet (was Flamel's disciple.)

Notes

I discounted John Dee...was taken in by Edward Kelly and duped so unlikely and Aliester Crowley who was more of a cult leader.

"I love Willox the Warlock," laughed Andy. *"He's great, what a name."*

"Well we seem to have some longevity among our alchemists starting with Merlin," Laura looked at the list again. *"Maybe one of them did find the philosopher's stone and live forever, maybe Merlin was/is immortal?"*

No one laughed, which surprised her.

"I know that Fulcanelli wasn't who he said he was. No-one really knew who he was. The letters of his name, she paused, they change to 'can lie full'," Emily said thoughtfully. *"Frater Albertus, who I discounted as well, his name spells 'rat fable ruser' so may not mean anything,"* she laughed. *"I discounted him because he definitely died in 1984 and he was a Paracelsian so not an independent thinker."*

"You are good at playing with words Emily. 'Rat Fable Ruser' sounds like a punk rock star. I bet you are good at crosswords," Laura smiled as she spoke, and then Andy joined in.

"The beast, Aliester Crowley was a rum bloke. Do you think he really was a devil worshipper?" The students both looked at Laura.

"Well, when he died he was living with his girlfriend and child in a flat in somewhere like Brighton or Eastbourne and living an ordinary life. But he did drive his assistant and one wife mad - they say - with his spell casting."

"Didn't they realise it was all show?" Emily looked puzzled. *"He did live by Loch Ness though, in Boleskin House...maybe he conjured up Nessie."*

"Nessie had been seen long before he arrived," put in Andy. *"Do you think he believed he was doing magic stuff?"*

"Well," began Laura. *"In those days people believed more in God and the Devil, and most of them believed - including Crowley - that behaving badly would let them conjure up some pact for power with the Devil. Instead, all they get is bad publicity and bankruptcy usually.*

Crowley didn't have the patience to do things properly; they say it takes 6 months' preparation for the ritual of Abramelin, which he used when he drove his assistant mad. He didn't wait 6 months. He probably thought it didn't matter so it went wrong. I don't know much about it apart from reading Dennis Wheatley novels when I was young, and stuff on witches or wise women in Gender Studies, but I do know any of these sorts of belief stuff requires months (if not years of study) , there are no short cuts."

"Hmmm, so really he started a cult and then went back to living a normal life after all the damage he'd done. Typical," snorted Emily.

"Unfortunately it's the innocents who always suffer and get taken in. Well you have done a good job on your lists Emily, a thorough one. Thank you. It will help a lot."

"It's a bit odd though all these people who may or may not be dead," Andy put in.

"Well, records weren't kept much apart from some parish records, years ago. Births and deaths weren't registered unless the local priest wrote it into the parish books. Most people couldn't write and probably they didn't see much point in recording things. It's not like today when you need documents to prove who you are. This also made it easier for people to re-invent themselves in those days."

"So really someone else could be using the alchemist's name and claim to be 200 years old and basically people will have believed him and there was no proof either way."

"Not only no proof. People were more afraid of magic and demons in those days and more

gullible. I suppose you would have to be, to believe someone could be magical enough to live forever," Laura was trying to be practical about this. She didn't want the students to think she was loopy.

"Shall I make some more coffee?" Emily said.

"Yes, good idea; and there are some cake and sandwiches on the kitchen side. I made them this morning. Bring them through as well. We will have a break and then look at Andy's stuff."

Emily brought in the three plates of food and some plates. She followed this with the tray of cups of coffee.

Andy handed them around his list as they ate.

"Nice sandwiches, Laura. What's this - tuna and sweetcorn?" Emily ate in small mouthfuls and could therefore talk between bites without being rude.

"Yes, my daughter's favourite, and we have chicken and green salad, and cheese and tomato. The cakes are just homemade buns with icing, fairy cakes."

"Well they will go down well in this quarter," Andy was always hungry but never seemed to change shape. *"Anyway this is my stuff I found."* He cleared his throat. *"Well there have been stone carvings since 1,500 years ago of a creature in the loch,"* between mouthfuls. *"And continuous mentions of water kelpies and beasts in the loch since the first recorded sighting in 565, when Saint Columba supposedly turned back the beast with prayers. Only that really took place in river Ness I think. Depends who you read. The river runs into the loch though and, well, look at the list I've made."* They all concentrated on reading Andy's timetable of events.

Timeline of sightings:

- **565** St Columba Beastie in loch poss. River Ness not loch
- **1527** Duncan Campbell said he saw 3 men killed.Terrible beast in the loch
- **1600 and 1700s** Many reports - no details. There may have been soldiers stationed near the loch. There was a warship moored on the loch supplying troops at this time. Floating islands reported but there are no mats of vegetation in the loch.
- **1771** Reported sighting no details - Great beastie

(N.B. there is no documentary proof to support the earlier sightings only stuff written many years after it happened)

- **1871** Dr Mackenzie reported to police Log-like then upturned boat

- **1879** Children reported to police - Elephant coloured creature small head on long neck turned head side to side. Waddled (on land)
- **1880** E.H. Bright and cousin - Long neck dark grey. emerged from wooded area and left a wash where it entered water (on land)
- **1885** Roderick Matheson to police - Forward moving in loch. Biggest thing he ever saw with horse like head.
- **1889** Not known. Strange creature in loch
- **1890s** Gypsy lady - Unknown except strange creature in loch
- **1895** 6or 8 people including a forester, a ghillie, anglers and hotel keeper. Reported to police a horrible great beastie in the loch
- **1898** McKenzie It appeared in the loch at times and then it seemed to go away
- **1889** No details only several people reported to police A beastie in the loch
- **1903** F.Fraser and 2 others - Hump in water like upturned boat tried to row closer but couldn't get a close look
- **1908** John Macleod Long tail eel like head 30-40ft lying on the surface of the water, quickly moved off Inchnacardoch bay
- **1912** 5 or 6 children including William MacGruer - Queer looking animal moved to the loch and vanished in the water. Described as camel like with long neck and humped back. (land)
- **1919** Mrs P. Cameron and 2 brothers Small head like a camel long neck humped back 4 limbs
- **1923**
  1) William Miller and D. McGillray. Like an upturned boat about 10-12 feet showing, moved off in an arc and submerged
  2)Alfred Cruickshank at night on land. About 20 to 25 feet long arched back with 4 legs and lighter underbelly skin elephant like (on land)
- **1929** Mrs Cumming and D Gillvray Motionless sank with a splash, hump - size of a horse's body
- **1930s** Several sightings :

Including 3 young men in a boat, Ian J Milne, Alec Muir and several school children. Exact dates not recorded. Described as 2 or 3 small humps, moved in an arc. One on land sighting which left a visible trail of squashed moss

- **1932** James Cameron. Hump like upturned boat
- **1933** 18 recorded sightings this coincided with the new road being built plus 5 land sightings All described humps, long neck fast moving.
- **1934** 11 recorded plus 4 land sightings . As above
- **1936** 1 sighting

"And then we get to the 50s and 60s and there were loads, so I thought I'd stop there," Andy grinned. *"There are probably hundreds more sightings but I took what I could find. I am sure there were loads more in the 1930s but they would be in some guide to Loch Ness or something. I couldn't find one, only history type books."*

"Blimey, I never realised there were sightings centuries ago," Emily put in. *"I thought it was a modern thing, so that TV programme that said the sightings only started after* King Kong *was on the cinema was wrong. The sightings started long before the media could pass on information."*

"Over 1,500 years and who knows before then, there may not be any record. The ones in the 1700s and 1800s were only recorded because of the military or police records," Laura continued. *"You see why I needed some help. I think it was Roy Mackal who said there had been 10,000 sightings and of the 3,000 he studied he found 251 he couldn't find an explanation for, other than there* is *something in the loch. There was also a film Tim Dinsdale took that was examined by air force people I believe and confirmed as genuine, and again he was an honest chap not a trickster."*

"Have there been a lot of fakes and tricks?" Emily looked at them both as she asked.

"Quite a lot," laughed Laura. *"Some included elephant foot prints, and a few faked photos. I knew one of the fakers, Frank. Met him when I was young, he's dead now probably. I think he wanted other people to believe because he did, and got carried away. Was too impatient to wait for evidence so made his own. There was a lot of animosity among monster hunters in the 60s and 70s particularly; each wanting to be the first to prove the beast existed. It broke out into violence sometimes."*

"There still is," put in Emily *"That Hayden Stark puts everyone's backs up. The stuff they say about him on the internet. I am sure half of it can't be true."*

Laura smiled. *"Well things always get exaggerated especially on the internet.* YouTube *has a lot to answer for. There are more UFO and lake monster videos on there than could possibly be seen at one time. Everyone is a film maker suddenly, the weirder the better."*

"So what's your theory, Laura?" Andy looked across at her.

"OK well it's a bit off the wall, but I think Merlin was somehow responsible for the monster or whatever it was people thought they saw, and the story or secret has been passed on via the alchemists, because let's face it Merlin was the original alchemist. I think a researcher has recently found evidence he was a real person who lived in Scotland but his name wasn't Merlin. As we have seen with Willox the Warlock, alchemists or wizards, whatever you want to call them, took on a new name. Plus our friend Willox was said to be found dead with a golden bridle that he used to ride the water kelpie. The only other question I have is when did Merlin die? As according to the information we have all alchemists lived a long time?

If he did *die. Who's to say this tale of them living forever isn't true. Well, if he was immortal and lived all these years under different guises? He has been recorded with different names,"*

Emily stared at the other two.

"That's a bit farfetched, Emily," Andy wasn't into myths and legends.

Laura looked thoughtful, *"Oh if it were true Emily, I hardly dare think it but it crossed my mind, what if he was Fulcanelli? What if he was Flamel? But I dismissed it."*

There was a knock at the door which made them all jump. *"It's John,"* laughed Laura. *"Come in you nearly gave us all a heart attack. We were deep in thought."*

"It will give you a headache," replied John.

"Is there any coffee going?" he continued *"I have news to impart."*

Andy offered to make it as long as they waited until he had done it to tell the news.

Laura asked Emily if there had been any news on Daniel.

"He'll be back after next week. His wife had a rough time, but they have a little girl. He is thrilled to bits and they are trying to think of names at the moment."

"Pam, his wife, was quite old to have a first child, so I am so pleased they are all OK. I think it was an unexpected - but very welcome - surprise." John took a coffee from Andy as he passed with a tray.

"Donald and I are just back from seeing the laird. We had an encounter with something on the loch. Large blip on the sonar and large shape in the water moving pretty fast. Some tourists on the bank saw it too. Henry looked very concerned. He said he knew it wasn't that eel we caught because that was a conger eel from the sea. There have been large eels caught in the loch before, but a different type. Anyway we have left it in his hands to deal with as he sees fit and we just wanted to warn you to be careful around the loch just in case."

"Bloody hell John, you sound so calm about it," Laura was taken aback by John's speech.

"Well there is not a lot I can do about it. Except avoid the thing when I am out in the boat," John smiled wryly.

They all started to discuss what should be done to protect people or find the monster.

"Maybe the loch should be drained so it can be sorted once and for all what is in there."

"I think that would be virtually impossible, Emily because the river feeds into it and the rainwater runs from the hills. It would be like one of those impossible tasks in Greek legends that you can't ever complete. Doomed for ever to empty the loch, doomed," the last few words John said in a gloomy Scottish voice which made them all laugh.

"So what is the next step in your research?" John wanted to change the subject.

"Well if I am right about Merlin, there may be the remains of an altar around the loch, or some sign he was here and practising druid stuff or alchemical stuff. So I thought a search might be in order, of the loch side that is accessible, bearing in mind it would only be the parts of the loch that have always been accessible on foot before the road was here."

Andy and Emily looked at each other, *"We are up for helping."*

"Thanks Scooby Gang."

"Well Donald and I won't be going out on the loch for a couple of days so we will help if you like."

"The more the merrier."

"That's settled then. Let us know when and where you want us."

"I'll text you all tonight when I have looked at the maps."

"Well we better be going and getting back to keep things ticking over for a bit," Andy said unenthusiastically. Laura smiled, *"Thank you, both of you. You've been a great help and tomorrow who knows what we might find."*

They departed somewhat reluctantly, and leaving John to finish off the remaining cakes with his coffee.

"So what did you find in your searches, Laura?"

"I am not sure John. I need to do more. It seems, however highly unlikely it sounds, that Merlin lived for thousands of years, or more likely that someone took on the persona of Merlin, each time he died. Took over the reins so to speak, so it seemed he was always live and kicking."

"The latter explanation sounds perfectly reasonable to me. Now you just have to prove it."

"Hmmm," Laura said. *"Not sure how."*

"Well I better go, see you sooner rather than later I hope," and with that John left her alone to her thoughts.

Laura got out the notes she had made. Merlin as Myrddin was at the battle of Arderydd which was in the 600s AD. That made him about 160 years old. There is something not right here. Laura decided to pay another visit to Henry's library. She had seen some old records there and some books about legends that might be useful. A puzzle indeed she said to herself, and one that I intend to try to solve.

CHAPTER 14
Dark Findings

The men in the dark suits with the American accents conferred in low voices over the meal in the hotel. *"We need to move quickly now; it won't be long before its public knowledge and the media turn up. It's unfortunate there have been the deaths to bring it to the notice of people and the tourists who say they saw something,"* said the shorter of the three men. *"We need to find the altar if we are going to bring him out of hiding."*

The other two looked at each other. *"Where do you suggest we start looking?"* said one.

"I think we need to get a map of the loch as it was before the road and see where it would have been possible to get down to the loch side, and in one of those places we will find the altar. I am sure of it," the first man answered.

One of the men continued: *"Tourists won't be taken seriously and the deaths were written-off as accidental. The other bodies weren't found. Sank to the bottom I should think. Probably have enough time before anyone takes an interest."*

The two other large men with him were identical except one was more intelligent than the other.

"The last of the line," thought Clayton to himself, looking at the dimmer one of the pair. He went on to say, *"So I suggest tomorrow we go and buy some maps or look them up in the library and start looking."*

The other two men nodded and continued to eat their meal.

The Scooby Gang, as Laura called them, (plus John and Donald) assembled on the beach at Dores. They were all dressed in warm clothes; the autumn was starting to give the mornings a distinct chilly feel. *"It appears that this has always been accessible so I thought we would start here."* She allocated them all an area each; on the diagram she had drawn on a rough map. Each area had a section of the shore and the undergrowth. Emily wanted section five as it contained the caravan where the local monster hunter lived. He'd been there for years and Emily would call in to see him and have a coffee. He was always happy to see visitors and she would buy a pottery monster from him to take home for her young nephew. *"Well,"* she said. *"I might as well make it enjoyable."*

Laura grinned and said, *"Now you are looking for a stone with a flattened top. It may be an irregular shape but on the top, probably very worn by now will be a square, with indentations to hold things and possibly some symbols. It will be much worn so you will need to brush-off the top to see it, as it will probably have lichen of some sort on it, or sand."*

"Or both," grinned Donald.

"True," said Laura. *"I have a sketch at the bottom of the map of what the symbols might look like and possibly written on the top of the altar, if it were clearly visible. I took it from a book on Enochian magic*, so should be similar. With five of us, it should be possible to cover the area thoroughly in about two hours. As it was a water beast Merlin was conjuring or contacting, the stone will be near the water."*

"I thought John Dee invented the Enochian magic stuff, long after Merlin was around," John put in after studying the symbols for a while.

"He did but they are based on much older Arabic and Babylonian symbols, so anything you find will be similar. It was just to give you an idea really."

"Looks pretty cool," said Andy, *"Right I am ready for the off."*

"OK people lets go to it and meet back here in two hours and I will buy lunch." They all looked at John.

"Have you won the lottery?" Laura said winking at the others.

"No, just got some tax back so we might as well make use of it."

"Cool," grinned Donald.

They all went off in various directions. Andy and Donald decided to work together and do their two sections as one.

About an hour and forty-five minutes later a rather bedraggled Laura appeared back on the

---

* **Enochian magic** is a system of ceremonial magic based on the evocation and commanding of various spirits. It is based on the 16th-century writings of Dr. John Dee and Edward Kelley, who claimed that their information was delivered to them directly by various angels. Dee's journals contained the Enochian script, and the table of correspondences that goes with it. It claims to embrace secrets contained within the apocryphal *Book of Enoch.*

beach. She had scrambled down a slope and back again to no purpose. She started pulling bits of greenery from her hair and clothes, and then saw John in the shallows on the loch. *"What are you doing John?"*

"I think I may have found your stone."

Laura ran into the water not caring if she got wet. John was bending over a stone that he was cleaning of greenery and was taking photos for her. Laura couldn't believe her eyes. There was a, very faint now, square marked into the stone. Hollows now almost worn flat in the corners and some symbols in the middle.

"My God it's real. I never imagined it would really be here," she gasped.

"Don't have an asthma attack on me!" laughed John *"I've taken photos from every angle, you can load them up to your laptop and study them at leisure."*

"John you are amazing."

"Awww thanks but I already know."

Laura splashed him and the sound of his shouts drew the others to look.

"You've found it Laura!" Emily was pink with excitement and from running down the shingle beach.

"No John found it, but yes it's here. I didn't think that the land will have shifted or even that it would be in the water but John did."

"Well I read some of your notes and to connect with the earth they stood on ground so it made sense to connect with the water you stand in the water. Talking of water I'm thirsty. Let's go get lunch and then we can load these up for you later." John gestured to the camera.

"I think we ought to cover it back up first. It will protect it a bit and we don't really want anyone else to know it's here yet," Laura looked around as she spoke, but there wasn't a sign of any sightseers.

"Wow a discovery, you will be famous Laura."

"You and your being famous Donald," laughed John. *"Come on, food first, talk later."*

"Well technically John discovered it so his name will have to be mentioned," said Laura as they walked along the shore to the local hotel.

They all trooped into the pub.

"Back again?" came from the landlord *"You university lot are becoming regulars."*

They grabbed menus and John ordered drinks after a bit of banter with the landlord. They settled at a table and began to discuss what Laura should do with her discovery. She thought they should keep it quiet until her paper was written, but tell Henry in case it was valuable. *"I agree"* said John, *"Otherwise it could get damaged by people coming to see it and so on."* Laura said she would take the photos to Henry when she had printed them out and leave it up to him to decide.

"After all it probably belongs to him anyway; it's probably his land or something." The others nodded and the subject was changed as the bar person came to take their food orders. They continued to chat about the loch and the eel discovery in case anyone was listening.

CHAPTER 15

Dark Doings

C layton was browsing old maps in the Town library when his phone vibrated. He went outside to answer, having been at the receiving end of the librarian's wrath before about his phone, and he needed to continue to visit the library as a resource. *"Yeah, Clayton."*

"It's me, Ed. You can stop looking at maps now; those scientists have found it for us. You were right to tell me to keep an eye on them."

"Jesus, do they know what it is for?"

"No they think it's something historical, but not what its use is."

"It's definitely the stone?"

"Yes in the water near the beach at Dores (He pronounced it 'Dor-res'), *with the symbols you said and everything."*

"Excellent. I will come and have a look see and we will have to try it out tonight then, in case they bring anyone else along to look."

Clayton shut his phone and smiled that awful smile. This is it guys now or never. You could perform the greatest service ever; he spoke to himself in his head. He went off to get the car thinking of the future. The glorious future there could be.

Laura studied the stone's markings in the photos John had loaded up for her. They looked like a combination of the Enochian magic John Dee had advocated and written about in great detail, and druid symbols. I suppose, she thought to herself, Edward Kelly would know about druid stuff and Merlin's magic and as he could read, used that when he dictated to John Dee. She had a detailed description of an Enochian altar somewhere and she was sure it had these four corners with hollows to hold candles or goblets. She would have to hunt it out. The question was, of course, what had Merlin used the altar for, and was it connected with the appearance of Nessie?

The fact they had found it without much problem suggested it was meant to be used again, or it would have been destroyed.

Was it used in an attempt to create a beast, or to control one already there? Too many questions, she said to herself, I am not sure I want to know all the answers. It worried her that they had found it so easily and that meant that others could too. It may need to be protected by the National Heritage people or something.

The phone rang at that moment. It was Henry inviting her, and also he said would be asking the others, for the wine tasting session tomorrow. *"That will be good, thank you. I can tell you where we've got to with the research. We have had some exciting developments."*

"I will look forward to hearing about it. See you at 2:00pm. Goodbye." And Henry was gone. She wondered about Henry, had he been married or did he have a girlfriend or boyfriend? She resolved to ask Hamish next time she saw him. It was too personal a thing to ask Henry in front of the others. She would like to think he was happy, such a nice man.

The cats reminded her it was time to eat so she went through to the kitchen, and sorted their bowls and then looked to see what she felt like for dinner. There was a supermarket in Inverness that delivered so she always seemed to have something in the freezer.

It was very dark and along the shore very quiet. Whispered voices and the slow procession of three torches along the loch side announced a presence. *"There it is, Clayton."* The torch shone down on the stone. Clayton took the bag from Joey and first cleaned the stone and then set a cloth upon it. His hands were shaking, not from the cold but with excitement. On the cloth he placed four goblets in each corner of a square. He put on a cloak from the bag and instructed the other two men to stand away from him. *"OK guys we may not a get a result first time and it may take a few days but here goes."*

The men stood back respectfully as Clayton raised his hands and started to mutter words not heard for many centuries. They knew Clayton had been training for years for this. After an hour and a half the men were shuffling their feet, when suddenly waves started to lash against the shore almost knocking Clayton off his feet. This momentarily stopped him in his chant and the waves immediately died down. *"Oh frig!"* he said. Then they all turned, they could hear voices. It was some people on their way either to, or from, the local hotel. He quickly gathered up the cloth and goblets and took off the cloak. *"You did say it probably wouldn't work first time,"* Joey reminded him as he passed him the bag. *"Yeah I should have been prepared for that. No worries, we know the invocation works. The loch was starting to boil. Let's go."* The men hurried away in case they were spotted by the people they had heard, or a fisherman on his way to the jetty.

CHAPTER 16
Dark Drink

They all met up at the end of the drive to Henry's house. Autumn felt like it was well upon the Highlands already and they were all in coats and scarves. Laura had bought herself a wind-proof/water-proof/could-be-used-in-the-Arctic-type parka before she came. Having once spent a miserable Easter week in the Highlands with a friend with a car with no heating and house with not very good electric storage heaters, she was well prepared this time. They had to drink whisky to stay warm; she had never been very fond of whisky.

Emily was similarly clad, only in white and pink and the men in the sort of multi-layer ramblers' waterproof s with fleece insides. *"This should be great,"* from Donald. *"But if I drink too much and get silly someone stop me won't you?"*

"Stop you?" laughed Andy. *"No fear, it will be on my 'phone and on You Tube tomorrow."* They all laughed on their way up the drive. Gordon was there as usual and suggested they may want to keep some outer garments on, as the cellar was chilly in places. They all opted to keep on their woollens and scarves, but divest themselves of their coats.

"This way please," Gordon walked ahead and they followed through to the hallway and down a passageway. A heavy oak door stood ajar and Henry appeared behind them.

"Hello hello, is everything ready Gordon?"

"Yes milord, and I have provided torches should the lights fail. One never knows."

"Indeed. Thank you Gordon. Follow me, ladies first, be careful of the stone stairs they are very worn in places."

They all clattered down the stairs behind Henry into the dimly lit room below.

"The cellars go on for some way but I thought we would start here with a whisky to warm us through and then proceed through the rooms, white, rosé, red and then brandy and liqueurs. There are some light refreshments as well...we don't want anyone falling in the loch on the

way home," Henry beamed. He obviously was going to enjoy taking them on this tour.

"For those not fond of whisky...yes there are people, Donald, who don't like it, there is a liqueur made with whisky and cream they might prefer to try." Donald had not realised he had looked astonished at the suggestion someone didn't like whisky.

The women and Andy chose to try the liqueur; the others had a 26-year-old Glenlivet. *"This tastes as if it is cream,"* John smacked his lips as he spoke. *"I will see you get a bottle, John, when you leave, in fact if anyone has a particular favourite, let me know and if supplies allow you can take a bottle away with you."*

"Cool," from Andy.

Laura gazed around the cellar room, it was very solid looking as if it had been carved from the granite hillside, but then she reasoned it probably had. The room was lit by wall lights so they were shadows in corners and between racks of bottles. They were getting their drinks from a tray on an upturned cask. It was as you have expected she thought and wondered if Henry put this on as a show to visitors. There were plates of canapés to help soak up the whisky. Laura tried one and found they were very good. It seemed to be some sort of pastry flavoured with chilli. They drained their glasses.

"Well, if you are all ready we will move on to sushi and white wine."

Emily's face lit up. That was more her sort of thing.

The next cellar was cooler and rows and rows of racks and bottles, but as you got closer you could see little labels with years and types of wine on each row. *"Gordon spent hours sorting out the wine cellar for me, but he enjoyed it. He used to be a wine merchant you know but the eighties recession killed off his business and he trained to be a butler. He is a very good butler I have to say."*

They had a choice of sweet or dry white wine. Laura chose dry, the others sweet. Emily was enjoying Sauternes even though it was too sweet to go with sushi. *"I am not over fond of white wine, Henry, but this is really nice,"* John held up his glass and looked at the very pale liquid. *"It's South American; they are really coming into their own with wine production these days. Thought we have lots of very old wines I like to include some new world ones."* There was a selection of Chablis, Chenin Blanc and Pinot Grigo for them to taste as well.

"I really like Argentinean and Chilean wines." Before Henry could reply to Laura, John cut in: *"You like anything red that comes out of a bottle."*

"That's not true and you know it, there are lots of wines I won't drink, some taste like sheep dip and I can't bear tomato sauce - that comes out of a bottle."

"You in the habit of drinking sheep dip then?" countered John and they laughed as Laura hit

him with her scarf.

"I bow to your superior knowledge of sheep dip Laura, but I agree with what you said," said Henry smiling broadly. Laura noticed the men hadn't touched the sushi. They will regret not eating something later she thought.

After trying a few more sips of different wines and Emily declaring the Sauternes the nicest she had ever tasted, they headed off again. *"A right turn here I think,"* Henry steered them.

"Should we have brought a ball of string?" Andy grinned.

"It's alright, all the walls are marked and Gordon will find us if we get lost. He made a map of the cellars after I spent 20 minutes trying to find my way back once."

There were lights at regular intervals along the walls but Henry had given them all a torch each as well, as the electricity could be unpredictable and the house generator took a while to start in the case of a black out.

"Now Laura, you will like this, a rosé from Pinot Noir grapes," Henry handed her a glass as he spoke. There were grapes, olives and potato snacks to have with the wine. *"This is fizzy,"* said Donald. *"Like champagne."*

"Lots of rosés are fizzy," Laura smiled at him. *"I have no idea why but I am sure Henry or Gordon could tell you."* Henry at that moment was deep in conversation with Emily over the reason for the different colours of the rosé wine, some were very dark and some without almost any colour, and were the palest pink. He was explaining how rosé had gone out of fashion but was now back and that a greater variety was now available.

Andy and John were quaffing it as if it was lemonade. *"They'll be sorry later,"* whispered Laura to Donald. *"It's just as strong as any wine."*

They set off again with Henry in the lead, and Andy and John getting louder and the others giggling at them. Henry seemed not to notice. He turned suddenly, *"The first of the red cellars and we have a choice of two Pinot Noirs, a Shiraz, Cabernet Sauvignon and an old Claret. Laura you must try the Claret."*

There were cheeses and biscuits and oatcakes this time. Laura steered the men towards them. Both herself and Emily had been very careful what they drank and simply tasted some wines and did not drink the whole glass.

"This Claret is nice," said Emily. *"I usually find red wine too sour."*

"It depends on the type of grape and the cost of the wine and how old it is. New wine which is usually cheaper is often quite tart and can catch in your throat," Laura was enjoying the claret too. Henry came over: *"Would you like a bottle of the Pinot Noir to take back with*

you?" Laura replied without hesitation that she would. *"I think John and Andy may have had a bit too much rosé,"* she said nodding at them. Andy was trying to balance an oatcake on his nose. Henry laughed, *"They are fine. Let them enjoy themselves. There is only one more stop after this."*

They set off again and Laura realised they had come around a square and were next to the room they started in. *"We have sherry and brandy, or a liqueur if you prefer, and some bowls of nuts."* Laura decided on a glass of the fine pale sherry Henry had in his hand, Emily went for mint liqueur, and the men the brandy.

"They are going to try and throw and catch peanuts in their mouths aren't they?" Emily sighed.

"They will be lucky, these are almonds," laughed Laura. *"More likely to take an eye out."* They both giggled as Henry tried to restore the men to some sort of order.

"Well everyone, I think coffee in the sitting room is in order." Henry very adroitly steered the men out and up the steps. *"You've done this before,"* said Laura.

"Many times dear lady, many times."

Once they were all seated with coffee and mints, Henry asked Laura how her research was going. *"Well it's all a bit fantastical but..."* and she told him about her theory and about finding the altar stone.

"I am impressed Laura. You have certainly found out more than most people have for centuries."

"Well it may all be just hearsay and the altar stone could be anything, but it will make some evidence for my paper I shall write. Probably along the lines of Merlin did exist in Scotland and may have lived for a very long time. I don't thing academics will wear the live forever thing."

"Well perhaps not, but the stone may help confirm he was here and that should be enough to provoke thoughts on other themes. I would like to see the paper when you have written it."

"Of course and I shall mention your letting me use your library."

"Anytime, dear lady."

"I have one worry though" Laura continued.

"And what is that?" Henry smiled.

"The stone. I think if it turns out to be genuine, it should be protected historically or something."

Henry looked thoughtful. *"Leave that with me my dear. I have contacts and I will find out what the procedure is. Ah, here is Gordon with everyone's choice of bottles and Hamish is bringing the people carrier to get you all home."*

"You are too kind Henry."

"Nonsense it's my pleasure. I get little company these days; we are a bit cut off here and I have enjoyed the banter and the oat cake balancing. Perhaps I should suggest it for the next Highland Games"

Laura laughed.

Hamish insisted on seeing them all to their respective doors, and - had Laura thought about this more clearly - she would have asked why, but presumed it was politeness. As John and Donald alighted, she called to them not to drink the bottles of whisky they had received from Henry or they wouldn't get up in the morning. Donald said something that might have been Sassenach woman; she wasn't sure but just grinned to herself.

CHAPTER 17
Dark Morning

S he slept fitfully that night and put it down to the mixed drinks. And the dark shapes in the loch flitted through her dreams again. Morning dawned in cat-time and the more elderly cat Aristotle appeared on her bed. *"I am sure it is too early, but I am getting up"* in answer to the plaintive cries and the paws poking her eyes. *"I have never known a cat with such pokey paws,"* she grumbled to herself as she staggered to the bathroom in her dressing gown and then down the stairs. Kettle on and cats let out (she kept the cat door shut at night) then fed and watered, she tried to wake herself up and think about the day. She decided she would go back up to the big house library and see if there was anything about the altar stone. Henry had some very old books in there that she hadn't looked at before because at the time they didn't seem relevant, but now they might be. *"I'll ring later at a more reasonable time and see if the library is free to use,"* ruffling the old cat's ears as she spoke. He purred because he was full and getting attention so he didn't care what she was talking about, and anyway it was sure to be something nice about him, after all he was a cat!

She had another thought and after she got dressed she rang Emily. They arranged to meet on Wednesday to go shopping in Inverness as it might be the last chance they had before Daniel returned. He would want to catch up on lost time and Emily may not have the time later. Christmas would be here before they knew it and Laura wanted to get some little gifts to send to friends and family, plus a birthday present for her sister. Then she rang Cragneghil Castle. Gordon informed her on the 'phone that the library would be free all day so she told him she would be up after lunch, but if the library were needed just to ring and let her know, she had no wish to abuse Henry's hospitality. She set about some domestic chores and then settled down to go through her notes.

Donald and John had headaches to contend with, and John suggested they went through sonar readings and sample reports and then write up an interim paper .He said to Donald it would help them find out where they were up to and what was left to do before the end of the study. He had no wish to go out in the boat today, not just because of the hangover, but because of what might be lurking in the loch, and it might be hungry. John wasn't easily shaken but something had been under the boat and shown up on the radar and they weren't the only ones to see it. He had seen the body of the boy, Campbell, and had no wish to end up chewed.

Henry had not mentioned anything about the loch the day before in the wine cellars, and John, thinking Henry didn't want to alarm anyone, had done the same.

Donald made a large pot of black coffee and they sat at the table, the results spread out in front of them, and began to work their way through the pile of papers, making notes as they did so.

There was no sign of anyone when she got to Cragneghil and Gordon appeared after she rang twice. *"I am so sorry Ma'am. I was in the cellars."*

"That's OK Gordon." He took her coat and left her to go to the library herself. She found a book she had seen but not thought relevant on her previous visits. It was about Arthur and the knights. Then she found a small volume on the Templar knights, so she took that down as well. Laura was so absorbed in the old book, she didn't hear Gordon enter the library. Gordon gave a discreet cough and she jumped.

"There is a gentleman arrived who has permission from the laird to use the library. Will he be disturbing you madam?"

"No, no problem Gordon, please tell him to come in." The man immediately appeared as if he knew she would not object.

"Clayton Blome-Grant at your service," said the American-sounding stranger proffering his hand.

"Laura Loomis," she smiled trying to look welcoming. *"Are you looking for anything in particular? I have an idea where you can find some materials if it will help?"*

Gordon withdrew and Clayton replied, *"I am looking at the history of Loch Ness, the monster in particular, and also I am tracing the history of the Grant family."*

"Well you are in luck, I know where a lot of the books are." She led him over to the shelves where Andy had been. "And over there on the right," she pointed to the far side of the room as she spoke, "there is a history of the Fraser-Grants which might be useful to you and two shelves along, you will find stuff about the loch and the monster."

"Been looking into it yourself, the monster that is?" queried Clayton.

"Sort of, as a side line to my main research. I thought the monster might be the questing beast of Sir Pellinore."

"So you are looking at the knights of the round table. I wish you luck with that. There must be lots of information to go through," and with that he turned and started browsing the books.

Laura returned to her place, she wasn't sure why she hadn't told him her real research but she just knew somehow not to trust him. He made her feel creepy. She eyed him over the top of her book, he appeared not to notice, but she felt like he had eyes in the back of his head and knew she was watching him. At 4:00pm, she left a note with Gordon to say thanks again to Henry and the titles of two books she had borrowed, having carefully replaced the other books she had used back on the shelves. She marked the places with pieces of paper to make sure she put them back properly. Clayton was still in the library when she left, head buried in a book. She had called goodbye, but didn't know if he had heard. Had she looked through the window after she left she would have seen him go to the shelves and look at the books she had put back there. As they were all about knights and questing, he was satisfied Laura was no threat. If he had seen the books she had taken, one on Enochian magic and one on alchemists, he may have thought differently.

Laura went to see John and Donald before she went home. They offered her coffee with a shot of whisky, which she gratefully accepted; it seemed colder than ever today. *"So guys, how's it going?"*

"There is a great big thing in the loch, that's about it," said John with a heavy sigh. *"And I am not keen on going back out there at the moment."*

Laura laughed, *"Seriously though how is the rest going?"*

"It's going OK. We have some idea of fish numbers and habitats and food stocks. Enough to nearly write a paper. How about you?"

"Well I am making some headway but not as much as I'd like." Laura then went on to tell them about the creepy guy in the library and John told her he had met him as well. *"Do you think he is the guy that's always watching us with binoculars?"* put in Donald.

"What guy?" both replied at once. Donald told them how many times he had seen someone in a dark suit watching them on the boat, and how there always seemed to be one of them around.

"Maybe the FBI are interested in you John, or the men in black...they think you talk to aliens," Laura laughed and Donald grinned and John pretended to sulk.

"It's still weird," said John.

Laura left shortly afterwards and went home to her cats and resolved to make a fuss of them as they had been neglected of late with all the visits to the big house.

The men in dark suits in question were sitting in a restaurant in Inverness eating Chinese food.

"So she's no threat then Clayton?"

"The big woman? No she's the usual potty historian, like we get back home. Wouldn't know what the stone was for, probably thought it not important."

"Good we can work undisturbed."
"The man is pleased we have done so well. There will be a reward when we go to the base."

"Women? Medals? Gold?" said Joey all ears for once.

"Anything you want Joey, if we succeed," though Clayton privately thought Joey may not last that long. He seemed to be deteriorating lately.

As a waiter appeared they returned to empty tourist chat about the loch and the monster. The waiter looked at them. *"Twins?"* he said to Joey and Ed.

"Yes, identical," replied Ed and ordered some dessert and coffees for them all.

CHAPTER 18

Dark People

Henry sat deep in thought in his study. He jumped when Gordon coughed and handed him Laura's note. *"Has the American left?"*

"Yes milord, do you require anything?"

"No thank you, Gordon. I'll ring later if I need anything."

Gordon melted from the room as silently as he had come in.

"What does the American want?" Henry thought to himself. *"I know he tried to use the stone but why? What use could he have for it, it is fixed to the loch, cannot be used as a weapon anymore. I made sure of that."*

Henry decided to look up Clayton and his background via a contact at the American embassy and went to his computer.

The reply was not long in coming back and contained a warning about Clayton and his allies.

"Oh dear, this is not good, not good at all." Henry asked for more details on specific things that had been mentioned. He asked how Clayton had got into the UK with this background, to be told that as he had no criminal convictions there was nothing could be done to stop him entering the country as a holidaymaker going to Scotland. The FBI had sent on information to MI6 but there was not thought to be a threat. He was not arranging any gatherings or rallies. His informant went on to say that the organisation had lots of money but no one knew where it came from and thought it must be secret donations. *"I have a good idea where it comes from,"* said Henry to himself. He rang for Gordon whilst he waited for the reply. Gordon brought him a whisky and Henry printed off the second reply and showed it to Gordon.

"Oh dear, milord. I take it it's you he wants."

"Yes, or part of me, and he is using the stone to force me to reveal myself."
"I won't allow that to happen. It is my quest and has been my family's quest for many years to look after your safety. I shall call to my fellows for assistance. Do not worry, no one shall

harm you". With that Gordon left the room.

"No they won't harm me seriously," thought Henry to himself, *"but what use they could make of me? I will be a danger to others as long as the American is around."* Henry thought of going away for a while but that would leave things unguarded and split the fellows between him and the loch. *"No, I have to stay and hope that it can be dealt with."* He went to change for dinner.

Gordon had been sending emails before serving dinner. He was worried; to have those people here he shook his head. The replies came back before he left the room; the knights were on their way. He informed Henry after he served dinner that by tomorrow evening the house would be secure and that everywhere Henry went knights would be with him.

"Thank god for Arthur, and for quests, Gordon. Please have a brandy with me." Gordon poured two brandies and sat where Henry indicated.

"Until tomorrow night you should stay in the house milord. Just to be sure. Though I expect they will try each night to drag you out to the loch."

"Yes, you are right Gordon, thank you. To us" he said, raising his glass and Gordon repeated the words and action.

As the night grew dark and a mist started to settle on the hills around the loch, Clayton and his cohorts once again went down to the stone. Clayton put on his ceremonial robes and set up the altar. This time he added a wax tablet carved with symbols. He was wearing gumboots and a rope from his waist with two ends held by the two men on shore. He was determined not be taken by surprise this time and hold his feet. Plus, if he fell into the loch there was no telling what would happen. Being dead was not part of his plan. He started chanting. The mist seemed to grow and come down to the water. The water started to agitate and waves, small at first but then getting larger, crashied to the shore. *"It's working,"* whispered Joey grinning *"Shush, you will distract him,"* from Ed. Something was starting to happen in the loch, something was rising through the water, dark and large and a whirlpool was forming.

Henry tossed and turned in his bed, the sweat stood out on his brow. He suddenly shot up and yelled, *"No!"* and started to mutter in an old archaic tongue. Gordon came running into the room turning on the lights. He shouted to the housekeeper who had been awoken by his foot-steps running past her door to: *"Bring brandy, the laird is having a funny turn"*.

With previous lairds in the area having had funny turns, including wearing women's clothes and one bicycling around the house nude, she didn't argue and ran down to the dining room to fetch it. She had heard many a queer tale from fellow housekeepers in other parts of the Glen and hoped her laird wasn't going funny in the head. Her slippers made loud slapping noises as she raced across the tiled hallway and grabbed a decanter from the side table in the dining room. She arrived breathless and panting, and handed it to Gordon and then remembered she hadn't brought a glass. There was always a decanter of water and a glass by the bedside so she grabbed that and handed Gordon that as well.

At the loch the water was trying to keep moving but another whirlpool was forming and suddenly the whirlpool sucked the water back and all went quiet again on the loch. Silence and the darkness once again descended and not a ripple reached the shore. Clayton laughed out loud, *"He knows we are here, he won't be able to stop me tomorrow night and he will have to come down to the loch to control the beast."*

The men on the bank grinned at each other as Clayton returned and stowed the items and his cloak in the bag. They set off back to the car.

Gordon forced brandy down Henry's throat, making him cough.

"I will be fine now, just a nightmare, I will be fine" Henry repeated, seeing Mary's scared face.

Gordon waved the hovering housekeeper away.

"Go back to bed, Mary. It's OK now, panic over, and you have your hands full preparing for guests tomorrow."

She nodded. *"If you are sure you do not need me to ring Dr McBride,"* Gordon shook his head and she departed back to bed with a sigh. She would have felt better if he had let her ring for the doctor.

"This was bad Gordon, a bad dream," Henry wiped his brow as he spoke. *"The beast was loose. The Nazis were controlling it."*

"The matter will be dealt with tomorrow milord. Don't worry about that."

Henry nodded and lay back exhausted. After seeing Henry was calmed and didn't need anything, Gordon returned the brandy to the dining room and then went to his own room. He knew they would have to act before tomorrow night or Henry would go to the loch to protect others.

In the early hours of the morning the thwack thwack sound of a helicopter slowing to land was heard. No one in the village took any notice, just turned over and went back to sleep. Police helicopter, oil workers returning home, pleasure seekers; the village was used to them passing over. It landed in a field behind the big house and Gordon went to meet it. Several bags were thrown out of the machine, then seven men descended from its bowels, and immediately after, it took off again.

"Hello Gordon, old man .Things tricky eh?" one cheerfully called. Gordon nodded.

"Yes, you came in the nick of time. We have to move fast before it gets light."

The men nodded, and one answered, *"Show us the way, and it will be done."* He heaved a large bag of something heavy that clinked together onto his shoulder as he spoke. Various other bags were strewn on the ground.

Gordon handed him a piece of paper. *"I'll see to the rest of your things, go and do your work."* Gordon then started to pile the bags onto a trolley behind him and the men silently set forth.

CHAPTER 19
Dark Delights

Daniel was due to return the following day, so Laura and Emily made the most of their shopping trip. Inverness had a selection of a modern shopping centre, and an indoor Victorian market where Laura got her hair cut in a tiny shop with three barber's chairs, and the usual tourist type shops selling tartan and jewellery etc. John had Donald drop them off on his way to collect the new camera and optic cable from Aberdeen, and they arranged to meet him to get a lift back.

They bought Donald some chocolate and John a whisky cake to say thanks. It didn't cost that much on the bus, but the convenience meant they could get some food shopping as well. Inverness had most of the big names of stores found in other cities. Laura took Emily to *Monsoon* to look at earrings and hats. After some trying on of styles and giggling, Emily found a suitable one; Fair Isle pattern with ear flaps for on the boat, to keep out the cold.

"It looks Tibetan," Laura said. *"And very cute".*

Laura bought some long earrings, she loved earrings but only the long dangly sort. Then they spotted the rail of ankle length dresses. The usual discussion over the long dresses occurred along the lines of , *"It's lovely but would I ever wear it?"* that must go on all over the world when women shop and then the friend will say, *"Go on treat yourself, live for today. If you come back and it's sold, you'll regret not buying it."* As a result Emily's bank account was lighter but she had a wonderful dress for formal dinners back at college. After exhausting the shopping centre, they had usual the coffee and muffin in the American style coffee shop and then went to the station where Donald would pick them up.

Emily said how much she'd enjoyed the shopping with Laura as neither of them were big on shopping, but they had frequent stops and only browsed when they knew they wanted something. The hairdressers where you could wait as in a barber's shop, and have your hair cut intrigued Emily. She had never seen it before. *"Neither have I,"* laughed Laura. *"But I remembered it from last time I was here. It's great idea. I think you would have to book if you wanted anything other than a straight cut and blow dry done."*

"Normally you have to book well in advance for hairdressers. I don't often..." Emily started

to say and then, *"Here's Donald."*

Much gentle teasing about the size and amount of their shopping bags from Donald kept them all laughing until they got back. Laura presented him with his chocolate and the cake for John and he went off grinning.

Emily came in with Laura for a cup of tea and they sorted out their purchases.

"I hope we get chance to go again Laura, I have enjoyed your company."

"Me too," said Laura. Emily, Laura discovered, had more about her than the frail appearance and girly pink look she paraded to everyone. She was quite a tough young woman on the inside, and Laura thought of her as a friend now.

After Emily left and the cats were placated with some goodies from the Marks and Spencer's food hall, Laura decided to go for a walk down to the shore to look at the stone again, maybe take a rubbing if it wasn't too wet. The loch was calm and she waded out in the couple of inches of water to the stone. Then suddenly she almost lost her footing and fell in. There was a great hole where the stone should be. She walked back and checked it was the right place, puzzled and thinking that she had misjudged the distance. The stone had definitely gone. *"Why on earth would anyone pinch the stone?"* she said to herself. *"It was heavy and of no use to anyone. Unless someone thought it was worth something or took it for their garden."* She wasn't sure what to do. Should she inform the police? She rang John on her mobile. He was as incredulous as she was. He suggested she took some of the photos of the stone to Henry and told him about its disappearance. *"I'll do that tomorrow. It's getting dark and he may be busy. Thanks John."*

"Thanks for the cake by the way, much appreciated."

"You are welcome," Laura smiled as she put the phone down. Academics everywhere liked free food and free drinks even more. It was a standing joke at the university if you opened a bottle, a line would form outside your door before you put the cork in the bin. She used to get people to come to lunchtime seminars by putting on sandwiches, it always worked. She made her way home puzzling over who would take the stone.

The men in suits arrived at the loch many hours later, when it was dark and quiet and they would not be disturbed. Clayton splashed his way to the stone this time in waders and then suddenly disappeared giving out a yell. The other two men rushed to him as he struggled, dripping, to his feet. The water in his waders made it difficult for him to regain his balance. *"Shine the torch, shine the torch,"* he snarled. They all followed the torches beam to a hole and a swirling of water where the hole had been. Clayton let out a yell of anger, almost inhuman in sound.

"They have taken the stone, the bastard has beaten us. This isn't the end," shaking his fist in the air he trudged back squelching to the car. The other two men looked at each other, grinned, and then, stony faced again, followed him.

CHAPTER 20

Dark Morning

The next morning Daniel had the students up early and got the boat ready. They had drunk a glass of champagne the night before to wet the baby's head. Flora Danielle Woolf, 7lbs 5ozs (about 3.4 kilograms to the rest of us) in old money, as Daniel put it. Mother and baby were now doing well and at home with maternity nurse and grandmothers in attendance, so Daniel had returned. He said he was reluctant to do so, having waited for this for so long. Fatherhood and his project being sponsored at the same time had rather overwhelmed him and his wife had made the decision he should return to Loch Ness.

They set off in fine spirits to do some soundings in the first turn of the loch. Emily was singing softly to herself and Andy was setting up the machinery. Daniel was at the helm of the boat. The loch seemed quite calm and despite the approaching winter chill in the air, it was a clear and pleasant morning. The readings seemed to indicate nothing abnormal on the first run and they started the second. The run seemed to be going well when, *"There must be some activity near that side of the loch,"* shouted Andy above the noise of the boat and the water, and he pointed to the left. Daniel turned the boat and they headed for the spot. *"It seems to have gone quiet again,"* said Andy puzzled. Daniel came over to see. Suddenly the boat tipped from under them. Daniel grabbed Andy and the side of the boat, *"Hang on everyone! Hang on!"* he yelled. The boat righted itself just as suddenly.

"Bloody hell must be some activity has blown up a water sprout or something," Daniel looked up as he spoke. *"Where's Emily?"*

They both rushed to where Emily had been. There was no sign of her. *"She must have fallen over board,"* Andy's voice quivered as he spoke.

"Did she have her life jacket, please God man say yes?" Daniel's eyes looked frantically at Andy and then he realised he was holding him by the arms, so let go quickly. Andy looked shocked and then went silent for a minute.

"Yes she did," then with more conviction. *"Yes she did,"* he said realising that meant she would float back up. They scanned the water around them. *"There she is. I can see the orange jacket. She's not moving!"*

Daniel swung the boat around, *"Grab her. Use the boat hook . Get her back on board."*

Andy was able to grab her with his hands and struggling dragged her on board, she was still and white.

"I think she's dead," he sobbed. Daniel felt for a pulse.

"No, she's still with us. It'll be the cold water and shock. Try to keep her warm, I'll radio ahead." Andy ran for blankets to wrap her up. They always had space blankets, the silver ones, on board for emergencies.

"This is Mary Scott 2 *calling the coast guard, emergency.* Mary Scott 2 *calling the coast guard emergency. Over."* The answer came back almost immediately.

"Go ahead Mary Scott 2. *What is the emergency? Over."*

"Woman overboard. We got her back on the boat, but she's hardly breathing. I think she's in shock. Over."

"Give your location Mary Scott 2 *over."*

Daniel gave the bearings as near as he could.

A few minutes later the reply came back as Daniel anxiously waited. It seemed like half an hour to him.

"Emergency services notified, and on their way to Temple Pier. Can you make it there? Over."

"On our way thanks. Over."

Daniel spun the boat around and headed for the pier full-pelt, hoping no one would get in the way so he had to slow down. Temple Pier was a private pier, but the nearest and Daniel presumed they had permission to use it in an emergency. Emily's pulse had been very thready. A colleague had lost a student in caves once and the body had been recovered days later, he never got over it, and Daniel did not want that to happen here.

The ambulance was waiting when they got to the jetty, the paramedics' efficient and re-assuring, as they lowered Emily from the boat to a trolley stretcher.

"She's still with us, she'll be OK."

As they worked on her, Emily started to cough and then she opened her eyes and started to scream and wouldn't stop. The paramedic stepped back startled for a moment and then gave her a mild sedative into the drip his partner had set up in Emily's arm.

"What's wrong with her?" gasped Daniel.

"It's just shock ye ken. We'll take her to Inverness. She'll be OK, it's just the shock."

Andy rang Laura when they were on their way in Daniel's car trying to follow the ambulance. She ran to John and Donald, and luckily they were still in the house. John snapped into action and gave Donald the car keys.

"Take Laura. Tell Daniel I'll go down and see to the boat, and bring it back. Ring me if anything happens or anyone needs anything."

"Thank you, John." John squeezed Laura's hand seeing her worried face.

"She'll be fine."

Laura nodded and ran out to the car where Donald had already got the engine started.

The journey to the hospital seemed to take forever and they got lost twice on the way. *"Bloody one way system, and stupid signs,"* muttered Donald. At last they made it and found their way to the reception.

"A student, Emily Coutts, just been brought in, fell in the loch. Where is she please?"

"Are you a relative?"

"No. I am....." Laura paused for a moment. *"I am her supervisor, here is my university identification badge."* She flashed her old staff badge at the woman, hoping she wouldn't realise it was a different university. Luckily it was still in the back of her purse, she had forgotten to remove it.

"Ward 3, follow the signs. You won't be able to see her yet though."

"Thank you." Laura grabbed Donald and ran up the corridor before she questioned them further or queried who Donald was.

Daniel and Andy where pacing the corridor outside a side room as they got there.

"Any news?" Laura looked at the strained faces.

"Not yet," Andy just shook his head.

"Come on let's sit down, there's some seats here." She lead them to some plastic chairs.

"Donald, take this," handing some money over *"and get us all some coffee. We passed a machine on the way here."* Donald nodded. He disappeared and returned about 15 minutes later.

They all sat in the corridor drinking something that once might have been called coffee from plastic cups with paper handles.

"They say when someone is born someone has to die, one replaces the other, you don't think ..." Daniel let the words trail off into thin air.

"Don't be silly," said Laura. *"She's not dead by a long chalk."*

The nurse came out and the sea of faces turned to her, *"You can go in now but not too long. She had swallowed a lot of water and had a bad shock."*

They all trooped in behind Daniel. Emily was sitting up in bed, an oxygen cannula attached to her nose. She looked more pale and ethereal than ever. She held out her hands to them. *"I thought I'd never see you all again,"* in a whisper.

Laura grabbed one hand, Andy the other. *"Thank God you are OK,"* from Daniel.

"I thought you were an atheist?" grinned Laura. Daniel glared at her and Emily smiled. *"That's better,"* Laura winked at her.

They stayed and chatted for a few minutes until the nurse pointedly looked through the door.

"We have to go, I'll bring you some things tomorrow. If you think of anything else get them to ring me," Laura gave Emily's hand another squeeze. As they were leaving, Emily called Laura back. *"Girl stuff I expect,"* Daniel muttered to Andy and Donald. *"Lets wait outside"*.

Emily waited until they had left the room. *"I saw something, Laura, in the water. A great big eye looked at me and I was knocked off the boat by a tail of a large beast. I saw it Laura, I saw the monster."*

"You might have been concussed. Are you sure?"

"I am sure. That is why I was so shocked. It was so enormous and I was so scared I must have fainted."

"OK, well, we'll keep this to ourselves for now. When you get out of here, we will talk about it. In the meantime, write it down and draw a picture of what you can remember and then forget about it until you get out of here. Otherwise you won't get better."

"OK," Emily smiled, and Laura left before the nurse came back and threw her out.

With everything that had happened, Laura had forgotten about the stone until the next day. She decided she would go and see Henry after she'd been to the hospital with Emily's things. Emily's face lit up when she saw her. The oxygen cannula had been removed and she had some colour in her face. *"I can leave tomorrow if I am OK."*

"That's good. Do you want to stay with me for a couple of days until you feel stronger?"

"Oh, that would be nice. Thank you. I don't want my parents trying to get me to go home."

"Well you are in with all men aren't you, and a bit of home comforts will do you good. They will try to look after you, the blokes, but they tend to stress you out more by saying and doing the wrong things."

Emily giggled, *"Yes you are right about that. Here, I wrote everything down and drew a sort of picture. Will you take it and keep it safe?"*

"Of course I will." Laura then told her about the stone going missing to distract her from her worries. *"Any ideas?"*

"I will think about it whilst I'm stuck here. You never know I may come up with something. I remember a detective story where he solved the crime from his hospital bed."

"Go girl," said Laura grinning.

By the time Laura left, Emily was smiling again and looking less frail.

CHAPTER 20
Dark Deeds

After returning to the cottage, she printed off a couple of photos of the stone and set off to see Henry. If he wasn't in she would leave a note with Gordon, and she would go do some more research in the library. Henry was at home according to Gordon, when she knocked on the big wooden door, and would be happy to see her. Henry welcomed her in the sitting room.

"Dear lady, what can I do for you? And tell me is Emily recovering. I heard she fell into the loch. Please take a seat."

"Yes, she's fine now. Should be out tomorrow. It was mainly shock. I wanted to show you this," Laura handed him the photos and then went onto tell him about finding the stone and it's disappearance.

"It could be tourists or some sort of relic hunter who will sell it. All I know is, it's not there now and I have no proof."

Henry smiled. *"Come with me."* She followed him across the hall to the library bemused. In the library there was a door concealed as a book shelf. It had been locked when Laura was there last. Henry opened it and there, in a sort of priest's hole, was the stone. *"But how?"* she gasped. *"Sit down Laura; I have some things to tell you."*

"You may remember the American gentleman who you met in the library."

She nodded.

"Well the man and his compatriots are not good people. He is the son of Hans Blome, an infamous Nazi who was taken by the Americans after the war under Operation Paperclip to work for them on germ warfare. He had previously been a doctor in concentration camps, notoriously so. However, the Mossad, the Israeli secret service, kidnapped him and he spent his remaining years in prison in France after standing trial. His son, brought up in America, continued his work. He must have found out about the stone, he is a very intelligent man, and thinking it valuable was trying to steal it, so I had it removed and brought here. However, you must tell

no one except your fellow academics and they will have to keep quiet too, until the man has left. You can come and study it anytime; indeed, you are very welcome to. As laird I see it as part of one of my duties to care for the loch and it's antiquities. The stone will be placed in a museum at some later date where it can be guarded, but for now it is safe here."

"I am so glad. I had this horrible fear someone had taken it for their garden or something, a tourist, and it would end up as a bird bath."

Henry laughed. Laura looked thoughtful, "Come to think of it, Donald said the man had been watching us through binoculars at various times. He must have seen us when we found it."

Henry inclined his head, "I have no doubt and then he came to the library to look for information. Found it could be valuable and vowed to take it back to the USA with him. Now I have some business acquaintances staying. Would you like to stay and have tea with us? I am sure they will be delighted to meet you. After all, you found the stone."

Laura said she would, and Henry took her through to the sitting room. "There will be one more for tea, Gordon."

"Very good milord."

"Just before we go into tea, Henry, there's something else." She told him about Emily and what she said she had seen, and the drawing she had made. The drawing looked like a dragon with a long body. It reminded Laura of a story of The Lambton Worm, it had looked like that in the illustration.

"What do you think Laura?"

"Well she could have been concussed, but I am inclined to believe she saw something that frightened her."

"I think you may be right. There is something in the loch causing problems. If it is a practical joker, they will be severely dealt with, and if it is a large fish or an enormous eel, it will be captured or disposed of. You have my word on that. Come let's go into tea. I have some friends I'd like you to meet."

Laura followed him into the drawing room where tea was being served. It was high tea, with small dainty sandwiches, scones, biscuits, small iced cakes and a large fruit cake. The cakes and scones were on tiered cake stands and the sandwiches served on the old-fashioned square shaped plates with fancy edges that she remembered from her childhood. A real old-fashioned tea she said to herself.

"Gentlemen," said Henry, and the buzz of conversation stopped. "I would like you to meet Laura Loomis, the finder of the stone that resides in the library."
Seven men turned to smile at her.

"Let me take you around and introduce you my dear."

"These are all business partners of mine. We have a shared interest in old things. Rafe here is a dermatologist"

Laura shook hands with a tall blonde man, with blue eyes and a smile that lit up his face, as if the sun shone on it.

"A pleasure," he said.

"Zaph here is a jeweller." Laura turned to shake hands again with a small dark man with quick brown eyes. He shook Laura's hand firmly though and commented on her earrings. *"An admirer of dangly earrings I see. I must show you some of my designs some time."*

"I'd like that very much" said Laura.

"Here we have Cam. Cam is a professional soldier."

Cam was tall and strong, and Laura could see the bulge of his muscles through his shirt. The hand that shook hers was not rough though, but quite gentle.

"This is Zak, our legal person."

Zak was stocky and square looking and shook her hand with a grin, *"At your service."*

Laura smiled back and then was introduced again, *"This is Hani. Hani is a psychologist. You and he will have a lot in common."*

"I sometimes teach psychology at the university," she explained as she shook his hand, a large untidy looking man with a typical air of academia. *"Cool,"* he said. *"I'd be no good at teaching, too many questions at once, you are a brave woman."* Laura laughed.

"Ah this is Mike. Mike is a chemist and does a lot of research."

Laura turned to shake hands with Mike, who gave her a lop sided grin and said, *"Nice to meet you."*

"And last, but not least Gabe, who is an astronomer."

Gabe turned out to be tall and gangly, and very serious looking. As Laura shook his hand, Henry continued. *"These are my Angels of the Talisman or my knights, whatever you wish to call them, and they look after my interests. Now then Laura let's get you some tea."*

Henry led her to the table and got her a cup and saucer, *"How do you like your tea? We have Earl Grey or Indian."*

Earl Grey please, just black."

"Good for you, I can never understand why people put milk and sugar in, spoils the taste."

Hani appeared at her elbow, *"Come and get some sandwiches and cake, Laura, and tell me about what you teach."*

He led her to the other table and handed her a plate. It was china with a pattern of small roses. She loved old china. Hani offered her the sandwich plate and she took a couple of cucumber sandwiches, the others were probably anchovy or smoked salmon, she remembered these old-fashioned high teas. He then offered the cake plates and she took a piece of what looked excellent fruit cake. *"Come let's sit by the window."* He had several sandwiches on his plate and two iced cakes. As soon as they went to sit down the others filled up their plates. *"Don't be shy gentlemen,"* said Henry. *"There is plenty more if you require it."*

Between mouthfuls, Laura told Hani about her teaching and about her research, and he told her about his practice in New York and how he was paid lots of money to, as he put it, listen to people. He was good company and they were joined by Gabe, who told her about his work and the stuff he had done for NASA and the time he spent at Jodrell Bank.

It was 5:00pm before Laura realised it and getting quite dark, and she went over to Henry. *"I'm afraid I have to get back. I have two hungry cats at home and am expecting Emily to stay, so have the bedroom to get ready."*

"No problem my dear, it was nice to have some female company among all the men. Hamish will take you back." As she started to protest he put up his hand , *"It's on his way home, so we will hear no more about it,"* and then he smiled. Laura smiled back and said, *"Thank you."*

The men called their goodbyes as she left the room and went into the hallway.

Gordon fetched her outdoor things and she went out into the night and got into Hamish's Landrover, which was parked outside the door. *"You ready lassie?"*

"Yes thanks, Hamish." With a jerk, they set off back to the village.

Hamish enquired about Emily and asked Laura to pass on his best wishes. Then he told her about people on the loch who got into difficulties, because they didn't realise it wasn't just a calm lake but stormy, almost tidal, water. She was back outside the cottage before she knew it and thanking Hamish for the lift. The cats set up their crying as soon as she opened the door so she set about seeing to them before going to make up the bed in the spare bedroom, and put out clean towels and anything else she thought Emily might need.

CHAPTER 21
Dark Dealings

C layton sat nursing his whisky deep in thought. Ed sat down beside him, while Joey remained standing. *"Joey had something he wants to ask you."*

"Go ahead Joey. I am open to all suggestions at the moment."

"If you could make another stone would it work?"

"Well it wouldn't be as powerful but it would do the job of bringing him here. Why?"

"What would you need to make a new stone?"

"Measurements, photos everything would have to be exact or it could go badly wrong."

"That big woman, the history one, she's got photos and measurements."

"What?" Clayton's head shot up. *"How do you know? Are you sure?"*

"When Ed went to tell you they found the stone, I was watching them and listening. The guy took photos and she measured, and the guy said he would load the photos on her laptop."

"Joey you are a genius. I don't care if you are the last of the line, you are a genius," Clayton slapped him on the back and sent Ed for more drinks.

"Now my friend, how do we get hold of this stuff?"

"The lady is at the shop. I saw her go. The house is empty," Joey grinned as he spoke, he liked to feel useful.

"Then we must be swift before she returns." Ed came back to the table, drinks in hand, and they downed their whiskies in one. *"You drive, Ed. I don't want to be stopped by the police, you have only had one."*

John and Donald stood with Daniel examining Daniel's boat. *"Same marks you had John. There must be something getting thrown up by seismic activity in the loch."*

"A bit worrying though .That's two of us suffered damage to equipment and one student hurt" Daniel looked thoughtful. *"You don't think it's sabotage do you?"*

"But why, Daniel? Who would want to sabotage our studies? It's not world shattering stuff." Donald said, *"I was reading about the history of the monster hunters, and they used to sabotage each other's stuff sometimes and I think a student got fire bombed."*

John looked at them both, *"You don't think Hayden Stark?"*

"No, the man is a self important publicity seeking unqualified jackass out to make money. He's not nasty though and it's in his interests to have people study the loch."

"You like him then," laughed John.

Daniel grinned, *"You know me and people who claim to be experts. When you have spent years studying and working on short-term university contracts to get recognition, and then some twit who spent a few years living here calls themselves an expert. Humpf."*

"Well let's take her for a run and see if the damage is just surface stuff. I will follow in our boat. Donald can ride shotgun with you. I take it Andy is at the hospital."

Daniel nodded, *"Yes he's visiting Emily, and if she is OK, will take her to Laura's this evening."*

"She's a good sort, Laura. Emily will be better there for a few days until she is fully recovered." John went to his boat as Donald cast off for Daniel.

The run went without incident. Laura was on the jetty on her way back from the shop and stopped to see what was happening.

"Everything OK?"

"Everything is fine thanks Laura. And thanks for taking Emily in. It helped reassure her parents. I had to ring them and tell them she had fallen in the loch." Daniel sighed which indicated to Laura it had not been an easy phone call. She patted him on the shoulder.

"Well, daddy, you will know how that feels now, to worry about your child."

"I have some photos, would you like to see them?"

"I would love to see them I thought you'd never ask."

She cooed over the photos whilst John tied up his boat. Flora was a dainty little thing with dark hair and eyes.

"Ah women and babies. You get no work done if someone brings a new baby in to visit the department." Laura just laughed at John and called him a misery guts. *"Actually why don't you all come over tomorrow evening for a bite to eat, bring a bottle and we can entertain Emily, if she is out of hospital, cheer her up."*

"That's a good idea. She might feel more like company by then."

Daniel nodded, *"Thanks Laura. Do you want me to bring anything besides a bottle?"*

"Not really, unless you want crisps or after eight mints. I will just do a buffet, jacket potatoes and stuff. Won't take much doing. See you all about 7ish then tomorrow?"

Lots of yeses and nods. She decided she would tell them about her visit to Henry's tomorrow.

As soon as she entered the cottage, she knew something was wrong. The elderly cat was agitated and Buzbi was nowhere to be seen.

"What is it Aristotle? What has upset you?"

Nothing seemed out of place. She hadn't been burgled; the laptop was where she left it. She flipped it open, no everything seemed fine. She decided another cat must have been in the house through the cat door, she left it open during the day. Buzbi appeared from upstairs where he had been hiding under a bed. *"For a big cat you are a terrible coward Buz,"* she fussed them both and gave them treats.

Had she looked out she might have seen Ed climb over the fence and go to the back road where a car was waiting. He had a pen drive in his hand as he sidled into the car he said, *"Got it copied, the lot. No one will ever know I was there. Damn cat scratched me though."* His hand was pouring with blood as he bandaged it with his handkerchief.

"Serves you right, you shouldn't have gone near it," laughed Clayton.

"It appeared from nowhere and seemed friendly enough, but as soon as I tried to leave it went for me," Ed nursed his hand grumbling. The car drove off with Clayton clutching his prize.

Aristotle prided himself on guarding the house. He once chased an electricity meter reader up the garden path because he had come to read the meter without knocking on the door. Ed would bear that scratch for a long time, Aristotle made sure of that, coming in his house touching his owner's things. The scratch was very deep, and long, and would take a few days to heal. He washed himself feeling he had well deserved his treat Laura had given him on her return.

Emily had settled in quickly and had slept well the night before, after her arrival from the hospital so was more than happy to hear the others were coming over. She sat at the kitchen table helping

Laura cut up salad and laughing at the cats' antics. Buzbi was chasing a piece of cucumber around the floor and having a great time, whilst Aristotle ate his with great relish.

"OK, that should be enough I think, Emily. We have jacket potatoes, sausages, salad, chicken legs and two types of cheese for the potatoes for veggies. I've made two apple crumbles and have two cartons of cream, and a squirty can in reserve."

"I bet Donald and John can eat it all by themselves," grinned Emily.

Laura laughed pleased to see her more lively.

"Why does Aristotle like salad? It seems unusual in a cat."

"He was a stray for a while before I got him and probably ate out of bins and as he was in a town centre probably the remains of burgers with the lettuce and stuff in them. He likes pizza too, and sausage rolls and adores pork pies. Funny old cat aren't you?" she said, tickling his ears. Buzbi skidded to halt by the table leg and Emily laughed and tickled his chin.

"They are lovely cats Laura. I can see why you are so fond of them."

By the time Daniel and Andy arrived, the table was full of food and plates and cutlery, ready for everyone to help themselves. John and Donald, who had arrived early, were champing at the bit, Laura refusing to let them start until everyone had arrived.

"Hi, I've brought After Eight mints and Pringles," said Daniel waving a bottle in the air as well. Laura took the bag from him, handed him a corkscrew and told them all to help themselves.

Emily was ushered forward first and Andy insisted on helping her and sitting her down with her dinner and a glass of wine before he got his own. When they were all sitting down and eating, John insisted Laura tell them her name theory.

"Laura has some wonderful and weird theories, you must hear them."

"Only if no one takes offence, but I think some people, like some people are the same star signs and are supposedly alike, I think some people's names reflect their personality, from what I have observed of certain people with the same name. So whether having a certain name makes you behave a certain way as a reaction to the name I don't know."

"Give them some examples Laura," grinned John.

"You are asking for trouble, but here goes. Johns never grow up," John took a mock bow and grinned. Laura ignored him and continued, *"Ians are philanderers, Stuarts are lively fun people when young (I don't know any older ones), Peters tend to be solid but lazy and a bit opinionated but a loyal friend, Adrians are full of their own importance and usually a bit useless, certainly should never be left in charge of anything, Daniels are also a bit full of themselves and a bit*

prone to having more than one woman, Kierans are immature and exaggerate, the classic buffoon. Toms are boring and stolid, the sort of man that could talk a glass eye to sleep." Giggles from Emily at this. *"Women called Elly or Eleanor tend to be a bit manipulative, and cover their mistakes by blaming other people, Jills with a J are usually trying to be something they are not, pretending to be a better class of person than they are and tend to be a bit useless work wise, full of ideas but can't carry them out and take the credit for the ideas of others, not good at managing people, power goes to their heads. Annes tend to be dependable but easily upset, Pamelas are moody, Emilys tend to appear frail but are quite strong underneath, Sallys tend to be feckless, Jans and Jens tend to be good workers and good at handling things that happen and cheerful in the face of adversity, Kates tend to be fun loving but good workers, Traceys are self centred, Sharons tend to get top jobs but once there turn out to be bad managers and sometimes bullies. That will do I think,"* Laura looked waiting for the protests.

"Do you know I think you may have something there, maybe you should write a paper on how people react to their names and if they changed their name would it change their personality?" Daniel seemed to have not minded what she said about his name.

"Well maybe my next project" smiled Laura.

"Tell them the ginger one," said John laughing.

"No, oh well alright then," Laura was laughing herself at this point.

"OK I used to work with a psychiatrist who had some interesting theories, one of which was one I always found to be true. She said never trust people with light eyelashes especially if they are ginger. I have found that right on more than one occasion. Her name theory was that lower class people called their children strange names like the names of pop stars or places because they thought they wouldn't get anywhere in life, so the name would get them noticed. That bit I don't know about, but she had more experience of life than me; I was only in my twenties then."

Daniel laughed *"Laura, you gingeriest, you."*

"Possibly, but I also have a thing against short people. Not very small people but men especially who are short. Knee biters...they will bite your knees in a fight because they can't reach to hit you."

This caused more hilarity especially when she added, *"Small people send shivers down my spine. I am talking about the 4 feet to 5 feet type here."*

"Now you are having us on. The secretary you had was only small and you thought the world of her," John put in.

"Ah well she was the exception to the rule...remember there's always one."

"Always one what?" said Andy puzzled.

"In any study you do with people, I have come to the conclusion there is always one that doesn't do what you expect or just behaves oddly. I keep meaning to write a paper on the rule 'there's always one'."

More laughter especially when John put in, *"Yes, but Laura, you are usually the one, who does something different from what everyone expects."*

The topic changed to the damaged boats and everyone speculated on what was causing it. Emily said nothing and then she mentioned the missing stone to change the subject.

"I have the answer to that. Henry has it locked away for safe keeping." Laura then went on to tell them about her visit and being invited to tea with Henry and his business colleagues. *"If I can remember them all correctly there was Rafe a dermatologist, Zaph a jeweller, Zak head of a law firm, Cam a soldier, a commander I think, Hani a psychologist, Mike a chemist and Gabe an astronomer. They were all different ages but fit looking and quite sort of charismatic. They apparently all have an interest with Henry in some sort of business, and called themselves the Angels of the Talisman. They were the ones who got the stone out and brought it up for Henry to keep safe."*

"Why did it need to be kept safe?" Donald looked puzzled and Laura told them about Clayton. *"I knew he was watching the boat,"* Donald then looked at John who sighed and nodded.

"I won't hear the last of this will I?" Donald grinned.

Laura went to get the apple crumbles from the kitchen and Andy came to help her carry things. Donald's face lit up when he saw the dishes.

"Pudding too. You are an angel Laura never mind Henry's friends being angels."

Something struck a chord with Emily and later when the others had left in high spirits she asked if she could look something up on the internet whilst Laura was tidying up. Laura had refused to let her help saying: *"You are a guest this visit so not expected to help. If you come again to stay with me you are a friend and can help if you wish. Saying that I have a friend who has stayed with me many times who never lifts a finger."* She laughed and left Emily with the laptop.

When Laura came back Emily called her over *"Look at this."*

The page had the title the Talisman of the Angels. There was a diagram of a circle of metal with a six pointed star and on it the names of angels and planets. The motto said *"Invia Virtuti nulla est via."* Laura said, *"I think that means There is no way barred or not passable to virtue, a bit vague."*

"Look at the angel names Laura, remind you of anything?" Emily pointed to the screen as she spoke.

- Raphael - the Sun,
- Zaphiel - Saturn,
- Zadkiel - Jupiter,
- Camael - Mars,
- Haniel - Venus,
- Michael - Mercury,
- Gabriel – the Moon.

Laura gasped, *"Raphael is Rafe. The sun, a dermatologist, makes sense. Let's look at the others."*

Emily and Laura made a list:

- Raphael - the sun - Rafe is a dermatologist, sun damage to skin I suppose.
- Zaphiel - Saturn - Zaph a jeweller - the rings of Saturn.
- Zadkiel - Jupiter - Zak the lawyer - Jupiter was also Zeus the law giver king of gods.
- Camael - Mars - Cam is a soldier - Mars was a god of war.
- Haniel - Venus - Hani the relationship psychologist - Venus a goddess of love.
- Michael - Mercury - Mike the chemist, and mercury is quicksilver used by alchemists.
- Gabriel - the Moon - Gabe an astronomer - the moon, it makes sense."

Emily sat back in the chair, *"That is just weird."*

"They must have adopted the names or my theory is correct about people reacting to their names." Laura laughed at herself, *"Come on let's go to bed and sleep on it. We'll have another look at this in the morning."* Emily yawned and went up to her room. Laura bookmarked the page before shutting down the computer and then checking on the cats, locked the doors and went to bed. Strange she thought as she drifted off to sleep, angels and knights and magic and Merlin, all seems so normal here.

CHAPTER 22

Dark Makings

C layton paced about waiting for the stonemason to finish. *"It's done,"* said a voice. Clayton turned *"Are the measurements exact?"*

"Yes Mr Grant and the decoration carved exactly as you wanted it." The mason was a small muscular man with an honest open face.

"Thank you. Let me have your bill, and I shall pay it whilst I am here and take the stone with me."

The stone mason totted up the bill, price of the stone, hours worked and handed Clayton a piece of paper. Clayton looked at it and never said a word but he signalled to the men in the car.

"Ed you and Joey come and get this stone."

Clayton paid the stonemason whilst the other two men loaded the stone into the boot of the car, grunting and groaning with the effort. The stonemason looked at the cash in his hand. *"You've given me too much, Mr Grant."*

"The extra is for the speed and fine work. Good day sir."

Clayton left before the man had time to ask questions, the car almost getting caught on the cattle grid as the boot was so low with the weight of the stone. The stonemason shrugged his shoulders. Americans are strange he said to himself, an exact copy of an old stone that wasn't particularly interesting, it will cost a fortune to ship too. You could have got a nice gargoyle or a stone Nessie for a quarter of the price. He always had one or two of those ready for tourists any time of year.

The car sped off back to Drumnadrochit. The stonemason didn't ask why they had come all the way out to the Black Isle when they could have had it down locally, he was glad of the money and it might lead to other work if the Americans took it back with them and people liked it. He would keep the design just in case. When he looked for the design the Americans had brought, he couldn't find it anywhere. Puzzled he resolved to have a good search for it tomorrow; he had other work to finish today. Gravestones were his bread and butter work and he had two to finish before tea. This time of year there were always deaths, the cold seeing off the old and the odd accident on the roads with the poor light. The extra money from the American's job would come in handy for Christmas. He made a living, but his wife had to work as well. Extra money was always welcomed.

Henry was talking to the assembled men in the library. *"Your presence here is very reassuring,"* he began *"But I may need your help for something that I may need to do which will be quite dangerous."*

The men looked at each other and nodded *"We are here to do your bidding."* said Rafe. *"Whatever the cost."*

"Sadly, the cost may be more than we all can bear. But if the Nazi magician tries to summon the beast again. I will have to go down to the loch to send it back, and in the process perhaps destroy myself."

"The beast will not harm you," from Zak.

"It's not the beast we have to worry about, but the Nazis," put in Gordon quietly from the back of the room. *"They want the laird for their own ends, for things I dare not think about because it would be the end of the free world as we know it."*

A hubbub of talk grew up and Henry answered the questions as best he could. He could only tell them what the folly of his youth had brought forth, and how he hoped to avoid more deaths. This had haunted him most of life and the cost had been dear; he couldn't let the Nazi's win now.

Outside it was dusk and something restless stirred in the loch. A lone fisherman on his way back to the jetty, rowing as fast as he could to get back before dark, found himself in a whirlpool, his boat spinning around. In his frantic scrabbling to get free, he lost an oar and then started to go around in circles. He hung onto the sides and started to pray, but those creatures who do not believe in God or the Devil are not affected by prayer, and when the boat was found floating out on the loch next morning it was empty. No sign of its occupant or what happened to him, just a lone oar banging against the jetty as it got caught in the slip stream left by the coast guard's motorboat as he towed the little fishing dingy ashore. The coastguard sighed, there were always deaths this time of year and he hoped a family were not waiting for news. At least he didn't have to deliver that news, the police did that. He radioed through to start a search around the loch for whoever had been in the boat.

Laura and Emily had passed a quiet day, going for a short walk and calling in the village shop and then reading for a while. Laura was glad to see Emily more like her old self.

"Before we make dinner Laura, I need to talk to you."

"OK, what's on your mind?"

"First of all thanks for having me. I will go back at the weekend if it's alright with you, so I can catch up on the work."

Laura nodded, *"It's been no bother, you know that, and I am glad you want to get back to it after the shock."*

"That's the other thing I need to talk to you about - the beast - and then I can get it out of my head. Do you still have the stuff from the hospital I wrote?"

"I'll go and fetch it."

Laura returned with the papers and sat down expectantly.

Emily looked at the shaky lines she had written in hospital.

"What can you remember?" Laura prompted her.

"Well I remember the boat started to rock and Daniel shouting and then I looked over the side to see if I could see anything rising from the loch bed, even though it wouldn't show until the last few feet, the water being like it is. I saw a large eye looking back at me, like I suppose a dinner plate sized cat's eye. I jumped and then stumbled over the ropes coiled up because I was going backwards to get away from it. Then when the boat rocked again I lost my balance and fell in. I was terrified, and then this big tail or a fin knocked me through the water and I was so scared I must have passed out."

"I think something hit you on the head, and that is why you passed out. But although the tail bit could be the shock and concussion, the big eye can't be. You weren't expecting anything. The drawing you made is not a known animal. It could be something prehistoric but unlikely. It looks like a giant slug with a dragon's head." Laura had looked up any known animal dead or extinct to compare with Emily's drawing, but had drawn a blank.

"You believe me then?"

"Yes I do because of all the other things happening around the place just now. Whilst you were getting served at the post office I was listening to the gossip. A fisherman is missing. His boat was found empty this morning. No sign of what happened to him, so he could have been knocked into the loch and no one was there to fish him out. I doubt he had a life jacket on, the locals tend not to."

"On my God," Emily stared at Laura, *"should I tell someone, warn people. Will they think I am mad?"*

"I've already told Henry. Things are in hand. Those friends he has staying are going to patrol

the loch with some of the locals to try and prevent another tragedy."

The ping of the cooker alerted them that dinner was ready, so the conversation stopped for a while, as culinary needs came first.

Laura hoped Emily was comforted by her assurances from Henry, but as Laura herself hadn't been too reassured, she doubted it.

CHAPTER 23

Dark Mistakes

I n the early hours of the morning, when they were sure the coast was clear, the Americans unloaded the stone and carried it down to the shore. Their feet sank into the shingle with its weight added to their own.

"Shall we put it in the same place the other one was?" a stage whisper from Joey.

"Yes if we can," from Ed. They splashed into the shallows and found the hole still visible so placed the stone in it and then stood on it for good measure. It seemed firmly situated. The ritual began as before with the implements laid out on the cloth on the stone, and Joey and Ed hanging onto the ropes so Clayton was not swept away.

Henry stirred in his sleep, but this time didn't waken. Cam and Zak watched impassively from the undergrowth ready to intercede if necessary. They knew something that Clayton could not have foretold. Clayton donned his robes over the rope this time so the back slit was either side of the rope making it look like he had two tails. He held up his hands, closed his eyes and started to mutter.

The chanting became more intense and louder and then the loch began to boil. This time however it was different, no large wave hit the shore but a whirlpool started to form. Clayton sensed something was wrong and started to falter. A huge wave suddenly hit the shore, knocking him off his feet, and as he surfaced spluttering, a massive bulk passed by him to the shore. There was a yell from Ed, *"Don't run Joey, stand still."*

Too late Joey froze in terror mid-stride, as he was enveloped in darkness, and the stench of something rotten made him retch. There was a swift movement; Joey was gone and a huge dark shape disappeared under the water. Ed and Clayton stood in shock for a few moments, not knowing what to do. They started to shout 'Joey' and run along the shore shining their torches. *"Jesus man that was one horrible damn thing,"* said Ed. Clayton just nodded and continued to shine his torch about the edge of the loch and the beach.

Clayton and Ed searched for an hour and then gave up. Joey was gone.

"We will send for a replacement. I knew something was not right. I could feel it but it was too late to stop."

Ed nodded grimly, *"Let's go back. There is nothing else we can do until it gets light."*

The two Angels of the Talisman, faces set, watched them leave and then returned to Henry's house to inform the others what had occurred. They knew what had happened to Joey and that the bottom of the loch held the secret of his whereabouts. It was unfortunate, but if you were on the side of bad, you had to expect consequences.

Clayton's failure had not gone down well with his masters. They recognised, however, he had done all he could and sent not only a replacement for Joey but four others as well. If necessary they would take what they wanted by force. Two days later, Joey's replacement was dropped in via parachute to avoid detection. The others came by the normal route through immigration and customs and arrived at Inverness Airport on a scheduled flight from Heathrow, after disembarking from their flight from the USA. The man Ed picked up from the shore and helped out of the parachute looked like Joey. They hid the parachute as best they could, among the stones and shrubbery near the loch side. *"What about your things?"* said Ed.

"The others are bringing them with theirs. Plus some of Joey's stuff will fit me and there is always shopping." Ed nodded, and they set off up the shore to where a car was parked.

"Must be triplets," muttered Rafe to himself. He watched them go. The lights Ed had lit to help the landing had attracted Rafe to the shore to watch. No one else was around at that time of the morning. The lights were extinguished as Ed and the other triplet left. The loch was fairly rough tonight and as Rafe met up with Mike they got splashed by the waves. On hearing about the triplets Mike decided he should investigate this further. They continued their patrol until it started to get light.

Henry was up when they got back and over coffee they discussed the night's happenings. *"So four men arrive via the normal means albeit in a private jet, and one look alike parachutes in."*

"I've wondered about it and think the only reason can be to disguise the other man's death and the third triplet will pretend to be the missing man and go out on his passport." Mike looked at the other two.

"They must be identical triplets," from Rafe.

"Or something else," Henry looked at Mike as he said it. *"Homunculi perhaps?"*

"Clones?" put in Mike.

"I thought that we hadn't advanced that far?" from Zak as he entered the room, and started helping himself to coffee.

"Organismal cloning has a long history. Early embryologists in the late 1800s and early

1900s looked at it. In 1902 Hans Spemann cloned a salamander using a hair from his son's head." They all looked at Mike. *"So I am a science geek,"* he smiled.

"The men don't seem exactly alike though, the one that was killed was definitely backward in some mental functioning."

Rafe answered Zak before Mike did, *"The progressive shortening of chromosomal telomores that occurs during successive rounds of cell division causes ageing. If the donor is 46 years old then the baby's cells will be 46 years old even though it is newborn, and it will age inside prematurely."*

"So that's why Dolly the sheep died young. The donor sheep was 6 years old I seem to remember," Zak was fascinated.

"Well that's the theory anyway," Mike smiled. *"And the more clones, the more the deterioration as the line goes along, if you see what I mean."*

Henry looked grave, *"That man Clayton, is not the son of Hans Blome at all, he's a clone. To all intentional purposes, he is Hans Blome. My God what a frightening thought. How many more Nazis have been cloned? Even Hitler himself could still be around."*

"He would be in pretty poor nick by now. He would have to have been cloned a couple of times." Mike suddenly slapped his forehead, *"Of course, how stupid of me. That's why they want you. Combine your DNA with the clone DNA and it may live a lot longer."*

"They must have been searching for you for years, and somehow found out how to draw you out. They were big on myths and legends and - of course - they know about you." Cam put in having recently entered the room with Gordon.

"What about the ethics of it though, and the legal position?" Zak was the lawyer after all.

"Since when did Nazis concern themselves with law or what is right or what is wrong?" Cam sighed and shook his head. *"I can't understand their obsession with Hitler. They could appoint someone else leader surely?"*

"Because my dear friend Cam, their motto has always been 'Ein Volk, Ein Reich, Ein Fuhrer' One people, one empire, one leader." Henry looked grim as he spoke.

"Madness," Cam shook his head. *"We need to have a council of war I think Henry."*

Cam continued, *"You two get your sleep. We will have a meeting this evening before the next patrol goes out and decide how to handle things. Especially now four more of them have arrived."*

"Looking, and I quote 'like Teutonic soldiers' from the village gossips," Added Gordon, appearing silently in the doorway. "Breakfast is served in the dining hall."

CHAPTER 24

Dark Waters

Not aware of any of the intrigue going on, Daniel and John arranged to go out in the boats together, taking Andy and Donald, but leaving Emily onshore with the radio, so she could summon help if anything should occur.

John decided to do some trawling to get some sample fish. They hopefully could be fairly near the surface so should be safe enough and the fish would be returned once they had been measured and tagged. Daniel would take readings and follow in their wake. keeping just enough distance so their boat trail would not affect his instruments.

Donald and Andy both had cameras ready in case anything should appear, after all Andy said a good photo of the Loch Ness Monster would be worth a fortune. They agreed to split the proceeds if either of them got a photo that was legible.

The morning passed quietly apart from a start from a flock of birds rising suddenly into the air, which made them all jump. They laughed at each other nervously, but come lunchtime they headed back to the jetty gratefully, and met up with Emily to go get something to eat. The weather was starting to turn; sudden storms often blew up on the loch and it was spitting with rain by the time they got to the hotel.

Over lunch, Emily told them about the knights or Angels of the Talisman.

"Well there is something called business angels that helps young entrepreneurs I think, maybe it's something like that," Daniel was as ever practical. Emily nodded, but wasn't convinced.

"The missing stone was weird though," from Donald. *"I'm glad Henry rescued it. Laura said if we want to see it before it's shipped off to a museum, it's in the library. We are welcome anytime."*

"Where is Laura today?" said Daniel in between mouthfuls of hot food.

"She had some stuff to write up I think, and was going back to the library," said Emily.

"I might go have a look around Henry's library. It sounds like there's a great collection of old books," Daniel smiled at the others. *"Pity I missed the cellars."*

"Maybe he will offer another tour, now he knows you are back. Though I think the others may be on water not wine." Emily laughed at the others' faces. *"Oatcake balancing, is all I can say."*

Daniel looked mystified, but no one enlightened him.

They split up after lunch and went away to crunch results and write up. Daniel wanted to get on as he felt two weeks had been lost whilst he was away. He was glad Laura had kept the students busy though, and they hadn't got bored and gone home or worse, got drunk, and been arrested. He did have a bunch of students one year that were quite riotous and it had been an exhausting business keeping them in check. Twice he had to return the Loch Ness Monster model to the hotel in Drumnadrochit. Luckily, the owners had taken it in good spirit.

CHAPTER 25

Dark Research

Laura decided she needed to know more about Merlin and his history, and also about Henry's lineage, as the family must be very old. There were books in the library on the family history. She rang the castle and Gordon answered as usual. He said she was fine to use the library despite Henry having guests. She thanked him, and decided to take her laptop so she could write her notes directly onto it.

It was starting to rain as she set off and she was glad of her waterproof coat. She arrived at the castle in a flurry of rain and wind which almost blew her through the door. Gordon took her coat and offered to bring her some tea in a short while for which she would be exceedingly grateful she told him.

It didn't long to amass the books she wanted to look at, but she kept the family ones hidden under the others until Gordon had left the tea and gone back to his own domain. Laura presumed he was in the kitchen or cellar when not needed. The term "below stairs" always amused her, as if people squatted in the under stairs cupboard, though to be fair in a house this size there was probably room.

She started with the history of the lairds of the area. The Grants appeared to be the lairds since the 12th C and the Frasers followed in 1420, by marriage. *"Hence Fraser-Grant,"* she thought to herself. Before that it had been the Marmaers of Moray.

She knew there had been a lot of cruelty against the highlanders during the clearances and there were some less than nice references to the Duke of Cumberland, who had been part of this period of history. In the early 1700s was a reference to Ambrosius Fraser-Grant being accused of witchcraft. This was one of the names Merlin had been called by. She started to look for more information. Perhaps there were links between Merlin and the Fraser-Grants.

Ambrosius Fraser-Grant had been taken to trial and been forced to endure the trial by ducking stool, in other words drowning. He was proven innocent when he subsequently died. *"Oh dear,"* she said to herself, *"not nice at all".* If you survived and floated you were a witch and hanged, if you drown you were innocent, but too late to do anything about it.

1800s, Willox the Warlock, Andy's favourite she laughed to herself. Willox was a cousin of the Fraser-Grants. She continued on muttering to herself as she read. Blimey, alchemy and witchcraft fairly gallop through this family. She shook her head.

Stuart Fraser-Grant was considered a great medium in the late 1800s, Queen Victoria's time. *"Hmm, they were into séances etc., in a big way. I never could understand how an intelligent man like Conan Doyle could believe in that stuff. After all he was a doctor, saw death all the time, maybe that was his way of coping with it."* She remembered Conan Doyle had even written a story or two about spiritualism and tried to show it was a real phenomenon, something called the land of the mists or something like that. She continued on with her research.

1900s, she tapped into her laptop, and consulted her books: Clan Chief Fraser killed at the Somme. Son Iain takes over and dies in 1940s. World War Two pilot, without issue. He was at the Battle of Britain. This family doesn't have much luck does it, she sighed.

Cousin Samuel takes over, dies in his 90s and Henry becomes laird. Henry has resided in England for a long time from what he said. Will try a Google search on him at home, I don't think there will be wireless internet in here, despite Henry's talk of improvements. She turned to the family portraits at the back of the book. After looking at three, she leafed quickly through the others. They all look like Henry she said to herself. That's weird.

She also noticed something in the corner of one of the photos and, when she looked closer, realised it was the talisman that Emily had showed her. So the angels must be relatives she thought. Makes sense, family business I suppose. On closer examination, quite a lot of the photos had the talisman somewhere in them. Maybe it's the family motto. Then she picked up one of the other books she had gathered in her search. It was about the Knights Templar and their links to Scotland. She knew about Rosslyn Chapel, that strange piece of architecture. No one seems to have got to the bottom of that one she thought to herself. As she looked through the list of references at the back, she noticed the talisman of Saladin. The chapter said Sir Walter Scott had written about it and it had the power to heal. Talismans everywhere she muttered.

It was getting very dark in the library now and the storm was abating so she decided to call it a day and take her stuff home to look through. Gordon appeared in the hallway as she went to fetch her coat. *"Everything alright ma'am?"*

"Fine, thank you. Thank Henry again for me please, for the use of his library."

"Certainly."

"Oh Gordon, is there anyone local who is an expert on the history of the area, especially the families, do you know please?"

"Well you want to talk to Lady Cameron. She used to live in Aldarrie House, family been here for generations, five hundred years I think. Death duties after her husband died forced her to sell it. It's going to be a conference centre I heard. Anyway, she lives in Inverness now, her

address is in the phone book. I am sure she would like to see you to talk about the area. She used to do guided tours around Aldarrie and so forth, so very knowledgeable."

"Thank you Gordon. I will do that."

"Are you sure you will be alright walking back alone? It's getting dark."

"I will be fine, Gordon. I can always stop the bus if I see it, especially if the weather turns nasty. Good bye."

"Goodbye, ma'am." As Gordon shut the door she hoisted her laptop bag further on her shoulder and set off down the drive.

CHAPTER 26

Dark Plans

L ater that evening a solemn looking group of men met together after dinner in the library at Cragneghil Castle. Henry sat at the large desk facing the others who were scattered about the room. Henry cleared his throat and said: *"Well I think we know what these people are after and I fear as their numbers are increasing in the village, they may try to take me by force. The question is should I stay here? Or move away to protect the local populace?"*

"You are better served staying here. We can protect you better and the locals are unlikely to be involved. The household staff have worked for the family for years. Their ancestors fought against all types of marauders. You have no worries there," Rafe looked at the others as he spoke and they all nodded.

"What I would like to know is where they are coming from. Where is their base, where they are all created or whatever? Are they created or born?" Cam still wasn't too sure about this whole cloning thing.

"There was supposed to be a secret Nazi base in Queen Maud's region of the Antarctic. There were lots of tales about them finding green pastures and hot springs, like in Iceland. I know historically there have been exploratory missions in that part of the Antarctic since the 1830s. Quite a lot of them set out from South Africa I believe." Hani looked around surprised to see the others hanging onto his every word.

"There are others who say there's a base in the Arctic - a sort of portal. It's something to do with the hollow earth theory and other internet conspiracy stuff, but a team was supposed to go out in 2007 to explore this supposed entrance to the earth's inner world. I believe they said it was about 400 kilometres north west of Ellesmere island, but I don't know what happened or even if they went."

Cam shivered, *"Ellesmere Island, there's a military station there, Canadian I think. It's dark for 19 hours a day and the temperature gets down to -45 degrees. If you go for a walk you get followed by Arctic wolves. Beautiful creatures but scary all the same. I can't imagine anyone going there by choice."*

"Well," said Gabe. "Sounds a bit farfetched to me. It's more likely to be in South America or even in some small town in the USA where it's under the guise of the local factory or chemical plant. Plus I think they are born, Cam, in that they are implanted in a womb and born, but not conceived."

"Science fiction stuff alright," Cam muttered. *"And in the old films no good comes of it."*

Mike and Gabe smiled. *"It's not all gruesome stuff, Cam. Cloning could have benefits for those in need of organ transplants."* But as Mike said it, he knew he also felt uneasy about it. Cloning was fine in a test tube, but to grow another human felt wrong, like playing God. It was because it was being used for a bad reason and ethics and science didn't always make good bed fellows, sadly he thought to himself.

"There was that underground city discovered, was it Leavenworth? It was found when they were digging drains or something; there was even a parade of shops. Probably miners or rail workers had lived there at one time. They might have somewhere like that," put in Hani.

"I think it's in Salt Lake City," quietly came in Mike's voice. *"I had heard about it but until now didn't believe it. A lot of people in the scientific community heard rumours. It's a bit like Area 51 type of stuff, you take it with a pinch of salt."*

"Really?" said Henry *"What have you heard?"*

"Well, the men in the dark suits we saw would make perfect looking Mormons I suppose. They say there is a lab there that is used for research into embryology but it's a front for cloning, and that people go in and don't come out. No one ever sees the workers out of the bounds of the compound it is set in. Barbed wire fences, you know the sort of thing. There are women who go missing that they say are held there to produce babies."

"But where do they get the money to finance something like that?" Zak ever practical.

"Alchemist's gold, or Nazi stolen treasure from the war. Lots of it was never found. Plus the rise of Hitler was said to be funded by American bankers, who may still fund things for their own ends for all we know. Get as many details as you can, Mike, and I will pass it on to the appropriate authorities. If there is any truth in it, we may be able to get it shut down. They will probably have other bases, but each one less is less of them." Henry stood up.

"I think yourself and Gabe are on patrol tonight. The rest of us will secure the house as best we can. The quest is upon us, Gentlemen. Good luck to us all."

"Alchemist's gold?" queried Gabe, as he and Mike got ready to leave.

"It's quite a possibility. A particle accelerator could change the surface of lead into gold. Who knows what the Nazis might have. They were way ahead with their experiments of all sorts during the war, and they have had over 50 years to improve on that. Henry's relatives in the past were said to be alchemists who made their own gold. Anything is possible these days

my old chum. Science is basically trying to prove your guesswork, after all, and there are no real truths, just correct guesses. Alchemists were the first scientists. Henry still has a lab in the west tower of the castle. You ought to go have a look some time. He won't mind."

Gabe shook his head as they set off to the loch, at the thought of alchemy, and the discussion continued for some time about what science was as they walked on their patrol route.

Mike brought up the subject of gold again, *"There were lots of paintings and treasures were never found that the Nazis took, some of that would be gold. They could still be using stuff they stole in the war to finance themselves."*

"I guess you are right. Well look at the years people have spent searching for Nazi treasure and never found it. It must have gone somewhere. A bit like Templar gold that was never found was it, well at least not by the King."

Mike grinned at Gabe, *"Too true my friend, too true, de Molay might have been an old man but he hoodwinked them in the end."*

Gabe suddenly spoke up, changing the subject. *"You know I bet they have a base in Argentina, close to the Antarctic and a safe haven even these days for them."*

Mike nodded, *"You could be right, its maybe worth further investigation after this is all over."* They carried on their patrol in thoughtful silence.

CHAPTER 27

Dark Walks

L aura sat with one cat upon her knee and the other lay next to her. It was quiet again without Emily. She was studying the photos of the stone and realised that there were other markings on the one in library, which they couldn't see under the water line. I must go have another look she said to herself. The Angels of the Talisman also intrigued her. That was something else she could investigate. She put down her notebook and was trying to decide what to do next when the phone rang. It was John. "We are down at the hotel, want to join us?" She pleaded an early night and tiredness as an excuse because she realised what she wanted to do was go for a walk by the loch in the dark. It might inspire me she thought.

Wrapped up with scarf and gloves, and her weatherproof coat and a good torch she set off. The sitting room lights were left on so that the cottage looked occupied. The silence and darkness seemed to envelope her as she reached the loch side. Standing on the shore looking out at the loch her imagination ran riot. Was that a shape in the water? Was that the sound of a large creature coming up the beach? What was that splash? She turned startled at a sound behind her, to see two of the angels from Henry's tea party approaching towards her. As they drew closer, she recognised them as Gabe and Mike.

"Hello Laura. What are doing here?" Gabe seemed taller in the dark.

"Just getting some fresh air. It's very fresh too!" she added grinning. *"You two out for a walk?"*

"We are patrolling for Henry. We all take turns to keep an eye on the loch for anyone in distress. Another fisherman is missing." Mike scanned the loch as he spoke.

"So I heard in the village. What do you think about this monster? Do you think it is real?"

The men looked at each other. Gabe spoke first, *"Well something is happening in the loch, who knows what."*

"Maybe someone having a joke. Sudden squalls often blow up on the loch and people get caught out, even people who know the loch well. Either way, if we keep watch we will catch whoever, or whatever, is going on."

"Walk with us if you like," said Mike.

"Yes, we would like the company, if you aren't heading back yet."

Laura smiled at Gabe. *"Thanks I will. It's a bit creepy out here, your imagination runs riot."*

"That's why there is two of us," laughed Mike. *"One, to stop the other imagining things."* They continued down the beach, chatting about the weather and the village.

There was a splash out in the loch and all three looked at each other, and then hurried to the shore.

"Can you see anything?" Laura peered out.

Then Gabe lit up a large searchlight type torch and swung it around over the water. Something moved in the water and Gabe and Mike instinctively stood in front of Laura to protect her. She tried to see through the gap in their shoulders. It wasn't easy as they were both taller than her. Then she wished she hadn't. There was a dark shape coming towards them and she felt herself starting to shake.

Suddenly a man ran past them into the water screaming, *"You don't exist!"*

And then a splash as his foot must have caught in something and he fell. The men and Laura rushed to help him up and drag him from the water. Whatever was in the water disappeared without a sound leaving a huge wave, which followed them to the shore and sprayed them all. Gabe shone his torch in the man's face as he was hauled up onto the beach. He flinched and Laura recognised him. *"It's Hayden Stark,"* she told the other two.

If Nessie exists he'll be shown up to be a bigger fool than he already is, she thought to herself.

"What are you doing, man?" Mike yelled at Hayden. *"Trying to get yourself killed? If there is something in the water, you will be eaten and even if there isn't there is a sheer drop 50 yards out off some of these shores. They drop to 500 feet straight down. You are an idiot."*

Laura laughed to herself. Couldn't have put it better myself she thought. She decided to intercede before things turned nasty.

"I'll take him to the hotel to dry off. John and the others are there."

"Are you sure, Laura? What if he runs in the loch again?"

"I'll let him drown," she grinned. *"Come on you, let's get you dried off before you get pneumonia."* She grabbed Hayden's arm, and he didn't resist and was marched off into the night.

"What a fool!" Gabe was angry that he could have endangered them all, and distracted them from what they were doing.

"No harm done, Gabe. Let's continue on. Laura will be OK if she is meeting the others and I am sure she is quite capable of handling Mr Stark."

They carried on silently along the shore.

Laura's arrival at the bar with a dripping Hayden Stark caused some commotion and a lot of tittering behind hands.

"What's all this?" asked the landlord.

"Hayden fell in the loch," said Laura. *"And I had to help pull him out. He thought he saw Nessie."* The landlord got his wife to fetch towels and gave Hayden a whisky. People moved so he could be near the fire. *"Are you OK lassie?"*

"I'm fine Thank you."

"Your friends are over there if you want to join them. Drink on the house for the lassie," the landlord Jim said to the barmaid.

Laura joined John and the others, who were all agog to hear what happened, but she told them only about Hayden running into the loch at something he thought he saw in the dark, and how Gabe, Mike and herself had pulled him out.

"The sight of Hayden, kilt flying, and screaming you don't exist was not pretty I can tell you, not with those legs and no knickers!" with that she took a large sip of her red wine that the landlord had sent over, free of charge for, as he put it, *"Bringing the evening's entertainment."*

The others howled with laughter at the face she had pulled, and the whole ridiculousness of it all.

"Long streak of donkey snot that he is," Laura said grinning.

"Don't you mean short streak, it was cold out there," John grinned back wickedly.

"What must those friends of Henry think," said Emily wiping her eyes, crying with laughter, the laugh had done her good. *"I bet Henry will laugh when they tell him."*

"I shall have nightmares," grinned Laura.

"Well at least Henry has kept his word and they are watching the loch," said John. *"What were you doing there?"*

"I was intending to go to bed early, but couldn't settle so thought some fresh air might help."

"Luckily those men were there to help, Hayden wouldn't have been so willing to be rescued by you, and might have cut up rough." Donald had a low opinion of Hayden.

"I think he would have been OK, but had he fallen and banged his head and been unconscious or something, I couldn't have managed him on my own," Laura turned her head. A further commotion was happening at the bar as Hayden had spotted Clayton and was haranguing him about something to do with American tourists inciting the locals to invent the monster. Clayton just stood impassively whilst the landlord urged Hayden to go home and offered to drive him. Hayden declined the lift in Middle English and flounced out.

"Did he say thank you to anyone for rescuing him?" asked Andy.

"No," came from Laura. *"Ill mannered creature that he is."*

Emily laughed, *"Brought up in a field, as my mother would say."*

They then went on to one of their silly moments where they speculated what Hayden would do if he met Nessie. Everything was suggested from throw a tent over it so no one could see it, to feed it a banana. It ended up with John saying he would run into the water screaming, 'You don't exist' and them all falling about laughing.

They decided to walk back with Laura as she had had enough shocks for one night and didn't need to run into Hayden again. Jim, the landlord, called goodnight as they left. They were becoming welcome distractions from the usual happenings at the hotel. He grinned to himself again at the thought of Hayden running into the loch. The locals would be buying more drinks tonight as they discussed the happenings of the evening. Good for business these university lot he said with satisfaction to himself.

Gabe and Mike, unseen, observed the small group pass, chatting and laughing away with Laura.

"I knew she would be fine," said Mike, and they continued on their way. The rest of the night passed quietly.

When the knights returned, Henry was sitting at his desk in the library drinking coffee.

"You are about early," Mike said popping his head around the door having seen the light on from the hall.

"Ah you are back. Come and join me for coffee. I couldn't sleep so decided to get up and do something useful rather than toss and turn."

Mike and Gabe sat down whilst Henry rang for more coffee.

"So how did the night go? You seem in good spirits."

They both grinned. *"You tell it Gabe, you do a better impression than I do,"* Mike said still grinning.

"Impression? You better tell me," said Henry looking mystified.

Gabe started to tell him about meeting Laura and then something in the loch, and then launched into a pastiche of Hayden running into the loch.

Henry let out a guffaw. *"Stupid man. He could have been drowned."*

Gordon, who had brought the extra coffee and cups, was grinning in the door way. He placed the tray on the desk and went back to the kitchen to tell the housekeeper, who would also enjoy the joke, leaving Henry and the others to their refreshment.

CHAPTER 28

Dark Readings

Laura couldn't get to sleep easily. She knew she had seen something in the loch. *"I'll go see Henry in the morning for my own peace of mind,"* she told herself. Hayden arriving as he did had caused whatever it was to retreat, but she knew she saw something, and so did the two men, Gabe and Mike.

Emily also set off to Cragneghil Castle early next morning, she too had questions. She told the others she was going to use Henry's library, which was true. She didn't tell them what she was searching for, and as she had been helping to write a paper with Daniel no one asked. They just presumed she had seen a book there that might be useful.

Gordon greeted her and said there was no problem, she was welcome to use the library. The books Emily wanted concerned angels, knights and talismans and the reasoning behind the same. She also picked up a book on seismic activity in the loch so should anyone enquire, she had an alibi as it were. After a couple of hours, she had quite a lot of information. The names of the angels were attached to planets as they had surmised before, but also to Enochian magic. In an old book dated 1674, the print almost faded away, she found a drawing of the talisman. It was similar to the one she had seen on the internet, but not as ornate.

One of the most powerful of all word talismans contained the names of the angels who controlled the seven planets. She read and took note. A charm which embodies these and which may be worn as a symbol of general good luck, is seen the below. The names of the angels and the planets they governed are as follows:-

- Zaphiel governs Saturn;
- Zadkiel governs Jupiter;
- Camael governs Mars;
- Raphael governs the Sun;
- Haniel governs Venus;
- Michael governs Mercury;
- Gabriel governs the Moon.

In this charm of general good luck is also included the Latin motto *"Invia virtuti nulla est via"* or *"There is no way impassable to virtue."*

So Laura's translation had been right, thought Emily. How strange it should be used by the friends of Henry though. Unless it's Henry's family motto and then Emily remembered Laura saying something about Enochian symbols on the stone. Magic of course and the Knights Templar were accused of magical practices. This led her back to the Knights of the Talisman and the Knights Templar. *"This is turning into a quest for me,"* she thought. There was a book on the Knights Templar in Scotland, she had seen it on her last visit so she sought it out and started to make more notes.

Knights Templar set up in 1128 or 29, there seemed to be some dispute about the correct date, so she wrote both down. You never know what might be important later she thought... The Order was dissolved by papal degree in 1312, but there was no order of suppression in Scotland so it was where some of them took refuge. In 1745 Prince Charles Stuart entertained Templars at Holyrood House. In 1807, not that long ago she added to herself, Alexander Deuchar became the master of the Scottish Templar, Master of Militia Templi Scotia.

The modern Knights Templar movement exists to help preserve history, and be the guardians of Scottish traditions and heritage. It is open to people of high ideals and those who hold other beliefs, though not Christian, may be admitted. She hit her forehead.

"Of course they came here to protect the stone."

That explained to her satisfaction she put the books away. *"The Talisman Angels or knights must be the special branch for preserving stuff in this area,"* she thought, or maybe of things of a certain age. I wonder if Henry is a knight templar as well. She felt better now, for some reason she had suspected something sinister, but she didn't know why. *"Probably the after effects of the shock I had,"* she said to herself *"making me think there is a plot around every corner."*

She decided to leave a note on Henry's desk to say she had borrowed the book on seismology in the loch and when she returned with it, no one would be any the wiser. The last thing she wanted was the others to think she still suffered effects from her fall in the loch, which they might if they knew she was researching angels. As she was leaving the library, she heard voices. It was Laura and Henry, and someone else. She crept across the hallway and nearer the door of the drawing room, not sure whether to go in or not.

"Gabe and Mike were there Henry; there was something in the water, something huge. John and Donald have seen it. Emily was nearly drowned when it hit Daniel's boat. What is it? What's going on? I know you have an idea what it is. I can tell by your face."

A voice Emily didn't know answered, *"If Henry could tell you he would. I promise Laura no one else will get hurt, we are here to help Henry sort this out."*

Then Henry's voice, *"I promise I will explain everything to you when I can. The less you know the better at the moment. Please I am begging you; keep this to yourself, or at least to you and your friends for the moment."*

"Well I shall have to tell them the little I know. They could get hurt, but I will ask them to keep it to themselves. I am not happy doing this though Henry, it goes against my social conscience that people could be in danger and don't know it."

Henry again, *"The locals know Laura, trust me on this. They are well aware of what goes on in the loch. The knights will patrol the loch to see that no one else gets into difficulty and I assure you it will be dealt with."*

"Now please sit and stay and have some coffee. You can chat to the others when they arrive and they will help calm your fears," with that Henry must have rung the bell as Emily heard a door open somewhere downstairs and knew Gordon would be shortly appearing. She ducked back into the library and seemed deeply absorbed in a book when Gordon arrived to ask if she required coffee.

"No thanks Gordon. I am leaving now. Pass on my thanks to Henry for letting me use the library please , and I have left a note of a book I am borrowing."

"Certainly, that's no problem," smiled Gordon and left the room.

Emily went to the hall to collect her things and headed back to meet up with Daniel and Andy. She decided to say nothing until Laura spilled the beans, but she knew she had been knocked off the boat by a large creature. She suddenly realised, *"I met the Loch Ness monster and survived!"* This made her laugh as she walked down to the village and then to the jetty.

About an hour later, Laura came down the same route. She came across Hamish as she walked back deep in thought and as she looked at Hamish's honest face and decided to confide in him. After all, he knew everything that went on at this end of the loch and would be trusted to tell her the truth if he could. *"Hi Hamish. How are you?"*

"Fine, fine, and yourself?"

"I am OK, but Hamish I need some answers. I've been up to see Henry and he says the locals know about the monster in the loch. Is that true?"

"Sit yourself down," Hamish indicated a bench. *"And keep me company whilst I have my break and I'll tell you. But by telling you, you are one of us and have to keep it to yourself."* Laura sat down feeling like it was story-time at school.

Hamish offered her some tea from his flask but she declined saying she had just had coffee with Henry and his friends. She was glad to have an excuse - the tea was thick and black and probably full of sugar. OK if you are in shock she thought but you would have to be in deep shock to drink that!

"You give me your word this is between ourselves? You'll not go telling folk at newspapers?"
Laura nodded, *"Cross my heart, Hamish. I have no wish to tell the newspapers anything."*

"OK Lassie, I shall tell you what I know about the loch. There has always been beasties in the loch. They keep themselves to themselves, occasionally coming up and frightening or entertaining the visitors, but they are harmless, dumb, bottom-dwellers who just live their lives as the fishy types they are. Not dinosaurs as such, but old certainly. Been around a long time. Some sort of ancient eel or whale they say, but I've not seen one myself. They are peaceful and don't harm nobody."

He paused: *"But then there's also the evil. It's not called 'Dark Ness' for nothing. The tale is that long ago, maybe hundreds, maybe thousands of years ago, a man came to the loch and created the evil beast. He was some sort of warlock or magician. Anyway he regretted what he done so he became a holy man and came back and sent the beastie back where it came from. That was St Columba. Trouble was, other evil men came and kept bringing the beastie back. Once it was created, it could be brought back. So, the laird's job is to see that the beastie is kept back and to protect the people, as his forefathers did before him. The laird has the doings to send the evil beastie back when the time comes. I don't think it has to be a full moon or something special for it to work."*

Laura sat there dumb struck. *"He's having me on, she thought."* Hamish looked at her face. *"You wanted to know the truth so I told you. You make of it what you will."*

"But people are dead, Hamish, and if what you say is true something needs to be done."

"No need to fret lass, they died accidentally like, and their families are taken care of and they will be honoured when the time comes. The laird will see to everything. He has them Germans to deal with first. The laird won't let us down. Well I have to get on." and with that he rose to his feet.

"Thank you, Hamish," said Laura because she didn't know what to say. As she watched him walk away, she realised what he had said. Germans? What Germans? Maybe he meant the Americans she decided, and got up and brushed down her coat. Better get back and feed the boys and myself for that matter. She shook her head, this is all too much, I wish I hadn't asked now. It gets more confusing, and what on earth is an "evil"? She walked back to the cottage in a state of mind that could only be called chaotic, as the thoughts went round and round in her head, each asking yet another question of herself that she could not answer.

CHAPTER 29
Dark Musings

On the two boats, things were going well. Both groups had agreed to go out together for safety. Daniel was making progress with his soundings, and John's camera was working fine and he was taking samples of numbers of fish and other life forms. In ecology, on land, to take a sample to estimate numbers of wildlife, fauna etc., you would throw a square of wood or metal down and count what you found in the square (usually wiggling things and bacteria). In the water, John had decided to draw an invisible square and count what was in it. They did this by using four cameras attached to the corners of their square and counting what they caught on the cameras. You can't count fish that are swimming away, so capturing them on film, John hoped, would give them some estimate of numbers. It was never going to be exact in these waters. The waters of the loch from a few feet down are black with peat particles washed down from the hills and visibility is very poor. By using infra-red cameras and lights he hoped to show some results. The cameras were very small and light by necessity and securely attached. If it worked, he had invented a new method of sampling.

The radio crackled to life. It was Daniel. *"I am reading a disturbance in the loch to the right of you. Pull your cameras in just in case."*

John thanked him and ran to help Donald get the cables up fast. He didn't want another chewed one. The university frowned on too much damaged equipment being claimed for. Donald had already started to pull them in when John had shouted and it didn't long to get them aboard. *"All present and correct."* Donald gave a mock salute.

The boat suddenly rocked. John and Donald looked at each other and they ran to look over the side. There didn't seem to be anything there. The radio crackled again. *"It's moving away get out of there."*

John didn't need telling twice and with Daniel just behind him he opened the throttle and dashed for the jetty.

As they tied up the boats, Daniel said: *"I think it was a seismic disturbance but I thought it best not to take any chances,"* in a lower voice he added, *"and Emily looked a bit white."*

John replied, *"I don't want to take any chances. There could be something nasty in there that is hungry. Anyway a seismic disturbance would blow our cameras."*

"I think we should have a council of war, man. Do you think Laura would mind if we all met up at her place? We could all bring something so we don't impose on her hospitality and friendship. It's just the hotel is kind of public and your place is too small for entertaining."

John nodded at Daniel's suggestion and got out his mobile. Laura had not long been in the house when he rang. She said she had things to tell them and would be glad of the company.

"7:00 pm at Laura's it is. Bring food and drink but knowing Laura she will have something made as well."

They departed their various ways, Emily went to the shop with Donald, and Andy helped in carrying equipment for Daniel and John back to the cottage to print out their results. The man on the shore with the sunglasses watched thoughtfully. He was observed by Zaph and Rafe. *"It gets more like the Cold War every day, us watching them, them watching someone else,"* laughed Zaph. *"Let's hope there are no double agents, then,"* grinned Rafe.

"Or that we are on Candid Camera!" adjoined Zaph and they both laughed.

Laura had made a large winter salad and a quiche, which was ready to come out of the oven when the others arrived. John said he and Donald would bring a couple of pizzas on their way back from town and Emily was bringing a pudding, the other guys would bring snacks. They all seemed to arrive at once and it was about 20 minutes before everyone was settled with plates of food and drinks.

The chatter was just general stuff until everyone finished eating. Emily produced chocolate cake and started off the council of war as it were. She told them about the knights and that she thought they were here to protect the stone as heritage, and that she thought Henry was one of them.

"Knights Templar, eh? Interesting," said Andy.

Then Emily said she had a confession to make and that she had overhead an argument Laura had with Henry and was very embarrassed about it, but Laura just smiled. *"That leads nicely into to what I have to say."*

Laura told them about her discussion, as she put it, with Henry and that Hamish had said that the locals had long known that there was something in the loch. She didn't tell them the tale of the two beasties, as she called it to herself, she had said she wouldn't tell and she kept her word.

The men joined in with the story of the jolting of the boat and the sonar again showed something large in the loch, though it could have been a blow out from the bed of the loch. John continued,

"Those samples we sent away, from the scrapes on the boat, came back indecisive. Marine animal of some sort, but not enough to determine origin or species. Having measured the bite out of the eel, Donald estimated it must be nearly 40 feet long to have a mouth that size."

"Mega mouth monster Johnus Donaldi," laughed Daniel.

"Very funny," grinned John. *"Though I have heard the monster was thought to be a hybrid of an ancient whale of the Georgiacetus genus. It had fins or feet and a tail, but has not been around for 40 million years."*

"Well people always bring up the story of the Coelacanth at this point. Supposed to be extinct but found alive and well in the Indian Ocean," put in Andy.

"I wish we could prove it was real. We'd be proper scientists," from Emily.

"You are a proper scientist Emily, and I am not sure I <u>would</u> want to prove it exists. The loch would be dragged, or even drained, and it would be hounded until it was stuffed in a museum or kept alive in a side show." Daniel was right, they all knew that.

"King Kong all over again," sighed Laura. *"I think we should do as Henry wants and let it be kept quiet for now until he tells us what has been done to sort things out. He seems to know what he is doing."*

They all nodded. *"And in the meantime be careful if you go out on the loch,"* she continued. *"Perhaps concentrate on the other end of the loch, it doesn't seem to be about there as much."*

Nodding heads. They continued to speculate about the knights and their role in all this. *"Well I suppose the monster is heritage as well."*

"More like tourist trap Emily, but you may be right," Andy looked thoughtful.

"Well, I think it is time we were going, Laura, we have abused your hospitality enough," John rose as he spoke. The others followed suit. Laura saw them off at the door and went back to tidy up a little. It was 11:00pm but she didn't feel tired.

She decided to go for a walk. After all the knights, or whatever, they were would be around so she would be quite safe. Settling the cats with leftovers from the evening, the old one loved pizza, she pulled on her coat, grabbed a torch and set off.

CHAPTER 30
Dark Battles

D eep in thought, she wasn't really thinking were she was going and found herself at the bottom of the drive to Cragneghil House. Looking up the drive, she could see lights on but also something odd, like people creeping about outside the windows. She turned off her torch and when her eyes got used to the darkness, she could definitely see figures circling the house.

Without hesitation she set off up the drive to warn Henry. If she went via the shrubs on the left, she could get to the door of the library without being seen by the intruders.

Spiders' webs caught her hair, normally she would have flinched but she was suddenly afraid for Henry; after all he wasn't a young man and if they overpowered Gordon and everyone else was asleep, it didn't bear thinking about. She hurried around the side of the house. No one was there, and with a sigh of relief she tried the library French windows and found them unlocked. She heard someone whispering and got inside just in time as shadows passed the windows as she hid behind the long curtains. Taking a deep breath, cautiously she walked across the room and opened the library door a slit. No one was in the hallway so she headed across to Henry's study where she had seen a light.

She pushed open the door, and opened her mouth to tell Henry he had intruders, only to see Henry gagged and being held down by 3 or 4 men and Clayton approaching him with a hypodermic. They looked up. *"What the hell are you doing?"* she exclaimed.

"Get her before she wakes the house," Clayton said in a hoarse whisper.

Henry was struggling to free his hands, but the men held him down in his chair. Laura could see Henry's eyes wide with alarm and her heart in her mouth she backed quickly out of the room to do something; she didn't know what, her heart was racing and her mind whirling.

She ran back into the hallway and looked for a weapon. The coat racks held only umbrellas and coats. The first one had a heavy handle in the shape of a parrot, so she grabbed the umbrella and then she saw the large gong, probably the one that was used to call guests to dinner. She hit it as hard as she could with the umbrella, and again and again, the sounds resounding around the house. The welcome sound of doors opening and someone yelling is it a fire, and then her relief vanished as she was faced with Ed, his scar making him look more furious. As he lunged at her she hit him in the stomach with the umbrella and then stamped on his toe. As he yelled and bent double, she ran in brandishing the umbrella and seeing Clayton about to insert the needle into Henry's arm, hit Clayton over the fingers. He yelped and dropped the needle. He went to grab her as Ed came stumbling back into the room, she went to poke Clayton in the stomach too, figuring it had worked the first time. Unfortunately for Clayton, he was smaller than Laura; she was quite tall and he was still slightly bent forward from trying to insert the syringe, so the parrot handle on the umbrella went up his nose.

"Oops," from Laura as he grabbed his nose and fell over backwards. As Ed went to grab her, four of the knights ran into the room in various stages of readiness for bed followed by Gordon in his stripy pyjamas and one arm in his dressing gown.

Laura felt some one run past her and she saw Henry was breaking free as his capturers ran towards the others who had entered the room. There was shouting and confusion, so she grabbed Henry and pulled him back behind the desk with her, out of harm's way.

She saw Cam give Ed a real 'fourpenny one', which gave a real smack sound like on a cartoon, and Ed fall backwards over a chair. She couldn't really tell what was happening and the shouting and confusion made her heart thump so loud that she thought everyone must hear it. She clung onto Henry's arm.

Then it was all over. It can only have lasted about 10 or 15 minutes but it seemed like hours. The knights and Gordon had overpowered the Americans and they sat them in a row on the ground hands on their heads, all except Clayton who was holding his nose with a large handkerchief as it gushed blood.

"Well, maybe we ought to add umbrella fighting to the Highland Games Laura, you'd win hands down!" Smiling, Henry giving her a large hug. He looked pale and Gordon was administering brandy as he spoke. *"I can't thank you enough my dear."*

Laura looked embarrassed.

Cam spoke, *"What were you doing here, Laura? It was a miracle you appearing when you did and the gong a stroke of genius."*

"I couldn't sleep and was out for a walk, and as I was passing I saw figures outside the house and I just knew somehow there was something wrong. I came up the drive into the library to tell Henry. And the gong, well I was looking for a weapon and saw it as I grabbed an umbrella and just thought in a split second it was the best way to rouse the house."

She suddenly felt very cold and her knees very weak. Her face must have gone white because Rafe grabbed her and sat her down, *"Brandy here too Gordon, I think it's adrenaline rush causing a bit of shock."*

Cam said he had rung the police and they were on their way. Zak had the men in the sights of a shotgun he got from the ghillie's gun cupboard, to make sure they didn't move.

"Lucky for us you did, we hadn't heard a thing and now maybe Henry you will let us turn the burglar alarm on even when you are in the house."

"The cats set it off and it's a nuisance sometimes." Henry explained to Laura.

"Why were the Americans trying to kill you?" Laura suddenly realised that it looked like they were trying to drug Henry.

"I am sure the police will find that out, maybe to steal the stone, I don't know."

With that the police arrived and confusion reigned again, with everyone speaking at once and the Americans protesting at their treatment. It took some time to remove the intruders and take them away, the local police thought it was a burglary gone wrong.

The sergeant was talking to Henry, *"The castle would have been seen as fair game for antiques and they probably thought everyone would be in bed, sir. You were lucky this lady happened by when she did and chose to act rather than just walk by. However we don't normally encourage members of the public to get involved. She should have rung us,"* with that he looked at Laura pointedly.

"By the time you arrived, Henry could have been dead," pointed out Cam. Cam looked annoyed as if he thought they should have been more grateful to Laura.

It took yet more time for her statement to be taken by a grinning policeman, who sniggered when she told him about the umbrella going up Clayton's nose. When she had signed it, she suddenly seemed to feel it was all over and she was so tired. Gabe motioned to Rafe and he came forward to suggest it was time Laura went home, she looked exhausted. The police had done all they could for now and the sergeant agreed, she should leave and get some rest. *"We will be in touch if there is anything else Mrs Loomis, we have your contact details."* Laura nodded.

Rafe drove her back to the cottage and said they would make sure the cottage was watched for a couple of nights to see she was safe in case there were any other Americans lurking. He watched her go in.

Back at the house Henry and Zak discussed the night's happenings. *"She was drawn here Henry, it's obvious she is somehow involved. Maybe her ancestors lived here or she has some psychic thing, women's intuition, I don't know."*

"Then we must protect her as well. She was meant to be here at this time perhaps to save

me ...serendipity."

Zak nodded and said, *"Time we were all in bed. Here's Rafe back. We can set the alarm. I will text the patrols and let them know in case they set it off on their return."*

"It will be interesting to see what tale Blome-Grant tells the police," said Henry grimly as he set off up the stairs. He felt very tired and old. Zak watched his retreating back and hoped that Henry would be alright. This had been quite a shock to him; to them all come to that. He grimaced when he thought of what could have happened. Thank god for women, he grinned to himself, and went round to check all the doors were again secure, before he went back upstairs.

The bed felt very good to Laura, the purring bundles that appeared shortly after she put out the light, made her feel safe. She hugged herself trying to get warm and calm herself after what she had been through. Eventually she slept, but in her dreams the dark shapes still swam and she woke up the next morning with a headache.

CHAPTER 31

Dark Talks

Henry had called a meeting with the main estate staff the next morning. They all gathered in the library whilst Gordon dispensed tea and coffee, and biscuits. Gabe and Hani stood behind Henry's chair. Henry held up his hand and the murmur of voices stopped. He looked around at the sea of faces, Hamish the salt of the earth, Mary the housekeeper a strong God-fearing Scottish woman, and the Stephen the estate manager, an honest hard working chap, and the others standing behind them in respectful silence. Henry sighed to himself.

"You will no doubt have heard by now about last night's burglary and the attempt on my person," he began, and a muttering arose about it being a disgrace and people not being safe in their own homes. He raised his voice slightly and continued, *"Although the police have detained those responsible, it has made me realise how lax we are on matters of security. There are many valuable things in the castle and I would have never forgiven myself if one of you, my staff, were hurt. So to that end we are going to have to tighten things up ,including putting on the alarm, even if the cats do set it off,"* he grinned as he said it.

The estate had quite a few house cats, who were ridiculously spoiled by Mary and Gordon, but despite that kept the mice at bay. They had a cat door on every floor, but would use the windows, and their comings and goings often set off the alarms. Henry was fond of the cats and they would often take turns to come in and sit on his lap by the fire at night.

"Also," he raised his hand again to stem the murmuring, *"there may be another attack yet on the estate. There may be others who - hearing of the near success of the men last night - may try their luck. So please be vigilant. If we need men to walk the borders of the estate, to secure the boundaries, they will be paid ghillie's rate, so please pass that on. Hopefully, they won't be needed. Now thank you for coming and if you have any questions, Gordon and Gabe here will answer them."* Henry rose with some difficulty from his seat. The others parted to let him through and Hani followed. *"Come into the study Hani. I could do with some company."* Hani nodded, understanding Henry needed to talk.

Henry's slow departure had not gone unnoticed and Hamish was the first to say, *"The laird has taken this hard, he looks old this morning."* A nod of agreement from all and Gordon said:

"Well we must do our best to help him get over it, even if it means locking the cats in at night so we can set the alarms."

"What's this about another attack?" from Mary. Then the voices rose and Gabe had to shout to be heard as the questions continued.

Henry, seated in his study chair, motioned Hani to the one opposite. He looked up as he heard the voices rise and then Gordon shutting the door. *"Don't worry, Henry, Gabe and Gordon can handle it."* Hani then looked at Henry and spoke more softly, *"What is it Henry? You look done in?"*

Henry gripped the arms of his chair. *"All this reminds me of when Margaret was killed."*

"No, this is different Henry. It is not your fault and what happened with Margaret wasn't your fault either. She went out on the loch in your Barbour coat and was mistaken for you. Your wife died because of someone else's wickedness, it was not your fault."

Hani paused as if deciding something, *"Have you heard from your son?"*

"Yes, he still refuses to have anything to do with me. His adopted parents told him the whole story, how I sent him to them for safekeeping, but he won't forgive me for his mother's death. I have three grandchildren now you know." Henry gave a tight smile, *"I get sent photos and letters with news by Samuel's wife. She does not understand his attitude, but does not know the whole story. All she knows is he blames me for his mother dying."*

"This is not the same Henry, this has not happened because of you being cursed or any of the other things you think. It is because there are people in this world who will hurt others to reach their goals." Hani looked at Henry, and knew Henry was thinking that it was his fault, because he had come back to the castle. There was a silence and Hani wondered if he should let Henry think or interrupt. Suddenly Henry slapped his hands down on the arms of the chair, making Hani jump. *"I will not let them take what they want. They killed Margaret and for her sake I will not give in to them. We must fight Hani, we must. Margaret would never have let me give in."*

"That's the spirit Henry," Hani was relieved to see Henry angry. This morning Henry had looked like a broken man and he had been afraid for his mental state. *"I may be older than, and not as tough as, I once was, but I can't let this go on. It is time they were stopped. I will certainly not let anyone of the staff get injured because of me. Come let us go look at our defences with Cam. We need to check that alarm for a start."*

Henry rose much easier than before, more upright and alert and Hani followed him from the room. As they passed Gordon in the hallway, Hani gave a thumbs up sign behind Henry's back. Gordon nodded to show he had understood and then they both grinned at each other. Their one worry was that Henry would go under, being reminded of his wife's death. If only his son was around thought Gordon, he sighed and shook his head; families are so difficult sometimes.

CHAPTER 32
Dark Occurrences

The girl, about 13-years-old, walked along the shore swinging a dog lead. In her wake, a young spaniel whose tail was wagging so much it's a wonder the dog didn't take flight like a helicopter. Fiona, the girl, also bounced as she walked. She was dressed in the normal teenage attire, jeans and big clumpy boots, her coat flying open despite her mother's protests that she would catch a chill.

"Come on Poppy. Leave the dead fish alone or you will have to have a bath. Mum won't let you in the house."

The dog ignored her, so she found a stick and waved it, to attract its attention and threw it along the shore. The dog bounded after it yipping with joy.

Hamish on his way to check out some nets that had been reported tangled by the shore, a hazard to wild life, smiled when he saw her. She was small and slim with red hair escaping from her hat and he stopped to talk to the girl.

"Hello Fiona, I see yon dog's as daft as ever!"

The girl giggled. *"Dad got her for a gun dog, but she kept going for the guns, barking at them, and not fetching the game, so she's my pet now."*

"Ach well some dogs are not meant for working. She makes a better pet." He fondled the dog's silky ears as it bounded up to see him. *"She's in beautiful condition; you look after her well lassie."*

"Thanks. I love to her to bits and mum says it does me good to get out in the fresh air."

"Take care to keep out of the water. There's been a few accidents lately with the blows up from the bottom of the loch."

"Aye I ken Hamish. Do you think we'll have an earthquake?"

"Nay lassie, there's always been activity in the loch, it's just the earth moving and twitching a bit like an old man stretching when he's stiff with sitting. Nothing to fret about."

She nodded trying to look wise. *"See you Hamish"* and with that she was off, the dog yelping at her heels.

Hamish smiled as he watched her go, nice wee lassie not like some of them; full of cheek some of them that got off that school bus. They daren't cheek Hamish though, they knew they would never have got away with it, one way or another he would have got them back. Further along the beach he found the nets tangled in the stones on the shore. There was a sea gull caught in one end, been trying to eat the fish that was still stuck there. Hamish put on his thick gloves and got out his knife. In a few minutes he managed to free the frightened bird despite its best efforts to peck him. He gathered up the nets, and pulled a black bin liner from his pocket and shoved them into it. Something had torn the net badly and it had come to the shore on the waves. Probably more stuff coming up from the bottom of the loch, he sighed to himself. A man's work is never done. Walking back it occurred to him young Fiona, hadn't gone past him on her way back.

"I hope that daft dog hasn't got her into any trouble," he grumbled as he set off back along the shore.

Then he heard it, the dog howling and the splash in the water. He dropped the bin bag and ran towards the sound. The fear of what he might find giving him speed.

The dog was quaking visibly and howling and whimpering and refused to come to him when he called. There was no sign of Fiona, only the dog lead on the shore. Two of the men staying with the laird came running along the shore attracted by the noise.

"Did you see it Hamish? Did it take the girl?"

Hamish went pale, *"The evil, please god not wee Fiona."* He prayed as he ran around the area calling her name and the two knights searched the bushes.

Then a shout: *"She's here. She's alive."*

Relief flooded through Hamish as he turned to the direction the shout came from. Zaph came running out of the undergrowth carrying Fiona in his arms. She was still, her face frozen and white but she was still alive. Zaph struggled to get a hand free and gave his 'phone to Hamish to ring for an ambulance. The wait for the ambulance seemed forever. Zaph wrapped Fiona in his coat to keep her warm, her small white face seemed to be admonishing him, for allowing this to happen. Once the paramedics arrived, seeing there was nothing else he could do, Hamish went to fetch her parents. Luckily they were both at home. What he didn't tell the parents was what the knights had seen, just that they had found the dog and then Fiona and that they weren't sure what had happened, and she'd gone to Inverness hospital.

Zaph rang Henry after the ambulance had departed. *"It's been seen in solid form. It was huge Henry more terrible then I have ever seen it. The girl was unharmed but in shock. We have to do something before more of them come and get it from the water to do harm. It's out of control again."*

He listened to the voice on the other end of the 'phone and then returned to his companion. They continued on their way and Hamish meeting them, returning to inform them Fiona's parents were on their way to the hospital, said he would take the dog home with him. Zaph handed the dog over gratefully. The parents had enough to deal with. Grim faced Hamish picked up the dog, which was still visibly shaking, and took it back to his house. Sadie would look after the poor wee thing for a few days.

Sadie never questioned him when he told why he'd brought the dog. She just said, *"I will put it by the stove and give it a drop of warm milk. Leave it with me."*

"I have to go see the laird," was all Hamish said. She just nodded and took the dog from him. Hamish never went to Cragneghil Castle unbidden, but today he went to have it out with the laird. Enough was enough, it's time he acted, the next time the child might not be found alive.

CHAPTER 33

Dark Messages

L aura sat with her notes going through her time-lines of alchemists. She had spoken to John on the 'phone and told him about the threat to Henry's life and her part as nose puncturer, which helped by giving the knights time to rescue Henry. He was at once amused and also afraid for Laura. *"You could have been killed or injured as well."*

"You don't think in a situation like that. I've never thought of myself as particularly brave but I just acted. If I had thought about it, I probably would have walked past and then called the police and it would have been too late. Will you tell the others for me, John, please? I don't think I can face repeating it all over again."

"No problem. Well you know where we are if you get worried or just need a friend."

"Thanks John. I'll catch up with you tomorrow."

She turned off her mobile as she had a feeling once the others found out they would ring, and she didn't feel she could go through the questions, nor the sympathy. Thoughtfully looking at her notes, she realised that if what Hamish told her was truthful in some respects, then Merlin could have been St Columba and it may not have been prayers that sent the monster back but incantation. How many local people would have understood Latin or any ancient language, it would all sound the same to them. And what about Willox the warlock she said to herself. What if it was set up to like the Flamels, nobody in the coffin, so to overcome that they put someone else's body in the coffin or weighted it down with stones. The horse's bridle thing could have been left to convince the locals it was Willox. People look different when they are dead and no DNA testing in those days. *"I am turning into a conspiracy theorist now,"* she laughed to herself. *"I will have to put it on the internet next to alien reptiles ruling the earth, Merlin is still alive and has lived for 2000 years."*

With a sigh she realised the cats were circling like piranhas. *"Its lunchtime again is it old chaps? Come on then let's go see what we have got."*

The elder cat Aristotle, despite being 17, was still fit and full of life. Woe betides any dog that entered his territory. He had once had two large dogs and their owners pinned to the wall outside a house they lived in, growling and spitting at them. The old boy had got out when the delivery man came. It hadn't helped the delivery man had said to the dog owners, *"You wouldn't think he was 17 would you? A game old cat isn't he?"* They did not reply. The dog walkers always took a detour after that. The younger cat, despite being twice the size of the elder, hid behind the settee and growled, Buzbi was a coward and was there for back up, as long as it wasn't needed. Laura gave them some packets of food and left them to eat it. Whichever bowl she put in front of them, they would immediately go to the other one, so she left them to sort it out themselves.

Henry was pacing the floor in the sitting room angrily. *"Are you sure? They haven't been charged?"* the words almost shot from his mouth.

Rafe nodded, *"They are being deported back to the States. Covered by diplomatic immunity apparently, but Clayton's "twin" brother Derek has arrived with a large cohort of men. They have taken over one of the larger houses to rent over on the Black Isle. Perhaps thinking we wouldn't find out,"* he went on to say. *"Thank you MI6 for your reliability."*

"I won't ask how you get this info Rafe, but it is useful. Damn and blast it." Henry hit his fist into his other hand as he spoke; *"I was hoping they would at least be in custody for a while but they are relentless and tricky. I should have realised they wouldn't do something like this if they hadn't thought they had some insurance to get away with it."*

Rafe shook his head and continued, *"My step brother works for the service doing electronic surveillance as required. It's usually stuff like drugs and people smuggling he is called in for, but he is kept in the loop and has access to certain networks. Even if they had been charged Henry, the others would have come over to sort it out. Probably would have caused a stink, which the government wouldn't want at the moment. The Prime Minister is not popular as it is and the friendly relationship with the American President would be something he would want to retain and not have the USA upset. These people will have powerful connections in industry and the government."*

"I remember Philip, your step brother, very intelligent when he was young but a little distant. And I know you are right, but it irks me all the same." Henry continued after a sigh, *"We can expect Hamish at the door next after what happened this morning."*

"If distant is a polite way of saying Philip probably has Asperger's syndrome you are probably right, but he's a nice guy despite that, and I can't say I blame Hamish. He will be angry it's gone on this long."

"Did you go to the Black Isle?"

"Yes we did Henry," Cam insisted. *"They are renting that big pink house that's set back, up the hill. The place with the funny name Politzfield? The only other things there are a few cottages and some smallholdings.*

They are mainly English people living there. The one who runs the smallholding was a miserable so and so. Cam swears he has seen him on 'America's Most Wanted' page on the internet," Rafe grinned as he spoke. *"The man finding they weren't there to buy anything or rent a cottage from him had been quite terse. They say the Scots are dour but either he had been here too long or left England because he was too miserable to stay there."*

Henry seemed not to hear and continued, *"I will explain to Hamish about the Americans, why they are here. He will understand. He won't be happy but he will understand. There are families here who have kept the secrets of the loch for generations and they will not fail me now."* Henry strode out of the room to the study to think on the new developments, leaving Rafe to stare after him. Rafe had never seen Henry so angry.

"Those Nazis," Henry raged to himself. *"Not content with one genocide they want another and innocent people are suffering because of their determination to be supreme. Aryans Pah! Barbarians more like."* He flung himself down in a chair to brood on the new developments.

When Gordon entered the study discreetly, Henry looked up and expected him to say Hamish was in the hall but instead he said, *"The Nazis are at the door milord, wanting to speak to you. Do you wish me to send them away?"*

"What! Damn cheek," Henry could not believe what he was hearing. *"How many of them?"*

"Six milord. Rather large gentlemen."

His first instinct was to tell Gordon to refuse to let them in, but then he thought they ought to size up the opposition and see what they wanted. *"Alright Gordon, get Rafe and the others, and give us a few minutes to move into the library and then show two of them in."*

Gordon nodded and did as he was told. Rafe and the others appeared through the door at the outside of the library, the one Laura had used that night, so they weren't seen by those in the hall.

"Go behind the priest hole panel and keep watch. Just in case. They surely won't be that stupid, but one never knows."

Henry motioned Rafe to stay at his side as he directed the others, and showed them the spy hole in the priest hole. With three of the knights hidden behind a panel in the library and Rafe at his side, Henry was ready.

The man who walked in was Clayton, but claimed to be: *"Derek Blome-Grant. We meet at last. You are not surprised by my appearance I see. I am the first born and more alike my father than any of the others."*

"Excuse me if I don't shake hands under the circumstance, and this is?" said Henry indicating Derek's companion.

"Another first born, Hans Goett, his father was an SS elite. However he does not speak English."

Henry introduced Rafe who also did not shake hands.

"I am here," Derek continued with the same snarly smile that Clayton had, *"to save us both and the local population some distress. I suggest you give us a blood sample willingly and we will leave you in peace. Otherwise, I am afraid we will take it by force and there is no doubt we will get it this time. Provenance saved you last time. It won't happen again I shall make sure of that."*

"Not provenance but a woman with an umbrella. I hardly think that ranks high on the Nazi list of great battles," laughed Henry.

Derek snarled again, *"Laugh all you want old man. Your time is over. It has been over for a hundred years. It is our time now. We are the new order; we are the magicians and the leaders. You had your chance. We will be back. Next time we will not fail and you may not survive."*

He turned on his heel followed by the morose looking Hans and pushed Gordon aside as he went to open the door for them.

"He talks like an old movie," commented Rafe, *"but the threats are real enough. So what now Henry?"*

"He is an old movie," came the comment from the panel as it opened. *"Remember his mind is still in the 40s, that's where daddy donor was from."*

Zaph shook off a cobweb he had managed to acquire from the panel. *"Could do with a dust in there Henry."*

"I will inform the housekeeper. It is not used often," Henry said without moving his face. He had a strange desire to laugh.

"So how strong do you think he is?" Cam looked at Henry as he spoke.
"Not strong enough, but he will cause havoc. We will have to decide where to hole up against his hoard and where I can fight back and not risk the locals being caught up in it. He will not strike before nightfall and will probably wait until the full moon. He will need time to prepare. It's what they believe in, ritual and magic, but that gives us time."

Henry rang for Gordon, "We need to get together with a map of the area and discuss our options."

The others nodded. Cam smiled. He liked a good fight and he had been rather bored of late. The scrap in the library hardly qualified as a battle.

CHAPTER 34

Dark Times

At the hospital, Fiona's parents waited anxiously for news.

The doctor came out from the curtains. *"We are going to transfer her to Glasgow as soon as they have a bed. She is in deep shock. Something must have happened to traumatise her, but until she speaks, we have no idea what."*

"She," began her father and faltered. He swallowed, *"She's not been attacked or harmed in any way?"*

"No she hasn't been abused if that is your worry." The doctor patted the father's arm, *"It was the first thing we thought of, but no there isn't a mark on her. That is what makes it all the more puzzling. What could traumatise a child so much and yet not harm her?"* He called the nurse at the desk over to leave instructions. *"You can go in,"* he said to the parents, *"maybe hearing your voices might help."*

As they entered the curtains they saw her sitting rigid, white faced, not moving. Just sitting as she had been left by the doctor. Her pupils were dilated as if in terror but nothing seemed to be going on behind her eyes. Her mother burst into tears as the sight of her and her husband tried to comfort her whilst staring in disbelief at his daughter. She was like a waxwork. He wasn't even sure she was alive, she looked frozen in time. *"Come on Mary, pull yourself together, we have to talk to her like. It works for coma people."*

His wife nodded and followed his lead. They both took one of Fiona's hands each and held them in both of theirs. Her mother started to talk, her voice quavering. *"It's me Fiona, mummy, Poppy is staying with Hamish until you get better so we can come and spend time with you. She is fine, the dog, just a bit scared. She will be missing you, but Hamish will take good care of her."*

"You will be able to take her back for walks down the loch shore again when you are better and home," began her father. The child began to shake and then opened her mouth and started to scream. It was the sound of sheer terror, of a person so scared they could do nothing else but scream. The nurses came running in, Fiona's mother put her hands to her face and then to

cover her ears, her husband had come around the bed and held her tight whilst the nurses tried to calm Fiona.

Hamish marched to the door of Cragneghil Castle and banged on the door decisively. Gordon opened it and welcomed him in, *"Come through to the study, Hamish, the laird has been expecting you."*

"Aye I bet he has," muttered Hamish.

The laird was sitting at the desk with a map of the area spread in front of him. He looked up as soon as Hamish entered. *"Hamish please take a seat and please take a dram with me. I know why you are here and I know you think I should have acted sooner."* Henry indicated a seat as he spoke. Hamish sat down. For once he didn't feel uncomfortable, he knew he was in the right to come and face the laird. Once Hamish had his whisky, Gordon made sure it was a 28-year-old Glenlivet, Hamish's favourite, Henry explained some of his reasons for not acting sooner and that the plan was to take the action away from the local vicinity and then once that was settled deal with the loch.

"I know it should not have got this far and I will make amends. I have arranged private care for the child and transport for her parents to visit her. She will be fine, I will give my personal guarantee and attention that she will." Henry signalled Gordon to top up Hamish's whisky as he spoke.

"Aye and I ken you looked after the relatives of Campbell and Angus, even though Angus probably was nothing to with things. He was probably drunk. I trust you but I am a feared of what will happen if you don't act soon."

"I will act as swiftly as I am able Hamish. How are the villagers taking things?"

"The locals know and will wait for you to act. They trust the laird. The incomers know no different so they will be fine. There will be a new laird no doubt when this is over."

"Hamish, you know more than most but yes I think it wise. Now please have some more whisky and we will drink a toast to the success of the quest and then if there is anything..." Henry's voice tailed off, *"You know what to do."* Hamish nodded and had another whisky. *"I ken they were Germans, from that last trouble, when you lost poor Lady Margaret. They were almost the same."* Henry nodded and rose. He signalled Hamish to remain seated.

"Finish your drink Hamish, God knows you deserve it." Hamish knew the wife would give him hell when he got home, drinking this time o' day. Once she knew it was the laird though she always changed her tune. Gordon showed Hamish out ten minutes later, and made sure he wasn't driving. Hamish left feeling better about things, though that could have just been the affect of the whisky, but he had done his duty and now he knew the full story he could understand. A few die to save the many, the way it has always been. They didn't know their sacrifice nor why, but future generations would survive because they had gone. He weaved his way back to his cottage, no more work today he decided, a nice nap perhaps if Sadie is out.

Chapter 35
Dark Changes

W hen Gordon returned from seeing Hamish out, Henry was back at the map on the study desk. *"I think we should give Hamish a pay rise, an honorarium for extra duties as it were. And check if he needs any work doing on the cottage, I am sure his wife would appreciate some modernisation. It hasn't been touched since when I last was here."*

"Yes milord," smiled Gordon. Sadie, Hamish's wife would be over the moon, being offered a modernisation, he knew that. *"There are a couple of other properties needs sprucing up and no one would think anything odd if they were all done at once."*

"See to it then Gordon; get that builder who normally does it. He's a good reliable chap and will see the work is of good quality. Tell him there is a bonus if he makes Sadie smile."

Gordon laughed. Sadie, Hamish's wife was a well-known local tartar. She kept the house spotless and was a marvellous cook, but Hamish had to do as he was bidden. Hamish loved her though, that was obvious and Gordon suspected that at home it was a lot cosier than outsiders imagined; otherwise Hamish would have left her years ago. She was a big handsome woman but stern faced and always dressed very smartly, but in dull functional clothes. However the postie once told Gordon that some fancy lingerie parcels got delivered to Hamish's house, so unless Hamish wore ladies knickers and suspenders, Sadie was glamorous on the quiet. Gordon left the laird contemplating his map and went to inform the estate manager about the improvements.

Stephen Prentice, the estate manager, was English and had been resented at first, but he did a good job of keeping the estate running smoothly, and was fair and had been grudgingly accepted by the locals, many of whom worked on the estate in some form or another. He was a tall well-built man, fit from working around the estate, going grey at the sides of his dark hair, even though he was barely forty. Most people with very dark hair seem to go grey early, Gordon had found.

Stephen gave Gordon a beaming smile when he saw him approach. They got on well together. He burst out laughing when Gordon told him about the builder's bonus and said: *"Do you think he would agree to our house getting a spruce up, since Janice had the youngest, she's found it harder to manage the old stove and the solid fuel heating."*

"I am sure he will be happy to agree. Just make your decision about what you want and speak to James the builder. Get James to do quotes for all the properties that need improving and then take it to the laird. Sooner rather than later would be good. We could get all the work done in the spring then if the quote is reasonable."

"Cheers Gordon. I'll get on to it right away. I'll make sure only necessary improvements are put down. Old Ma MacDonald wanted a whirl pool bath last time for her arthritis. She got a nice shower with a seat in instead."

Gordon laughed at the thought of old Ma MacDonald and a Jacuzzi. He must remember to tell the laird, it would make him smile. Gordon returned to the house. This would give the locals something else to think about than the loch. The laird was a clever man alright. There would be lots of discussion about who was getting what done and the incidents at the loch forgotten for a while.

Laura was just sitting down with her first coffee of the morning when her mobile went. Daniel's voice: *"Didn't wake you did I? Only John said you would be awake?"*

"No Daniel, you didn't wake me. I am not dressed but I am downstairs. Is something wrong? Is Emily OK?"

"Emily is fine. Well, the thing is, it's just that it's our last chance to take soundings before the weather gets too bad and well, well we need three and Emily, well I didn't want to ask her and John said you are quite capable ...well please pretty please, we need to go out today?" It all came out at speed in one breath.

"Haven't you got other students?" Laura was laughing now.

"Yeah, but they are not very good if there is an emergency and I need someone who doesn't flap and well someone I can trust. Plus I have sent most of them over to Loch Moray to take readings."

"Well if you put it like that, I will come. I'd like to go out on the loch anyway. It's a long time since I've been in a boat though. Give me half an hour to get ready and have the coffee on."

"Goes without saying. Thanks Laura, really, thanks. Good karma to you. See you at the jetty." Laura sighed, so much for her quiet day. She went to find some suitable clothing and hoped they had a life jacket; she hadn't swum for years either.

The cats would be fine, the house was warm and their dishes were full, and they ventured out less these days since the weather had changed. Just as well, she thought ruefully. Donald had been to visit after the last fine day and whilst he was there playing with the cats, he asked Laura where she got the big brown cat toy from. On investigation it turned out to be a dead rat that Buzbi had brought in and put in the cat toy box, to play with later she presumed. Luckily, neither her nor Donald were fazed and deposited it outside in the back garden, out of harm's way. Donald said a fox might eat it, so would provide supper, and not be wasted. She sighed and checked the cats were in and asleep.

When she arrived at the jetty, suitably clad in waterproof coat, warm jumper and jeans, John and Donald were preparing to cast off, and Andy was waiting for her grinning, mug of coffee in one hand, a life jacket in the other.

"Daniel said to show the screens you have to watch and how stuff works and then we'll be off." Grabbing the jacket she climbed aboard. She put on the life jacket, took a gulp of the coffee and got out a notebook and pen to write down anything she might need to remember. Andy showed what to watch for, when to tell them and which way to tell Daniel to steer the boat when she saw something.

They set off slowly at first and then speeded up to keep within hailing distance of John and Donald. Donald gave her a cheery wave as he caught sight of her on the deck. She waved back and starting humming Popeye the sailor man to herself.

Daniel's head popped into view, *"You OK?"*

"Fine. Quite enjoying the ride."

He gave her a thumbs up sign and went back down below to check on something. The first hour passed quickly and she was getting quite used to the screen and what to look for. Then something moved. She blinked and rubbed her eyes, no there was something large below them. She shouted Andy and he in turn yelled to Daniel. The boat stopped and John also stopped .She saw Daniel talking to John on the radio. Donald and Andy were both peering over the sides into the water. She went to look as well. At first she could see nothing only the dark water beneath her, she thought of how deep it was - over seven hundred and fifty feet they say and shivered. Then she saw a movement, *"Andy there is something moving."*

Andy ran to look over the port side where she was. Something large and dark was moving slowly under the boat. It was quite far down but the movement disturbed the water. There was no suggestion of shape just something large and dark. Daniel joined them. *"Is it still there?"*

"Yes but it's hard to tell what it is or how big," Laura said.

"You scared?" from Andy.

"No not really, more curious, but then I don't know what it is. If I did I might be." Laura replied. Then as she leant over further to look into the water, she saw an eye blink. She stepped back startled almost standing on Daniel's toe.

"It just winked at me," she looked at the other two. *"And if that is the size of its eye, unless*

it's all head, it must be bloody huge."

She held her hands up and drew a circle shape in the air, bigger than a dinner plate.

The radio crackled. John's voice, *"Whatever it is, it's moving away."*

"Thank God for that," said Laura. *"What the hell is it? It must be massive."*

Daniel shook his head and returned to the radio.

"Laura looked at it and scared it," Daniel said and John could be heard laughing at the other end. *"Actually she swears it winked at her, and because she didn't respond it's gone off heartbroken."* Laura hit him with the notebook she was holding. *"Ow ! Now she is beating me."* John's voice came back, *"Serves you right. I would have said something from this boat but not on your boat whilst she is there."*

They all started to laugh, *"Well its gone guys, do you want to do one more turn before we head back?"*

Daniel looked at Andy and Laura; they nodded, *"Yes we are willing if you are, man. It doesn't seem to want to attack us."*

The boats turned and did another sweep of the loch with Laura keeping a firm eye on the screen. She didn't want to see that eye again. It was cold, not like a cat's, more mean and reptilian somehow, she couldn't explain it. Cats could look cold but not like this, it was just pure predator and she could have been prey. She shook herself, *"Come on woman, stop thinking like that, it was probably just an illusion caused by the peaty water. I expect it was a normal sized eye for a large fish and the refraction of the light, being so dark in the water, made it look huge."* It was strange how they all just accepted that there might be something huge in the water and seemed to not be bothered by the fact, she mused, must be the whole 'familiarity breeding contempt' thing. We are now so used to the idea, it doesn't bother us anymore.

They carried on for another hour and just as Laura was starting to get really cold, she was grateful to hear Daniel say they were heading back. The jetty was soon in sight and Laura gathered up the readings she had printed out for Daniel and turned off the monitor. *"Right we'll tie up and collect the data together, you go to the pub and grab a table Laura and I will buy us all lunch. I told Emily to meet us there. She's been proof reading for me this morning. Here's John so we'll catch you up."* Laura nodded glad to be going into the warm.

The first thing she did on reaching the hotel, was run into the ladies toilets and when she came out and grabbed a table her ears were stinging as the warmth of the room started to permeate her cold limbs. She got a couple of menus and a glass of red wine, and ordered four whiskies for the others. The landlord was used to them by now, *"Who's' paying?"*

"Daniel said he would pay for lunch," she said.

"I will add the drinks onto the bill," he winked at her and she grinned.

The others arrived followed by Emily who decided she would have a red wine too. The men opted for meat pies with all the vegetables and chips and gravy; Emily and Laura chose curry. The one thing about Scotland, Laura thought, was they might say the food was unhealthy, but you can't beat good solid food on a cold day. She remembered going into a fish and chip shop in Aberdeen and seeing deep fried pizza and something called big foot which she presumed was a deep fired haggis or black pudding. That was unhealthy, this was just hot stodge which you need on an autumn's day, plus they had vegetables with it or rice with the curry. She knew there were people who never ate vegetables and in fact someone had written to the local newspaper in Aberdeen saying their family hadn't eaten vegetables in forty years or something. Mad she laughed to herself. The Scots are certainly characters.

They were silent for a moment whilst cutlery was distributed and plates sorted and served. *"Oh that's better, nice and warming,"* said Laura taking a mouthful. *"I can't believe how cold it gets on the boat."*

"It seems to seep right inside you," agreed Emily.

After the plates were nearly empty and the landlady came over and asked if everything was OK, Daniel asked for apple pie and cream all round.

"Oh and coffees, unless anyone wants another drink?" They all shook their heads with a chorus of coffee is fine.

"Well how did you like the boat?" Emily asked Laura. *"It was pretty cool actually, and I quite enjoyed it."*

"Did you cope with the sonar monitor OK? It can be confusing sometimes, too many signals and lines."

"You will have to ask the guys that one when they look at the readings," laughed Laura.

"Did you come across anything, you know strange?" Emily asked somewhat tentatively, though to Laura it had been obvious what Emily was leading up to. *"Well something large went under the boat but nothing happened,"* Laura spoke carefully, not wanting to spook Emily.

"She scared the monster away," chortled Donald.

"Really, did you?" Emily's eyes grew big.

"Very funny. I thought I saw an eye looking at me and stepped back and stood on Daniel's foot. Whatever it was left after that and they all say," Laura gestured to the men, *"I either scared it away or it was disappointed I didn't wink back."*

"What did you say?" gasped Emily.

"Aye Eye? What's all this then," giggled Laura, and they all groaned.

Emily laughed and they changed the subject.

At the next table, Derek had his back to them but was listening intently as he chewed his food slowly. So it's still there he thought to himself, the next move is ours I think. This could turn to our advantage after all. He raised his glass to the group unbeknown to them. *"Cheers and thanks for the info".*

The subject at the academics table had turned to Christmas and they were discussing who was going home and who was staying. Laura said anyone who was staying was welcome to come to her house for Christmas dinner as she was expecting her daughter so would be cooking anyway.

"Generous as ever Laura," said John and then they all laughed as she said: *"It goes with my size, generous is as generous does".*

They departed shortly afterwards with Daniel thanking Laura again for helping out, and presenting her with a box of chocolates he had bought in the local shop on their way to the hotel. It reminded Laura she needed to call in the shop to get some things. She would put the chocolates away for Christmas, unless she had a bad day, and then might be tempted to open them.

CHAPTER 36

Dark Sadness

L aura was going into the local shop, on her way back home, when she saw Fiona's mother approaching. The poor woman looked care worn, not like her normal self. She walked with her head down as if the weight of the world was on her shoulders. Laura grabbed a bouquet of flowers, nice cheerful yellow and orange colours and a box of chocolates, the sort in a proper box with a ribbon, along with her groceries. She paid for them quickly and as Fiona's mother entered the shop, she approached her.

"I am so sorry to hear about Fiona. I used to see her and the dog around quite a lot. A lovely girl."

She handed the flowers and chocolates to her, and continued, *"The flowers are for you and the chocolates for Fiona when she is feeling better."*

Tears welled in Mrs McDougall's eyes. *"Thank you,"* she stammered. *"Your kindness when you hardly know her…."* her voice trailed off and Laura gave her a hug.

She heard the shopkeeper saying as she left, *"A nice lassie that one. Always polite. And how are you dear? And any news on the wee lassie?"*

"She is still sedated but the hospital the laird got her into is very good. She is in a private room and there is TV and everything for when she feels better. He sends a car everyday to take us there and back."

"It's only right he should Mary, it's his responsibility to look after us. But he could have done nothing. There are those in the past would have done nothing to help. Anyway what can I get you and is there anything the wee one needs?"

"Well she is sedated, but she is having therapy now and not so sleepy, so maybe some comics?"

"Take what you like hen, a gift from me."

"People have been so kind," said Mary almost in tears again.

"Now, now no more of that. It's only right folks should help out. We are all neighbours ye ken and we all like the wee lassie."

Mary picked out some teenage magazines, that and the chocolates would put a smile on wee Fiona's face. Some more people came into the shop so Mary got the rest of her purchases, and left before anyone asked her anything and set her off blubbing again.

Laura felt guilty even though she didn't know why. She suspected it was because she felt responsible for letting Henry not do anything; she should have forced his hand. *"Too late for regrets now,"* she said to herself. *"The damage is done."*

Walking back, she met Hamish carrying something heavy in a sack. *"You OK Hamish?"*

"Aye lassie and yourself?"

"I am OK but feel like I should have said something sooner, you know ...little Fiona," she left the words hanging in mid air and didn't continue.

Hamish nodded, *"I feel the same lassie, but we have to leave it to the laird. I saw what you did, Mrs McDougall will appreciate that more coming from a near stranger than from a villager. It might restore her faith a bit ye ken."*

Laura smiled and bidding Hamish goodbye she went on her way back to the cottage. She decided she would contact Lady Campbell and go along see her as Gordon suggested, if she will see me she thought and went to look for the telephone directory. There must be one in the cottage somewhere she said to herself, if not there will be something online.

"Well gentlemen," Henry straightened up as he spoke. *"We have two choices as to where we take this now. I was going to say battle but that seems too grand a word for what basically is a defence of my person."*

The assembled knights and Gordon nodded.

"We could take it to Urquhart Castle and use the ruins, but it would have to be at night so no tourists. Or we could use Aldarrie House on the south side of the loch. It's closed for building work, being made into a hotel I understand, so would be empty at the moment and any damage would be limited by its present half restored condition."

"I think Aldarrie would be better in terms of avoiding locals getting involved, but Urquhart has been a stronghold for centuries - easy to defend and better in terms of isolation." Cam - ever the soldier - had already been and reconnoitred the area.

"But Aldarrie is further from the loch and they cannot call for help in that direction." Rafe considered Zaph's words.

Gabe decided he would make the decision. *"It has to be the old ruins, it's been the place of defence for decades and the nearness to the water is our advantage. If they try to approach by boat, we will have the advantage and know the area. We can easily call for help if needed from there and hold them off until it arrives. Henry you will feel at ease there, it's not the first time you have stood on those walls."*

A murmur of agreement and Henry nodded. *"Urquhart it is then. We will need to make provisions and I will contact the relevant people and get permission for us to be there star-gazing perhaps, or a monster-watch. That way there will be no curious onlookers wondering what we are doing there. I will see a notice gets put up saying castle out of bounds between 6:00pm and 6:00am as being used for scientific purposes. That should do the trick."*

They went their various ways to gather resources and organise their defence. Cam having already been to the castle, as a tourist, had the information they needed. Gabe wondered how he had managed to do it without being discovered, but then realised all tourists would take photos and no one would question someone measuring walls as they would think it all part of some geeky historian or archaeological thing.

Castle Urquhart, a good choice he thought, the current ruins were 17th Century but the site went back to the Iron Age and the 6th Century when St Columba visited the area. Its position for defence was excellent with views up to Inverness to the north and down to Fort Augustus in the south. Gabe went off to find Gordon and discuss what they would need in terms of rations for the evening. It would be very cold spending the night in the open so near the water. The wind off the loch could be bitter. There was a lot at stake here - talk about Armageddon, he smiled wryly to himself and he went down to the kitchens.

CHAPTER 37

Dark Questions

L aura put down the phone. Lady Campbell could see her this afternoon. She would be delighted to have her come for afternoon tea and discuss the history of the area and she had documents and photos she could show Laura. Laura had made a point of saying that she had been using Henry's library and that Gordon had suggested she talk to Lady Campbell.

Laura decided to get a taxi to the address Lady Campbell had given her as she had no idea where she was going. Luckily, the local shop had a cash machine so she was able to get more than enough money to cover her trip. She must remember to use all the Scottish notes before she went back to England as some shops wouldn't take them. The local taxi firm were available as it was before the school run time. She left a message on John's phone in case anyone worried if they came around, and she wasn't in and at the appointed time the taxi drew up.

The taxi driver asked where she was going and when Laura gave him the address said: *"Oh you going to see Lady Campbell?"*

"Yes, to ask her about local history."

"Och she'll like that, ye ken. She's a grand lassie, the Laird Campbell's widow. She will make you very welcome and will keep you talking. Give me a ring if you want me to fetch you back home."

He continued to chat all the way to Inverness and then they approached a road on the outskirts, which had houses and bungalows set back in large gardens. Reminded Laura of where she grew up, except the houses there were a lot older. The car drew up and as she alighted the driver said, *"Here's my card lassie. Just give us a bell if you want picking up."*

"Thank you, I will". Laura gave him a tip as she paid him, *"Keep the change."*

"Thanks lassie," and he drove off in a rush to get back to do his school run.

More and more these days children seemed to be getting taxis to school and back, she reflected. We live in a strange world where no one walks anymore. Getting more and more like the USA every day. She had seen on the news that they were going to introduce the yellow American style school buses in some areas for the school transport. She shook her head ruefully and walked up the drive to a smart modern bungalow surrounded by immaculate gardens and manicured lawns. It looked to be four or five bedroomed and quite large. She lifted the brass knocker which shone; it was the shape of the green man, leering at her. It brought her smile to her face looking at it and she heard footsteps before the echo of the knocker resounding through the house had stopped.

The door opened to reveal a young woman wearing an apron over faded jeans and pink rubber gloves, her blond hair tied back in a pony tail.

"I'm here to see Lady Campbell. Laura Loomis, I am expected."

"Ah yes, come in Bea is in the sitting room. I'm Leanne, the housekeeper." The Australian accent further surprised Laura.

"Hi," said Laura, not too sure what she was expected to say. *"I know everybody expects a faithful old retainer but you need to be fit to keep on top of this place. My partner Janet does the gardens and I do the domestic stuff."*

Laura laughed, it was an old butler or something she expected to answer the door, not this informal young woman. Leanne led her to a door off the long hallway where she knocked on the door. *"Bea your visitor is here."*

Laura followed her into a bright room with plain Berber carpet and solid furniture.

"Come in dear. I'm Bea, Lady Campbell. Fetch the tea things Leanne please."

The woman who stood up to greet her and shook her hand firmly was in her 60s, with short grey hair and sparkling blue eyes. She was dressed in a plain jumper and tartan trousers with a long padded waistcoat over, the sort Laura associated with her mother or with horsey people.

"Please sit down and call me Bea."

"Thank you". Laura smiled. The taxi driver was right she was indeed welcomed.

"Ah here is tea; we pour first, chat after. Do you mind having a mug? It's just the china cups don't hold enough tea and you have to keep topping up. Leanne introduced me to china mugs, wonderful."

Laura said she didn't mind at all. She couldn't stop smiling, what a delightful lady.

"Leanne and Janet have been my life savers. Janet is my cousin's granddaughter and has my

interest in gardening. They both came over from Sydney for a visit and stayed. I don't know what I would do without them now. They live in their own flat above the garage and attend my every whim."

"You don't have many whims, Bea. Thank goodness."

Leanne winked at Laura as she spoke, and put down a tray on the low table. *"There are scones and some biscuits to help get the tea down."*

Once tea and scones had been sorted and Leanne left the room Bea asked Laura what she wanted to know about local family history. Laura explained about her research, and how she found links with Henry's family and alchemy.

"So you want to know some of the history of the local families, and any links with Merlin?"

"Yes, how did you know?"

"It's what I would ask about," said Bea laughing.

"Well the story is that Merlin is the ancestor of the Fraser-Grants. However, the Fraser-Grants as a family are only 300 years old but are descended directly from the branch that Merlin headed as Ambrosius. Now, let me ask you something Laura. Who is this?" Bea said holding up a picture in a book.

"It looks like Henry."

"Look at the inscription underneath." Bea handed her the book.

The inscription read:

The only authentic portrait of Ambrosius Merlin known.

"Now do you see the connection with Henry's family?"

"Blimey! They could be twins."

"All the old families look alike, even through generations; you know that Laura, you have the look of your family. Oh yes, I recognised you as soon as you walked in the room."

Laura blushed. It was a standing joke that the "proper" members of her family all had the same nose and eyes and you could recognise them anywhere in the world.

"So now you want to know something of the history?"

"Yes please." said Laura glad the subject had turned from her, back to Henry.

"Well the story goes that Merlin had a wife and son, and that the family line was carried on in Scotland through the Lairds of Loch Ness. The Fraser-Grants were the last family to inherit the gene, before them it was the Morays. The male line has the same look about them. They have all been alchemists in their way. Henry was a chemist you know, long since retired of course but I believe he still has a little lab in the castle somewhere."

"Really?" said Laura *"Henry is intelligent, you can see it. I have often wondered about the thing about transmuting metal to gold. I can see Henry doing that or trying to."*

Bea laughed. *"Your own family have the same thing in the female line, you know. Ying and Yang in alchemy. There is usually a female and a male alchemist. I expect you know that though. There is a mixture of artists and scientists in your family isn't there?"*

Laura looked at Bea. *"How come you know so much?"*

"Didn't anyone tell you? I am a historian. I met Andy, Lord Campbell when I investigated Aldarrie House history. I was his second wife and younger than him. He needed an heir you see, his first wife died in childbirth, and I provided him with two, a boy and a girl. Once they went away to school and then university, I went back to history, my first love and continued to write a history of the area."

"My family have some connections with Scotland. There is even a song about one of my ancestors, not a very pleasant one though," said Laura laughing.

"Yes I know the one. So what else can I tell you?"

"I am not sure but, I think I can prove Merlin was here in Scotland and if I can continue the line down to the Fraser-Grants that will help."

"Well I can give you a sort of family tree, but of course records being what they were, it isn't complete."

"That would be helpful. Thank you."

"Do you have an email address and I can download it to you from my computer."

"That would be great thanks, here I'll write it down. I have my laptop with me at the cottage in Dores, so can pick it up no problem."

"Where else have you been researching Laura?"

"I tried a couple of local churches for parish records. Dunlichity Church was dedicated to St Finian, but the building there now was only built in 1758. However there is a baptismal stone set in the hillside that has been there for a few hundred years, said to be the original stone used for baptising, so that was interesting. Then I went to Dores church, or Durris in some

books. The current church again only dates from 1828 though there had been a church there since 1233. The Bishop of Moray gave the parish church to the Pluscarden Priory in that year, so there must have been a church. There were lots of Clan chiefs of the clan MacLennan buried there. It was lovely to visit them. Old churches and church yards are always interesting and peaceful but not much use for my research."

Laura handed Bea a slip of paper torn from her notebook. *"My email address. Could I have the details of the book, the one with Merlin's picture please? I shall try and get a copy."*

"This is the only copy I know of. It was a book by a member of the Campbell family from way back. The date will be in it of the original print somewhere. You are welcome to borrow it and you can post it back or drop it in when you are finished with it." Bea brushed aside Laura's thanks and handed her the book, *"Now in return dear you can tell me what happened at Henry's the other night when the police were called. I understand you were there?"*

Laura told her about seeing intruders and then rousing the house and Bea laughed out loud at the parrot umbrella handle up the nose of the Nazi.

"They got away with it though. Shame on our country they were allowed to go back without being charged." Bea was indignant.

"Well it was political I think."

"Politics, bah. It was politics and rules about tax that forced me to sell Aldarrie. I miss the garden. It's lovely here and Janet is a wonderful help but it's not the same. Though I do have all mod cons here." Bea smiled *"Poor Henry, that man needs a woman to keep him warm at nights. All men need sex whatever their age."*

Seeing Laura's face looking slightly shocked, she laughed: *"The advantage of old age is that you can get away with saying what you like, and be shocking if you want and everyone excuses it!"*

Laura laughed, *"Wear purple hats and chase young men?"*

"Exactly. And all anyone will say is: it's her age you know, can't help it, and then shake their heads and purse their lips. It amuses me sometimes to make them do so."

"I think modern society makes you feel more and more like rebelling but constricts you from doing so. You can't do anything these days without permission in triplicate from some local government department," sighed Laura.

"Yes, you see you notice these things as you get older. So much for the freedoms people fought for in the world wars," Bea shook her head sadly.

"If the government had their way we would not just be ID carded but microchipped and have

to pass border guards whenever we went out."

"With this CCTV stuff and Google being able to locate your house, we may be already. Someone could be watching us right now." They both looked at each other and laughed.

"You thought what I did then, didn't you, a rude gesture," said Laura.

"Too true." A giggle. The conversation continued for some time with Bea, telling Laura of the local area and the tales about the loch and that alchemy had been blamed for many of the problems around the loch in past centuries. Suddenly Bea saw the clock.

"Oh look at the time. It will be dark soon. How are you getting back?"

"I was going to ring the taxi that brought me."

"No need. Janet can drop you off she has to go and collect some things for me. It's only 20 minutes in the car."

Bea lifted up the phone and someone answered. *"Janet dear can you take Miss Loomis back to Dores. I have kept her far too long. She will have missed the bus by now."*

Bea listened for a few seconds and then replaced the phone. *"She will be a couple of minutes and then the car will be out front."*

Leanne came to fetch Laura and as she said her goodbyes and collected her things, Bea said: *"Please come again any time. It's been my pleasure."*

"And mine," said Laura. *"It's been delightful to meet you."*

Janet was tall like Bea but blonde with a surfer's physique, broad shouldered and still tanned. She greeted Laura and opened the door for her to get into the front seat of the old orange VW Beetle. The car was quite noisy so they didn't speak much on the way back, but when Janet dropped her off at the cottage, Janet said: *"Aunt Bea really enjoyed seeing you. You should come again. She misses talking about the history of the area, she used to love doing the tours of the old house."*

"I'll try," promised Laura. *"Maybe you should persuade her to teach an adult education course on local history. The courses are always popular."*

"That's a great idea," Janet smiled. *"I will look into it and mention it to her. Thanks."*

Laura closed the door of the Beetle and waved as Janet turned the car around and sped off. The usual cacophony of cat cries greeted her entrance and she set about sorting the cats out, her mind full of ideas and queries.

CHAPTER 38

Dark Tales

After dinner, she settled down with the book from Bea .She would probably never have looked at it, if she had seen it as it bore the title "Family Traditions and Stories of the Campbell Family".

It had originally been printed in the 1600s and then re-printed in 1926 by Bea's father-in-law, Lord Stuart Campbell ,with his own additions.

Laura took her time going through the book sorting out the stuff from the ancient writings and the more modern additions. She scanned into her laptop the picture of Merlin and the parts of the book she thought relevant.

The book could be posted back by registered post then, next week sometime, she thought.

She noticed an email from Bea and opened it quickly:

> Dear Laura,
>
> It was a pleasure to meet you today. I have attached a sort of Fraser-Grant family tree that might help.
>
> Obviously there are gaps as record keeping was not our ancestors' strong point.
>
> I hope we meet again very soon
>
> Regards
>
> Bea (Lady Campbell)

Abrosius Merlin 450AD
↓
  2 sons, one had issue, one became a monk
             ↓
         Myrddin 550 AD
          One son ,   and   one daughter
        Married Mertyna(600AD)   ↓
                       3 sons 2 daughters (all married well)
        ↓

3 daughters and 1 son   ↓
                Lost track but one of them became royalty
↓
8 grandchildren
1 grandson became an alchemist
750sAD
↓
800s AD reported to have two sons that became alchemists
↓
Both married clan chiefs' daughters
Became part of the Marmears of Moray

From here Laura you can trace the family to the present day. Sorry it is so vague but is a work in progress. All the men were called Ambrose or Ambrosias or Myrddin. I believe in Greek Ambrose means eternal or immortal.

Laura decided to look at the book first, and then compare her notes to the family tree and see if she could trace the family as Bea said. The book started off with some stories of the Campbell lineage and then went on to the strange tale of their neighbours the Fraser- Grants. The neighbours were said to be alchemists and witches. The text referred to the picture of Merlin as the first of the line and that the tradition of alchemy had started with him and been passed on through the generations. There were pictures of some of the lairds from the 1600s to the First World War. All of them had the same look, the long nose, the gaunt face and the piercing eyes.

"*So not only was Merlin in Scotland,*" she said to herself, "*but also left heirs according to this book, to carry on his work. Fascinating stuff.*" Laura could see her paper was going to develop into a book of its own at this rate. "*My theory is true, I got it right*" She grinned to herself. "*Merlin was in Scotland and did some of his work here. I must tell Henry when I see him.*"

Then she remembered the pamphlet she found about Dark Ness, that she had borrowed from Henry's library and got it back out. It had been written by Lord Stuart Campbell the Fourth, Bea's father-in-law's grandfather, she worked out. Looking at it again, she noticed something she hadn't seen before, a chapter on the local families. Previously she had been looking at things to do with Loch Ness so hadn't noticed it.

"The local tradition of alchemy continues the Frasers and the Grants being particular practitioners. It is only to be expected in view of their lineage but their wealth is being questioned by those who would bear them ill will. The current Laird Ambrosius is a good host and generous fellow and well liked about these parts."

"So even then people knew about Merlin being their ancestor. Why has it never been found before?" she puzzled over in her mind and then realised, that not many people will have had access to Henry's library or Lady Bea to acquire the knowledge she had been able to. The libraries of both houses were private and unless someone had been cataloguing them, no one would know what they contained or ask to see them. She suddenly realised how privileged this made her and how if she got published she would have to warn Henry that academics being what they were, more might come wanting to have access to the library. Mainly to try and refute what I have found no doubt she said dryly to herself.

Academics seem only happy in dispute. When she was teaching the students would ask her why this psychologist said this and this one the opposite and she would try to explain how experiments have to be replicable and if they can't be then the evidence is disputed. If other academics doubted the theory, or if it was different to their own, they would do another experiment to show it was wrong or try to show the thinking flawed. It wasn't unknown for people to fake results to prove their theory. She sighed, *"Oh dear, I will set myself up for a lot of stick, no doubt. I better get writing whilst I feel undeterred,"* and with that she settled down with the laptop to get a couple of hours writing in before bed.

CHAPTER 39
Darkness Afoot

D erek was also drawing up his plans, unbeknownst to the occupants of Cragneghil Castle, or so he hoped. He had taken the copy of the stone to use again and even though he knew he couldn't control what would be released, the release of it would cause enough commotion to distract from their main attack. Time was running out for them all, and if this failed the next step would be the short-term solution, which although feasible would not obtain the goal they had worked for. A lot of effort had gone into finding the right person and it would be hard to find another one still alive. There were other steps to be taken, other avenues to explore and the failure of this venture would cost only loss of face and loss of funds, but if he was triumphant, the world would change and he Derek, would be the main instigator and awarded the greatest of honours, to sit at HIS side. He smiled to himself and allowed himself a few moments of the imagined supposed glory, and then shook himself from his reverie and called the men to a council of war. They assembled before him in the huge hallway and he stood a few stairs up so he could see them all.

He was so like his father, the same ruthless streak, the same determination to succeed, the same disregard for those whom he thought inferior and those who stood in the way of the final solution. Derek was one of the few who knew what that really meant. Historians had their theories but only a chosen few knew what the solution really was and what it would mean. He and his comrades were part of it, but only a part, the real answer lay elsewhere in the world. *"If only the world knew,"* he grinned to himself. "They would surrender now. The glory will be ours yet. The time is coming when we will rule again." Then he corrected himself, *"When he will rule again."* It didn't do to have certain thoughts even to oneself, you never knew when your face might betray your thoughts and be seen by others. He cleared his throat and started to outline his plans to the assembled men.

The six of them sat around Laura's kitchen table eating homemade scones and cakes. *"I just wanted to do something to keep busy,"* Laura had said. *"The weather is too bad to go far as well you know, and I needed a break from writing."*

Daniel smiled: *"Yes we know."*

They all felt at a loose end, and had been glad when Laura rang to invite them over for coffee and cake. All of them had work they could be writing up, but things seemed unreal somehow and they all felt restless.

"So what are we going to do?" Emily said after swallowing a mouthful of butterfly cake. John shrugged, *"I don't know. I feel we should do something. I know we said we would leave things to Henry but nothing seems to be happening."*

Heads nodded around the table.

"What can we do?" from Andy *"I mean feasibly, what we can do?"*

"We could help patrol the loch," suggested Donald. *"That way we would be there if anything happens."*

"Not a bad idea," said Laura. *"We could go out for a couple of hours when it is dark and keep watch."*

John, his mouth full of cake, tried to speak and choked and had to be patted on the back and given more coffee.

"See, that's why you mother told you never to speak with your mouth full...because you choke," scolded Laura grinning.

When John stopped spluttering he put in: *"I was going to say before Laura's cake tried to murder me."* There was much laughing at that point and, *"you ungrateful so and so,"* from Laura. *"That we could split up and half use the boat or go to the Drumnadrochit side and half the Dores side."*

"No way I am going back on the water." shuddered Emily.

"Well I don't mind going in the boat. Anyway it's scared of me according to John," Laura grinned again.

"I don't blame it," said Daniel grinning. *"You scare the hell out of me sometimes."* There was more giggling from everyone including Laura.

"Someone said I was imposing and that I would suddenly loom behind people. I think they were joking though." No one replied to Laura's comment, John thought he ought to move the subject on.

"OK, then Laura and I, and Donald you game?" Donald nodded afraid to speak in case he choked as well. He was really enjoying the scones, shame to waste them.

"We will go in the boat and you three patrol the shore around Dores. We can go past Urquhart Castle and swing back and cover both banks."

"It's quite narrow just before the bay there, I know from the roadside stop near there you feel you can almost reach the far shore." Laura had spent some time one holiday stuck there when a friend's car broke down so she knew the spot well.

"Does the piper guy still set up shop there, I had my photo taken with him when I was younger?" put in Andy.

"I don't know," answered Laura. *"He was pretty cool wasn't he?"*

This led back to a discussion on legs and kilts and to Hayden Stark and his dip in the loch. They were soon laughing and it eased the tension.

"Well it's a full moon tomorrow night," said Emily looking at her little pocket diary, *"so why don't we start then? It's going to be too bad to go out on the Loch tonight."*

"Good idea." John followed by saying, *"Lets meet up at 7:00pm by the jetty and you lot meet on the Dores shore, and no detours to the bar mind, and we could meet up back at the hotel at 10.00pm?"*

"Sounds OK to me," said Laura.

They made their farewells and went their separate ways, leaving Laura to wash up and contemplate. The cats only appeared when it got near to dinnertime so she had no one to disturb her thoughts. The dark shapes floated through her mind again and then she remembered that eye and she shivered. She was surprised Emily had not mentioned the monster again, but guessed it was because she had put it from her mind in an attempt to get peace for herself. Laura couldn't imagine how it must have been, to be in the water and knowing that huge thing was in there with you, near you. She thought about little Fiona McDougall and realised that Fiona must have seen it and that was why she was struck dumb with terror. In an attempt to chase the dark thoughts away, she put on some music and sat down to read. *"A good whodunit will take my mind off things,"* she said to herself.

Sometime later there was a plop through the front door and going to investigate, she found the local free paper. Splashed across the front page was a headline, *"Where is Doris the sheep?"* a story underneath informed her that two pet sheep normally kept in a field near the loch had been reduced to one and no one had any idea where the missing sheep had gone. There was no sign that a car or van had been up to the field to remove it, and no sign that a boat had been drawn up to the shore. There was the usual photo of two sad eyed children and their mother holding a picture of the missing Doris.

"Oh dear," she said to herself. *"I guess it's getting hungry and bolder. Strange there were no marks or blood. Must drag things under the loch, but then how would it breathe and eat at the same time. Does it have gills?"* She went away to ponder on it and decided to do an internet search on strange water creatures. Afterwards she wished she hadn't. Several large predators roamed the world's waterways and none of them did she wish to see in the loch. The large

rays were beautiful and the sharks mean looking and some smaller creatures such as octopi could band together and kill you off. The teeth on the barracuda gave her shivers down her spine. There were also large catfish said to be responsible for pulling people under the water in remote parts of India and China. She went back to her whodunit gratefully, at least with that you knew it was make believe and unlikely to happen.

Meanwhile John and Donald were discussing their tactics in their cottage. *"We should decide what we are going to do if we see it and it sees us,"* said Donald.

"Well, we have a flare gun. That would probably startle it and give us time to head for shore."

"I hope you are right John, I was thinking of taking a net as well. We could always throw the net to slow it down."

"Good idea. See being around me is rubbing off on you."

Donald grinned, *"As long as it's the good bits that rub off on me."*

John laughed. He liked it when students felt confident enough to banter with him.

"How come Daniel only has two students with him this year, he usually has more?"

"Because the baby was due, most of his students are being supervised by Carol Foster on the Black Isle. Whale watching I think, for their voluntary work, and mapping out the landscape for their earth sciences bit. He knew he would have to go back home at some time."

Donald nodded. *"Makes sense. I did wonder. He's taken to being a dad hasn't he?"*

"It was a bit unexpected, having a child later in life, both he and his wife have always been travelling around doing research, so it just never happened I suppose and now it has he is a happy, happy man. And talking of happy shall we go Inverness for a take away this evening?"

"We could invite Laura; we are always going to hers."

"Good idea. I'll get the menu from the Indian, it's in the hallway I think and we can phone through and I can go pick it up whilst you fetch Laura and set the table. I'll go ring her now before she plans her dinner. She loves a Biryani."

John went to the phone while Donald dug out the menu, if he rang on ahead with the order it would be ready when he got there. They had an insulated box in the car, which they took on the boat; it would keep it hot until he got back. He perused the menu deciding what to have.

CHAPTER 40

Dark Trials

Hayden Stark was angry. He'd show them. Laughing at him, what did they know? His plans were almost ready. When he succeeded, their stupid monster would be no more and everyone would know it was a con trick. Visitors would still come but they would come to his exhibition about the nature in and around the loch, not one of the ones that claimed the monster existed. The exhibition he set up was high tech, the other one was a creaky old film and some old photos, and another all underwater vehicles, tangle with him would they? Ha, they would find out, these so tolerant locals, that he was not to be tangled with.

He carried on muttering to himself as he continued to work. No qualifications eh. Well qualify this and see where that leads you. He laughed to himself. Trying to fool him with that stupid shadow in the loch the other night. He knew it wasn't real. *Pah! They don't know what they are messing with. I'll give them tourist industry. I'll show you Dores and Drumnadrochit,* he said this out loud and then hastily looked around in case anyone heard. No one was about, the guests, mostly students, were all out and wouldn't be back until the evening. He carried on with his task.

The next day everyone seemed to be in a state of tension. At Cragneghil House, cars were being packed and men hurrying about with set faces. At Laura's cottage a meeting to arrange times and discuss safety measures. On the Black Isle men were also packing cars and Derek was fasting for his evocations this evening. Hayden was frantically working to get his plan finished for the evening; a full moon would mean everyone would see it. None of them except Henry, would have suspected how the evening would end, and even he would be surprised by some events.

As Henry watched the preparations going ahead at the house, his thoughts laid heavily upon him. If he lost another person to this madness, he would be distraught and he would never forgive himself.

"Buck up," Gabe slapped Henry on the shoulder breaking into his train of thought.

"Ever the angel, my friend" smiled Henry.

"You need to be positive, Henry. We all do. I know you feel the burden but none of this is your fault."

Henry said nothing because he felt it was. If only in the folly of youth he hadn't trod this path, but he had and now all he could do was try and make amends. The curse of vanity is stupidity he thought to himself, how right that was now looking back. He shook himself and went over to see if he could help the others in their tasks.

Laura was packing sandwiches and had asked the others to bring flasks to fill with hot chocolate and hot coffee. They would need it. She packed two large boxes with an assortment of tuna and sweetcorn, cheese and tomato, cheese and onion, and egg and cress sandwiches. Cheap and cheerful she said to herself and very filling, on wholemeal bread. She also added some chocolate biscuits and some packets of crisps and apples. Like a school outing she laughed to herself, I am the school dinner-lady. She remembered some of the horrible dinner-ladies from her time at school and decided she would have been the nice dinner-lady everybody liked.

Then she filled two flasks with hot chocolate and two with black coffee and the last one tea with milk. All set for an adventure - maybe we should have had ginger beer she grinned to herself, the six adventurers go to Loch Ness.

Derek had two men checking on Cragenghil House. They reported the cars being packed. He instructed them to follow if they left. *"So you are planning to leave?"* he chuckled to himself. *"That won't stop us, and where would you go where we could not find you eh? We have the only hiding places in the world not accessible by outsiders."* He continued to prepare for the evening as it might be a trick by the talisman group to make them think Henry was leaving. Derek was prepared for anything; nothing was going to get passed him.

Hayden Stark was checking his boat when Hamish saw him. *"Going out fishing Hayden?"* he said pleasantly. Like most of the locals they tolerated outsiders and Hayden was amusing to most of them. He was eccentric, but not dangerous and did bring in some visitors with his exhibition.

"I'm thinking of taking some night samples as there is a full moon tonight," replied Hayden.

"Take care then," said Hamish. *"Make sure your radio is working. You never know, there's been a spate of things lately, people going missing and so forth."*

Hayden nodded. *"I will Hamish."*

"Fool," he said to himself. *"There's nothing in the loch but a few fish. The locals are scared of their own shadow."*

CHAPTER 41
Dark Ness in the Moon Light

T he moon rose, bright and clear. There was a frost in the air and winter was almost upon the loch. The loch never froze, despite being a relic of the Ice Age, when the ice 10,000 years before had carved its way through The Great Glen. When the ice melted it left a deep lake, which they say is so large that everyone in Britain could stand in it and the water would *still* cover their heads. The waters from a few feet down were black with the peat particles that came down with the runoff from the surrounding hills and many a diver had been brought up white and shivering at finding him or herself in the black waters unable to see more than a few inches in front of them. No wonder it was a place of legend, a place where anything could hide in the eight hundred feet depths. Many had sought what they hoped was there and many had failed. Some - like Hayden - believed it was a scam by locals to bring in tourists.

As the first sightings of a beastie in the loch took place long before the word 'tourist' even existed as a euphemism for traveller, they could hardly apply to that category. Laura thought of the history of the loch and other things as she waited for John and Donald to call and collect her for the night's vigil. She hoped it would be uneventful; she was not afraid as such, but seeing the state Emily was found in, and hearing about Fiona, she had no wish to meet the thing unprepared. *"I wish I believed in something to pray to, it must have its advantages, faith at a time like this."* Instead, she rang her daughter for a chat and gave the cats a fuss. They were the things *she* believed in.

Derek scowled at the message he had received. So they thought to hide in a stronghold, the old castle. This was not the first time they, the Aryan race, had tried to turn the tide of the future their way in Scotland. There had been many stories told of rituals carried out by the Thule society and the SS on a Scottish abandoned island, or in a ruined church, to try to bring forth something to give them advantage. This may well have been over 60 years ago, but if this failed, it may be time to find that island and use the old ways. There was always the legend of the Thorn and the Blood, which may be worth another look. He would mention it when he returned. What the knights hoped to gain by hiding out in the castle, he had no idea. It was away from prying eyes in the main, but that would work to their advantage too, he smiled to himself. Then no one can see what becomes of them. The knights would suffer, he would see to that. Their interfering had gone on long enough and he would gain the upper hand. They were not Aryan knights; he heard some of them weren't even Christian. Knights of the Talisman, Knights Templar, they had no idea about real bravery, he spat on them in his mind. He barked orders to the men around him; the castle would be their target tonight. He could deal with the staff at Cragneghil House once the fight was over, and they had what they wanted. They would be easily silenced, and in time forgotten. Whereas we have *never* been forgotten, he thought, and never will be.

The cars bumped their way down towards the castle, the loch in front of them gleaming in the moonlight. A small entourage of a Land Rover, a gas guzzling 4x4, followed by a Ford estate and a Bentley. The tower would be the perfect choice for a place of defence. The walkways provided for the tourist trade, would make good vantage points and it would be easier to defend from attackers. Cam approved wholeheartedly of the destination.

They started to unload in the parking area and then turned off the car headlights. They barely needed the torches they had brought with them; the full moon made the night visible, but also threw up shadows that made them look warily into dark places for intruders.

The packs they hauled over to the tower contained everything from blankets, waterproofs and food supplies to swords and shotguns. Cam had raided the old armoury at the castle, the ghillie's gun cupboard, then the kitchen cleaning cupboard and gardener's shed to make home-made bombs. These he had kept hidden from Henry, as he knew Henry would not approve because of the damage they would cause. Cam reasoned that if it was a last ditch attempt to save Henry, Henry would forgive him any damage, even if it meant paying huge sums of compensation to the historical society and the tourist board. Henry watched Cam from his place of safety up the tower and smiled to himself, *"Cam, you do not change my friend,"* he thought, *"and I can only guess at what you have stashed in that pack that you don't want me to see, but if it stops the Nazis and their plans, it will be forgiven and you will be a hero."*

As they unpacked they kept their voices low and the torches and lanterns turned down to a glow. Gabe appeared at Henry's side, *"Well, Gordon has done us proud Henry, and your housekeeper; we could withstand a siege. Will they be alright at the house?"*

"I left Gordon with a shotgun and Mrs MacDonald has a meat cleaver." Gabe laughed at Henry's face at the thought of the housekeeper probably sitting in her dressing gown with her hair in plaits, nursing a meat cleaver.

"I believe that as well as Hamish, several men who work for the estate will be patrolling the grounds. Hamish is ready to fetch us by boat if things should get difficult and it is needed. They will know by now that we have left the house so apart from watching in case we return, they will not bother the staff unless things go very wrong for us here."

Gabe nodded, *"Things will not go badly Henry. We may lose one or two people, but good is on our side. And afterwards, well you know what to do."*

Henry patted Gabe on the back, and started to look for a place to settle for the long night ahead.

Hani was wearing some night vision goggles he'd borrowed from Cam, and was looking at everything through a strange red haze. He gazed out from his position turning to view each point of the compass to cover the entrance of any attacker. He felt quite excited and exhilarated, it wasn't often he got the chance to show what he was made of. The lessons and training with Cam had paid off, he wasn't afraid and knew he was equipped to deal with almost anything, but also knew Cam taught them all that over-confidence was also a killer. Always expect something to happen you didn't expect, he had said, because you can plan down to the finest detail but a small difference, a little flaw in a character, an animal running loose and if you are sticking to your plans, it will end in disaster if you can't allow for it. Flexibility Hani repeated to himself as he watched and waited.

Mike was making drinks on a small primus stove; he and Zak were making sure morale stayed high. Zak above them all knew what was at stake and he had prepared himself if it should end badly. His family would be taken care of, and his body buried in the special place. No knight was ever left to be scavenged on the battlefield, nor used for any other purpose, the past had taught them how the human spirit could be dark and nasty and they now took care of their own. He wondered if his son would want to succeed him when he was old enough and smiled at the thought. Mike handed him mugs of hot coffee to take to the others and then took one up to Henry. *"Thank you Mike, is everyone OK?"*

"Yes they are fine, thinking of their mortality I expect but you know how it goes."

Henry nodded and returned to his thoughts. He would have to pull off something quite fantastic to save them all if things went wrong. His thoughts were interrupted by Zaph. He was laughing, *"Cam has found the old trebuchet. He said it still works so he has lined it up to fire at any cars coming along the road. We've found some good sized rocks."*

Henry laughed too. *"Trust Cam."*

"It will be a defence against any attack coming in by boat or even the monster. Will you be calling it, Henry?"

"Only to send it back. I have other plans if things should go awry."

"Good because that thing frightens the shit out of me," and with that Zaph went back to check on Cam and the others.

Henry watched him go. *"Frightens me too Zaph, it is hard to control,"* he said quietly to himself. *"Though once it made Merlin the best magician the world had ever seen."* He went back to preparing for what lay ahead.

CHAPTER 43

Darkness Comes but once

Hayden set off from the jetty; he kept his lights off until he was well out onto the loch. He didn't want anyone to see him. It was a clear frosty night and the moon was rising full, he grinned up at it. *"It ends here, the legend will die, and I will be proved right at last."*

He planned to release his creature when he got near to castle Urquhart. It would be seen possibly, but most certainly found next day and then he would claim responsibility and the show would be all over. The waters gleamed black in the moonlight almost like black glass, and his boat skated across the loch towards the castle. Once he thought he saw a light but after straining his eyes for some time, he decided it must have been a passing car. Hayden stopped the engine and waited for a few minutes to check no one was around then he started to unpack things on the deck. This took some doing as there was more stuff than deck, but with skill that a twister player would envy, he wriggled around and over it frantically fixing this and that until it was ready. The strange looking Heath Robinson affair was then loaded over the side of the boat and as Hayden pulled on a pin, it started to inflate. It was something he was proud of, this thing, put together in very little time and he stood back to admire his handy work as the inflation of two life-rafts took the shape of the Loch Ness monster. At the front was a head made from a model Labrador's head and painted green, then a long neck which led to the two green humps made by the inflation of the life rafts sporting a frill on the tent like end. He got the rafts cheap at a sale of things from a decommissioned oilrig. The dog's head had been on a broken collection box outside a shop and he had given them a generous donation for it to help get a replacement. He then set up a small voice recorder to play continuously as long as the batteries lasted and popped it into the first life raft. After a few seconds a roar came out that made him jump even though he was expecting it. Hayden rubbed his hands with glee.

Laura was on watch at the stern of the boat; John was steering and Donald on the monitor. *"No sign of anything tonight, not even the fish are about,"* he said.

Laura was keeping an eye out as best she could, but the waves on the loch confused especially at night and sometimes she thought she saw something but it was just the wake of the boat. She didn't want to admit it even to herself but she was worried, if what Hamish said was right, this thing, 'evil' as he called it, might not be easy to stop. Hamish had seemed convinced

Henry would stop it but she didn't see how. Perhaps the locals thought he was a modern day St Columba, she said to herself. Maybe it comes with being the laird. Further out, coming across the loch, Laura and the others heard the roaring sound and startled, headed towards it.

"It doesn't sound right." said Donald. *"Sounds like something off* Jurassic Park *and we have never heard the monster make a noise before."*

"There's no blip on the screen." Laura pointed to it as she spoke.

John made a noise like harrumph. *"Someone is having a joke I think, but we will go see."*

"Do you think it's Daniel?" laughed Donald.

It wouldn't be the first time they had played jokes on each other, John once borrowed a bull dozer and drove it past where Daniel and his students were staying and then once the noise and vibration had woken Daniel, told him there had been an earthquake. Daniel had rushed out with his equipment in his pyjamas to John taking a flash photo, which he posted on the university intranet. Daniel had been trying to get back at him ever since.

"No," said John, *"not this time. We left them on the shore and he wouldn't joke about this. Not after what happened to Emily."*

John steered towards the sound. As they all looked out, straining to see across the loch, a large blip appeared on the sonar screen, unnoticed by them all and headed towards the noise.

Hayden was enjoying himself. He took several photos, which he intended to use for the media to discredit once and for all the myth. Suddenly the boat began to rock. He stood up and looked around to see if it was the wake of another boat passing. He shrugged, must be the current pulling on the model and rocking the boat. Then it happened again harder and this time he couldn't keep his feet and fell against the side of the boat. *"What an earth? Must be seismic activity,"* he said to himself.

Then he saw it, huge, black and dripping; pulling the model down and dragging the boat with it. As he yelled, the thing turned to look at him. Hayden swallowed and backed as far away as he could. It was the most evil-looking thing that he had ever seen. Its eyes were yellow and cold, bigger than dinner plates, and as it opened its mouth he saw rows of serrated teeth. It was no dinosaur, certainly not one he had ever seen in a book; it was something not quite of this world. All this raced through his head as he stood quaking before the creature. He felt something warm on his legs and realised he had wet himself in fear.

The next thing he knew he was upside down and in the water. Gasping as the coldness filled his lungs he struggled to what he hoped was the surface. His head broke through surface, and wheezing and choking he saw the boat being dragged beneath the waters of the loch. The predicament he was in then hit him, no one knew he was there, the thing was still in the water and it was freezing cold and dark. Just as he started to whimper he heard a boat.

Laura had screamed, she couldn't help herself when she saw the creature. Even from a distance she was afraid. Donald was praying and John, ever practical, *"Fucking hell! Whose boat is that? Has it got some poor bastard?"*

He speeded up towards the sinking boat even though everything in him screamed to turn around and head for the far shore as fast as he could. *"There's someone in the water,"* shouted Donald.

Laura ran to the side and saw a life jacket, she reached down yelling *"Hang on, I've got you."* Donald ran to help her and between them they pulled the shivering Hayden on board. Laura ran to get blankets and a flask of hot tea, which she knew was sweet and would help with shock. *"John,"* she yelled *"It's Hayden; we need to get him to a hospital."*

John turned to head back for the jetty but stopped when he saw the blip on the screen. *"It's between us and the jetty Laura."*

"Head for the castle," shouted Donald. *"We can shelter in the bay until it's gone."*

Laura forced the hot sweet tea down Hayden's throat and he coughed. He was shaking so much she spilled it. *"Are you alright, are you injured?"*

"I , I ...it was ..." and then he started to cry. Laura didn't know what to do but comfort him and try to dry him off and keep him warm. She looked helplessly at Donald who stood white faced.

"We are heading for shelter; the thing is between us and the jetty." Donald's voice shook, *"It's all we can do for now until it goes."*

Laura nodded and wished she knew how to pray. Even though she didn't believe in it, it might make her feel better.

CHAPTER 44
Dark Ness before The Dawn

A t the castle Gabe had tried to rouse Henry from his meditations.

"It's free again, it's attacking someone in the water, Henry come on."

Gabe shook Henry's shoulder; Henry was in a deep trance. He came out of it suddenly. Making Gabe jump. Henry snapped to attention .

"It's the Nazis; they have brought it out to distract us. Did it get anyone?"

"No, only the boat, John Draycott and his crew pulled out whoever it was, and they have headed for the bay for shelter."

"Sensible of them, but this means I have to act now. It also means I will be vulnerable."

"Mike has given the local police an anonymous tip off that someone is having a satanic orgy on Dores beach." Gabe grinned, *"So that should keep them occupied for a bit."*

Henry laughed. *"If he is dressed for the ritual, that will take some explaining, but it means they will come tonight."*

Gabe nodded, *"We'll be ready."*

Henry sighed and said, *"Let's get on with it then."*

Emily, Andy and Daniel could not believe their eyes. Alerted by a noise they had crouched down behind some rocks and greenery. They had been patrolling the shore when an entourage had appeared but they made enough noise to warn the three to keep hidden and quiet. The man at the front was dressed in a long gown covered in symbols and was tied by a rope to two others who stood on the shore whilst he stood in the water.

"Is it some kind of Celtic ritual?" whispered Emily.

"None I have ever seen or heard of and I've been coming up here every year for 15 years," whispered Daniel. Andy just watched tight-lipped, he had a feeling things were going to get sticky.

"I do hope they keep their clothes on," whispered back Emily. *"It's cold tonight."* This prompted a snort from Andy as he realised Emily probably hadn't realised what she had said. Daniel grinned and put a finger to his lips.

The man in the gown started to chant some sort of incantation, getting louder as he went on. After a while, and just as Emily thought she would have to stand up and risk being seen as her legs were aching from crouching, the loch started to get wild. The waves nearly knocked the man off his feet, but the two holding onto the ropes kept him steady.

"That explains the ropes," said Daniel to himself. He was a bit worried it might turn into a sex thing and he would have to cover Emily's eyes. It looked like it was some sort of ritual to the loch or maybe the water kelpie. Some local people still upheld Celtic traditions he knew.

The loch seemed to be boiling and then a dark shape appeared. Emily had to stuff her knuckles in her mouth to stop herself from screaming as the wind whipped past them, but there was no mistaking what was coming. Daniel grabbed the two students and tried to pull them further back into the undergrowth. The wind was now so strong they struggled to move back. The thing came nearer the shore and Daniel caught sight of a huge head and a slug like body, massive, it must be over 40 feet long. He felt Andy gasp and Emily buried her face in his jacket and began to shake and sob. The man on the shore changed his incantation and the beast, the monster, turned its head from side to side as if listening or was it looking for something to eat? Daniel hoped they were hidden from those horrible cold yellow eyes, but luckily they were fixed on the three men on the shore. It seemed like time stood still to the three crouched in fear as the man continued to chant. The beast at last opened its mouth and screeched a sound that set Daniel's teeth on edge. It was a sound like a hundred nails being drawn down a hundred blackboards. The beast then turned sending a huge spray on to the shore that even reached their hiding place and the smell from its foetid mouth still hung in the air making them gag.

The men on the beach started to congratulate each other but Daniel's first thought was to warn John and the others. He signalled to the other two to follow him and crept from the shore. Andy had to shake Emily and drag her to her feet. Her face white and eyes wide in terror, her face wet with tears she clung to his coat. At that moment there was a siren and sounds of running feet.

"It's the police," said Andy, *"Someone must have reported them."*

"Let's get out of here," added Daniel.

Andy dragged Emily by her arm and then pushed her in front of him, *"We must hurry,"* he said urging her on. As soon as they made the road, they set off running.

"We have to get to the boat, to the radio to warn John," gasped Daniel running faster than he thought he was capable of at his age. The other two were soon ahead of him but by the time he reached the car gasping and wheezing, Andy was already switching on the engine. They sped off ignoring speed restrictions and skidded to a halt at the jetty. Andy ran down and switched on the radio and handed the receiver to Daniel who arrived a few minutes behind, Daniel prayed that someone would answer the call and the boat was still afloat with all its occupants.

John's voice came back over the crackling line and they all breathed a sigh of relief. *"It obviously moves a lot faster than you lot,"* John cheerily began and then went on to relate the pulling of Hayden from the drink and that they were sheltering near the castle until it had gone. Daniel told John what they had seen on the beach.

"Blimey so it must be possible to call it," from John in reply, *"Unless it just heard the noise and came to investigate."*

"It may be heading back to the shore John for its reward or something, so stay put as long as you can. It moves fucking fast and man it is ugly and smelly and..." Daniel shuddered before he went on. *"It's got bastard big teeth."*

"I know and it's strong, pulled Hayden's boat down like it was a toy. I radioed the Emergency services that there had been an accident on the loch so they should be about."

Daniel replied, *"I think they might be busy with the guys on the shore. The police were arriving as we left."*

"Good. It might stop them calling it out again, over and out." John was relieved it meant they may escape unharmed if they waited until it was light.

John went up to tell the others what had happened and asked how Hayden was.

"Scared witless," was Laura's reply. *"Can't say I blame him. I am not feeling too brave myself."* John gave her a hug and Donald grinned.

"I don't think any of us are that brave Laura, what a horrible beastie, ...those teeth," he shuddered. John said, *"I am not giving you a hug too."*

Donald laughed. They decided to sit it out until it was light. There was a small bathroom on the boat and a few supplies, and plenty of blankets.

"Shall we put Hayden in the cabin? He will be warmer there."

"Good idea, Laura. I'll give you a hand to get him down there." John and Laura led the unresisting Hayden down into the warmth of the cabin and Laura checked him again for broken bones or serious injuries, but apart from some bruising and small cuts and scrapes he was OK, just still shocked.

"You stay with him," said John, *"and we will all take turns each hour. That way no one will get too cold or too bored."*

Laura smiled her agreement but muttered to herself after he had gone, *"Too bored? There's a monster on the loose. Too bored? The man is insane."*

Talking of insane, she looked at Hayden who just sat transfixed and did what he was told. That will teach you not to have an open mind she thought. She hugged herself and sat wondering if the night would bring any more terrors.

CHAPTER 45
To the Edge of Darkness

enry stood on the top of the tower as far as he could get to the edge, overlooking the loch. *"No fancy dress for Henry then?"* asked Zak.

"None needed. It's only trappings, but our opponents don't know that. Like the stone, Henry doesn't need it," replied Mike. *"He's had a lot of practice. The trappings just make people feel it's more magical instead of just being a bending of the law of physics and the fact that the creature answers to its name."*

"And I can guess who named it," grinned Zak. Mike nodded, straining to see the loch. After a few minutes a dark shape appeared and reared up in front of Henry.

"God, it's ugly" said Mike.

The creature was like a huge slug with a large, dragon-like head. Its body under the water tapered to a tail, and its fore feet, more like paddles, could be seen. The body undulated giving the appearance of humps and its yellow eyes swivelled in its head so it could see all around its proximity. A fearsome and fearless monster that had no mercy because it had no idea what that might mean. It was attack, kill or be attacked and killed. A creation that knew only survival.

"You are here then," Henry spoke softly.

The creature lowered its enormous head so Henry could look into its eyes. Near Henry it behaved more like a pet, in that it would not bite the hand that fed it or in this case created it. Henry looked at the creature before him and shook his head.

"You have to go back now. It was not your time. You were summoned too soon and not in whole."

He leaned toward the huge head and appeared to wave his hand over the beast. It turned and returned to the loch with a huge splash and vanished beneath the waves. Henry stood a long time and eventually Mike tapped him on the shoulder.

"Are you OK?"

"Yes Mike, sorry. I was just thinking. That creature, this is my fault. All the deaths and disruption are because of my vanity as a young man. Had the beast never been summoned in the first place, we would not be in this predicament now. No one would know it existed and had I not been so foolish as to think I could fool the Nazis well...." his voice trailed off.

"We all learn by our mistakes Henry," Mike said quietly *"and you have suffered enough for yours. Come down now. The night has a long way to go before it is over and the hardest task is yet before us."* Henry nodded and followed him down.

In the boat John, Laura and Donald had watched this open-mouthed. They had seen Henry call the beast and then send it back.

"I don't believe what I just saw," Laura shook her head as she spoke as if trying to clear it. John had called her up and told her to shut Hayden in the cabin, as there was something going on at the castle. Before she had time to comment more, a boat drew alongside and all three of them found themselves facing two men with guns.

"What the hell?" from John.

"Do as you are told and you won't get hurt," an American accent.

Laura realised these were probably friends of the Nazi guy. Donald said rather feebly, *"Never heard of pirates on Loch Ness before."*

"Is there anyone else on board?" When no one answered he pointed the gun at Donald and said: *"Speak or I will hurt him."*

"There's an injured man below. We pulled him from the water. He's in shock," John spoke calmly even though he could feel his heart thumping as if it would burst out of his chest. The man smiled, *"Good, I like well-behaved prisoners, saves on bullets."*

"Prisoners? What do you mean prisoners?" Laura's voice sounded several octaves higher to herself, but she tried to stop it quavering.

"You are the prisoners of the Fifth Reich until we get what we came for. Get the man below, you are coming with us," he gestured with his gun.

John went down and brought up Hayden, who offered no resistance, nor seemed to register the men with guns. After some discussion, the men decided to tow John's boat behind them and made Donald tie the boats together. They obviously didn't want the empty boat found. Getting Hayden onto the other boat wasn't easy; he got hysterical when they tried to make him jump to the other boat. In the end the larger of the two men picked him up, and heaved him across his shoulder and literally threw him onto the deck of the other boat. Laura and Donald ran and picked him up and put him on his feet. *"You inhumane buggers,"* she said. *"You can see the state he is in."*

"If we were inhumane we would have killed him when he refused to cross," the larger of the two men said.

"Not if you needed him alive or all of us alive for that matter," Laura snapped.

"Clever aren't you. You won't be so clever in the end. They never are."

John, who had just got on board, pulled her arm to stop her saying any more. She looked at John and then fussed over Hayden and led him to a seat. The boat set off at a great lurch and sped to the jetty, it was hard to see where it was. Once the boats were secured, they were once more taken off at gunpoint and bundled into a people carrier. Hayden barely seemed to register what was going on.

"What the hell do you think is going on? Don't they know the war is over," whispered John.

"I think they are friends of that other Nazi bloke that got deported," hissed back Laura, trying to talk out of the corner of her mouth as she was sure she could be seen in the mirror by the man who had got in the driving seat.

"They are going to try to use us to get to Henry, of course," whispered Donald. *"That's why they kidnapped us."*

John stifled a groan. *"This isn't good, not good at all,"* he whispered back and then shut up as one of the men got in the seat in front.

Laura fastened a seat belt around Hayden just in time as the car sped off around the loch. Before long she could see they were at the side of the loch bumping along the road to Drumnadrochit. The road was quiet, no one was around at this time of night so her thought of throwing something out of the window was a waste. She had hatched a plan to pretend to be car sick and ask for the window to be opened so she could drop something out while pretending to retch. The empty road though stopped that. They soon passed through the sleeping town and then she realised they were approaching Urquhart Castle.

They came to a halt and she saw they were at the lay-by near the castle. Two other cars were parked there and appeared to be severely damaged - one on fire. *"What the hell is going on?"* she thought to herself and saw John's puzzled face thinking something similar.

CHAPTER 46

Darkest in the Shadows

H ani had spotted the cars approaching and signalled to the others.

"Two cars and 8 men."

"Only 8?" said Gabe. *"How many were at the shore that the police picked up?"*

"Three, why?"

"That makes 11, there are two missing. There should be 13, keep your eyes peeled. The other two may be planning something to surprise us," Hani nodded.

Cam was loading up the trebuchet with Zak, who seemed to be doing a war dance. Henry watched puzzled, from his place in the tower and then realised Zak was actually throwing stones into the trebuchet sling for firing. The jumping about was the result of him dropping a large stone on his foot. Henry grinned, they always seemed to take things so light-heartedly the Angels of the Talisman; no matter how bad things were, they always joked. If you are not afraid of death, then I suppose you have no fear, he mused to himself.

The arrival of the cars had signalled an alert among them all but Henry sat silent and calm. *"Hani says they have guns."* Gabe's voice next to his ear.

"Thank goodness we are not at the house; the staff would have been injured or worse."

Henry nodded and said, *"Does Cam know how to fire that medieval weapon?"*

"I think he is about to find out" grinned Gabe.

The first shot whistled through the air and landed short of the cars, startling the men, who looked wildly around to see what the noise was. Cam adjusted the weights on the trebuchet. The second a large boulder, the one that had previously landed on Zak's foot, went over their heads and hit the hillside behind them causing an alarming fall of gravel and greenery. Again the men looked puzzled.

"This time I have it," from a gleeful Cam. He was like a child playing with a catapult. The third barrage hit the first car full on knocking it sideways and severely denting the bonnet and causing a cloud of smoke to appear. The men rushed to put out the flames but before they could gather their wits, a second boulder hit the other car, causing the rear of the car to buckle and a wheel fall off. There was a lull for a few minutes whilst Zak loaded some bricks he had found left from the building of the new visitor centre.

Then a people carrier drew up a few feet away behind the damaged vehicles.

"Get them out, show them their friends are here. They will stop when they see them," shouted Derek. The man in front motioned with his gun and Laura undid Hayden's seat belt and pushed him out in front of her.

"We have your friends here, if you value their lives stop what you are doing," yelled Derek.

It went silent whilst Hani relayed to the others that he could see Hayden, Laura, John and Donald lined up in front of a third car. Henry signalled Cam to stop and wait for developments. Laura and the others stood silently beside the people carrier wondering what was going on. Derek instructed one of the men to stay and hold them at gunpoint. The man with the gun grinned at them, *"Don't move or you are dead."*

The other men with Derek were making their way down the road to the castle, bent double to avoid being hit by anything else that might be thrown at them. Laura thought this is our only chance whilst he is alone. It seemed like the fear was making her brain move at a faster speed. She spoke up: *"What do you think this is? Some TV show? You can't hold four people up with one gun. It's not like the TV where only one person attacks at once, if we all rush you, one or two of us will get shot but the other two will over power you. We are English; we don't take kindly to being ordered about and treated like this. Didn't you learn anything from World War Two? We are stoic and will not surrender."* She crossed her arms and glared at the man.

He laughed: *"Oh yeah, I shoot the guys that leaves you, this other guy, he's not even awake properly. Nice try. Forget it lady."*

Laura spoke in Hayden's ear, *"That's him, the one who put the monster in the loch to frighten you and prove it is there. Get your own back Hayden, there's only us here, we won't stop you. Go on give him what for. He's ruined your plans and now he's laughing at you."*

Hayden stood for a moment and then he flung off the blanket he had around his shoulders and ran screaming at the man with the gun and grabbing him by the throat. The man was so shocked he didn't have time to retaliate. John quickly ran forward and wrestled the gun from the man's hand and Donald and Laura pulled Hayden's hands from the man's throat. When the man fell down as he was released from Hayden's vice-like grip, Laura sat on him, whilst Donald tried to calm Hayden down.

Henry!"

Henry was in the path of the rock fall as it went down to the loch and was swept away into the loch with a splash not having chance to utter a cry. Laura seemed to suddenly wake from a trance. *"My god, John we must get help. Can we start the car?"*

Laura started scrabbling around in the glove box but it was Donald who found a spare set of keys in the sunshade above the front passenger seat. John started the car and they backed up and started to head to Drumnadrochit to get some help.

"What about the man we left tied up?" Laura suddenly said.

"He was swept away with the cars," replied John, grim faced.

"Oh no!" Laura buried her face in her hands.

Afterwards they couldn't tell you much about the journey to Drumnadrochit. They ran into the nearest hotel that had a light on and the night manager, taking one look at their stricken white faces knew something bad had happened. John said there had been a rock fall near the castle and they had seen people and cars pushed down the hillside into the loch. The night manager immediately took charge. Rock falls had happened before, he knew who to contact and what to do.

They sat shivering in the hotel bar, given brandy by the night porter, and not speaking. The night porter looked sympathetically at them, the shock of seeing a rock fall and people being swept away was a terrible thing. Eventually the police arrived and after they were seen by a paramedic they were driven home. The police said they would contact them later for the details and to try to get some sleep. Laura and John looked at each other, not sure what they would say.

The road was closed for 4 days whilst it was cleared and the loch was searched for a week for bodies but none appeared. The story was that a rockslide had swept some American tourists to their deaths and also the laird who was at the castle watching the stars, astronomy was his hobby. It was supposed he had left the safety of the castle tower to help the Americans and had been caught in the landslide. The newspapers said some students and lecturers from a university had been returning from a night sample collection on the loch and seen the tragedy and reported it. The Americans were thought to be monster-hunters, having been days before seen asking locally about the monster and the loch.

The knights had been collected from the castle via a helicopter and winch before the emergency services got there, so no one knew of their presence. They had long since gone taking all their equipment, so it looked as if only Henry had stayed there, with his telescope watching the stars.

CHAPTER 48

Dark Ness Illuminated

There was an inquest on both the Americans and Henry. Laura and the others said truthfully that they had seen the rock fall and raised the alarm. No one questioned them further, no foul play was suspected. No one asked any details of why they were there, for which they were grateful. Laura wasn't sure she could have lied in an official court like this, even though she wasn't under oath. The Procurator Fiscal declared accidental death in all cases and that was it. Hayden wasn't called as he was considered unstable and had been quite ill since that night. The story was that the university people had fished him out of the loch when his boat had sank, probably due to the weight of the model monster he was towing, and set off to take him to the nearest town. Then they had seen the rock fall and gone to investigate, in case anyone was in need of assistance, as they were heading for medical help anyway. Finding there was nothing they could do at the site, they had gone to call the emergency services. Henry was thought to have been killed when he went to assist the Americans. Only two bodies of the Americans had been found buried under the rocks, the rest having been swept into the loch and not recoverable.

"The loch does not give up its dead," Laura thought to herself grimly.

The Procurator Fiscal gave permission for the Americans' bodies to be flown home; there was no need for an autopsy. A memorial service was to be held for Henry and a plaque would be erected in the estate church. They were all invited to attend and the wake following it. Henry would not want people mourning his death, but to celebrate his life instead. Laura and the others met up before the ceremony. Daniel and his students were going home for Christmas and so was Donald. John was staying on, and Laura invited him for Christmas as her daughter and a friend would be coming for a few days, so it would make it worthwhile making dinner with all the trimmings and perhaps help them get over their trauma. They had said nothing to anyone about that night, as who would believe them? And Hayden didn't want anyone to know the monster might be real. He wasn't sure himself what had happened, but he knew that *something* sank his boat.

On their way to the church they met up with the local police sergeant.

"How are you all?" he greeted them. Choruses of fine, ok, the way people do to be polite,

Dark Ness

rather than say they feel bad.

"I have been wondering," began Daniel. *"What happened to the guys on the beach, you arrested? With everything else going on, well..."* He trailed off.

"Oh you heard about them witchcraft lot. Well it's not against the law, but they got sent back to the States. We don't want to encourage that sort of thing." The sergeant straightened his tie, as he spoke as if to emphasise the point.

"No, quite," said Daniel. They reached the entrance to the estate and the sergeant bid them farewell and went off on his official duties.

"So that's that then," from Andy and the others nodded. The walk continued in silence.

The only room left to sit was at the back of the little church. It had been built on the estate centuries before and looked very old. They heard people say nice things about Henry as they sidled silently into their seats. The church was crowded with people standing in the aisles and at the back; the doors had been left open so people could shelter in the doorway from the biting wind. Strangely, the knights were not there, Laura looked for them but thought perhaps they were in the family pew and couldn't be seen from her vantage point. It was cold in the church and she huddled into her coat. It still didn't seem real somehow, everything that had happened.

The vicar talked about Henry's good works for the estate people and his many years spent abroad doing charity work, and then he spoke about Henry's service to the country during the Cold War. Laura and the others looked at each other.

"Seems Henry was a dark horse," whispered John. Laura nodded, for some reason *Smiley's People* kept coming into her head, a book about spies.

After the ceremony everyone was invited back to the house for a wake. Laura didn't stay long. She left and walked along the shore. Everyone was toasting Henry in a celebration of his life, which was what he would have wanted, but it didn't feel right to her. She felt strangely empty and stood on the shore gazing out and wondering about the creatures that Hamish said were there in the depths of the loch. Hamish had made a nice speech at the memorial service and had obviously been very fond of Henry. A sound in the undergrowth made her turn. She looked and rubbed her eyes and looked again.

"But you're, you're dead," she gasped. She felt suddenly quite dizzy and faint.

"Steady, dear lady, don't faint please," Henry smiled. *"As you can see I am very much alive. You see for once the legend is true; I cannot die whilst Arthur sleeps. My curse is that I have to be here when called to be at his side."*

"You are Merlin then?" her voice sounded high pitched and squeaky and she felt like she was hallucinating.

212

"Yes, as you had guessed that day after meeting the knights."

"But, but, what happened, we saw you swept into the sea?"

"A simple illusion, enough to fool any watchers and put the Nazis off."

"But," she started *"...the monster."*

"Yes again another illusion however a more solid form because others were involved. A sort of semi-hologram if you like, but it had mechanical parts and kept going off on its own when not contained. Merlin was a great engineer and designed it. It has been the lot of the Lairds of Loch Ness to be its caretaker all these centuries. We let it go each time they pulled off that stunt with the altar rock and the theatricals and let them think they called it, and it means the real creatures can rest in peace. I had hoped removing the altar stone would have stopped them, but somehow they had made a copy, so the charade had to go on."

"But what about that terrible smell?"

"Oh that was Zak's fault. He used fish oil to grease the thing and when it got hot it smelt terrible. However it seemed somehow appropriate it should do, so we continued with it."

"And what about the deaths, the disappearances?"

"Ah yes. Angus, the first death. He was - we think - killed, by the Nazis. He must have seen something he shouldn't. The water bailiff's boy panicked when he saw the creature and drowned before anyone could do anything; that was our fault and I shall carry that guilt for my life time. The fisherman was accidental, sudden squalls blow up on the loch, he got caught in one. One of the Nazis unfortunately got tangled up in the creature's mechanism and drowned when it went back in the loch. We couldn't do anything to help him, I'm afraid, so that also was our fault. Little Fiona, now happily recovered, was scared when she saw the creature and it caused some sort of post-traumatic stress condition. That again, was sadly our fault; I wouldn't have harmed the child for the world. The men killed by the rock fall, were not men as we know them." He looked at Laura to see her reaction.

She said nothing for a little while and then, *"Just a minute...you are teasing me about the Merlin bit aren't you?"* Laura looked at him sideways.

"Sadly yes, but for a while there you believed people could live forever. I am a relative, a direct descendant and do look like him," Henry smiled. *"I wanted to explain to you about why all this happened. I didn't want you to go away believing I was a wicked alchemist or not to know I was alive."*

"The rock fall?" she queried.

"Cam is an explosives expert. Unfortunately, he's not a geologist or volcanologist so couldn't

predict that the rock fall would cause so many deaths. It was not intended I assure you. The hillside was more unstable than he could have known."

Laura motioned to the seat half hidden in the undergrowth and they both sat down.

Her legs felt distinctly wobbly. She felt like she was asking too many questions but needed to know. She grabbed Henry's arm and squeezed it: *"You are real, it's not an illusion."*

Henry nodded: *"I am sorry to scare you like this, but my time is short."*

"Tell me why this happened then. What caused all this to start?" Laura looked at him; still not sure he was real.

"I was foolish when young Laura, like so many others I'm afraid. For a while during the cold war in the sixties, I worked as a double agent, for our side of course, but got accepted by the Nazis still operating in East Berlin, as one of their own. I did indeed almost become one of their own for a while, sucked in."

Laura nodded. One of her own family had been a spy during the early Irish Troubles, so she knew what Henry meant and how easy it was to fall into being that person, the one you played, the one you were essentially fighting against, but also acting the part too much.

"That evening when you saw them with a syringe, they were not trying to kill me, but take my blood. You see the Nazis still have Hitler's DNA and they want to clone him, but so far it has not been successful. One of the things they tried in the old days was to inject members with his blood to try to turn them all into bodies to carry spare parts for Hitler. The theory being they could clone him, and repair him and essentially keep him alive for many years, if not forever. The blood would form anti-bodies so, well the theory was, when the organs were implanted into Hitler, he would not reject them, as happens a lot with transplants."

"Blimey. A bit too sci-fi in its time, but these days probably feasible," said Laura.

"Indeed and they wanted my blood to test the theory out and maybe use me to clone Hitler, or some other purpose. I couldn't let that happen. Imagine the world had they taken it over. It is a possibility, they have the money and the support to at least take Europe and keep the rest of the world at war so they can continue their reign. They are the fifth Reich now, the sixth being the one that they expect to rule Europe."

"I understand now," said Laura and took Henry's hand and squeezed it. *"What a burden to carry Henry and why you have to pretend to be dead."*

"Your theory about Merlin is correct though Laura, he was the first of my ancestors and although he lived to a great age, because of the family likeness, it was others who took his place. He sadly did not live for thousands of years, nor hundreds, merely one hundred and ten. Long enough to pass on his knowledge and so it has gone on for generations."

"So, what now Henry? Or should I say Merlin?" she grinned. *"Where will you go? What will you do?"*

"Henry will do fine," he smiled rather tight faced. *"I shall return as the new laird in a few months, some slight changes of appearance, all my family have a strong resemblance, no one locally will question it. I shall not make the mistake I made last time of letting someone else take the reins whilst I stayed away. All this would never have happened if I hadn't stayed away so long. I let my guard down and forgot to watch for signs of the Nazis."*

Laura shivered as if someone had walked over her grave, *"I will be gone when you return Henry. I am glad you are OK, but I am a little afraid for you. It's all too much to take in at once. It sounds like some Len Deighton novel."*

"My dear lady, you will write your papers and there will be much academic discussion, but only you will know the truth. I hope you will come back and visit again. It gets lonely when you have to live as someone else and it is good to have friends."

"Maybe I will Henry, but should I tell the others?"

"That I leave up to you, Laura, but you may place them in danger by doing so. The Nazis don't like their plans known, so think carefully about it, and now I must go before the wake ends and I am found here. The knights are taking me to a place of hiding for the time being and then I will return as the new laird. Good bye my dear brave lady, I shall see you again, I hope."

And with that he stood up and turned and disappeared into the bushes leaving Laura staring at the space where he had been. When she stood up she felt as if she was dizzy or in a dream where things were unreal. Shaking her head to clear it, she walked slowly back to the cottage and later that evening, sitting by the fire hugging the cats, she thought how lonely Henry must be, and how sad to be kept here by a curse not of your own making. *"I wish there was something I could do for him,"* she said to Aristotle as she tickled his chin. *"Poor man"*.

Then a thought struck her, if everything was theatrical, what about the lightening? She saw it strike that man. Then there were other things, he hadn't explained, things perhaps he couldn't. She stood up suddenly, depositing a cat on the floor, who complained bitterly.

"I'll go ask him," she thought to herself. Then she sat down again. How could she ask him, he would be gone now?

"Until we meet again Henry, then I will find the answers," she said out loud as if he could hear her, and then shook herself and went back to stroking the cats, the deposited one having got straight back on her knee as she sat down.

CHRISTMAS
Light in the Darkness

John and Laura sat on either side of the fire, each sipping a glass of port. From the kitchen could be heard the sounds of Roz and her friend Vicki washing up.

"Damned fine dinner Laura. Thank you for inviting me," John raised his glass to her as he spoke.

"There is no way I would have left you sitting on your own on Christmas Day, John, and you know it."

"I had been invited to the castle to dine with the estate people and although Gordon said I should still attend...well," he hesitated, *"I was glad to have an excuse that I was coming here. It would have been awful somehow with Henry dead. I still can't believe what happened or what we went through. It just seems like a bad dream now."*

Laura handed him a box of after dinner mints and said, *"I still can't believe it happened. It seems like years ago now, not a few weeks."*

"Maybe the shock makes it seem like that. Our brain's way of protecting us from the bad things that happen."

Laura nodded and wasn't sure what to do, should she tell or not.

"What is it Laura? You look like you have bitten your tongue or something."

Laura looked at him. *"What if I told you Henry isn't dead. That I saw him"*

"I don't believe in ghosts and didn't think you did either. Were you dreaming or something?"

"No John I saw him after the wake."

"What...Is this a joke? If so it's not funny," John glared at her.

"No," she said softly. *"It's no joke,"* and she went on to tell him about meeting Henry by the loch.

John sat back looked totally bemused, *"My God, and do the estate people know?"*

"Oh yes, and they just accept it. In fact they were prepared, according to Hamish, for it happening. I was reluctant to tell anyone in case it put them in danger."

"Henry told you though, Laura, and I don't think he would endanger anyone. He was, is, a good man, a decent sort. Have you told anyone else?"

"No only you."

John nodded, *"Well I think we should keep it that way for now. I just hope I meet the new Henry or whatever his name is when he returns."*

Laura nodded, *"I get the feeling he intends that we should meet him again."*

John shook his head, *"All this is hard to take in."*

"I know. I have been wrestling with it for a while. I feel better for telling someone."

John suddenly said: *"So the memorial service was a suck up by the staff for when he returns."*

"No I think they really liked him and probably weren't sure then about his demise."

John looked into the fire at the flames, deep in thought, and Laura studied her glass. No one would ever believe any of this she thought, it's all too phantasmagorical.

"Why the glum faces? It's Christmas." Roz's voice in the doorway broke into their reverie.

"We were just remembering absent friends," said John smiling.

Roz and Vicki came and sat down, and the mood lightened and the noise grew as they laughed together and pulled the remaining Christmas crackers over nuts and sherry. *"Read the jokes! Mum always insists we read the jokes,"* shouted Roz.

"How do snails keep their shells shiny?" began Vicki.

"I know this one," laughed Laura. *"They use snail varnish."*

Groans all round, and Vicki yelled *"Yes!"*

Roz read the next one: *"What does the word minimum mean?"* and before anyone could answer she said, *"A very small mother"* and giggled.

"Doesn't apply to me then," grinned Laura.

Laura read hers out, *"What do you get if you cross a stereo with a fridge?"*

The others shook their heads.

"Cool music," she laughed.

"What has a.." Vicki began.

"No. No more," laughed John. "No more bad puns."

"Then you have to wear the paper hat," said Roz. *"It's the house rule."* John looked at Laura who shrugged her shoulders and laughed.

"I will put on the hat for an easy life." John donned the bright yellow paper tissue crown grumbling and Roz snapped his photo on her phone.

"Blackmail," shouted Vicki. *"We have the technology."*

Both girls fell about giggling and the dark days that Laura and John had been through receded further away in their memories as the laughter went on. Roz told the story of when she was about 8 or 9 and most of the family came to Christmas dinner. All the crackers had the same joke in them and Laura made them all read them out one after and another.

"By the time we got to granddad, people were begging for mercy," she laughed.

John made some comment about Laura should have been in the Spanish Inquisition and she tried to hit him with a cushion. Her aim was rather impaired by too much Christmas spirit and it went over his head to more laughter.

They didn't notice a face peering through the window, only Aristotle asleep by the fire raised one eye and made note. Gabe grinned to himself, he had promised Henry he would keep an eye on Laura as she still had a part to play, and she seemed fine. He went on his way back to the castle for dinner. The sound of the laughter from the cottage was still audible when he reached the gate. Yes, you will be fine, Laura, he said to himself.

THE CENTRE FOR FORTEAN ZOOLOGY
www.cfz.org.uk

STILL ON THE TRACK OF UNKNOWN ANIMALS

The Centre for Fortean Zoology, or CFZ, is a non profit-making organisation founded in 1992 with the aim of being a clearing house for information, and coordinating research into mystery animals around the world.

We also study out of place animals, rare and aberrant animal behaviour, and Zooform Phenomena; little-understood "things" that appear to be animals, but which are in fact nothing of the sort, and not even alive (at least in the way we understand the term).

Not only are we the biggest organisation of our type in the world, but - or so we like to think - we are the best. We are certainly the only truly global cryptozoological research organisation, and we carry out our investigations using a strictly scientific set of guidelines. We are expanding all the time and looking to recruit new members to help us in our research into mysterious animals and strange creatures across the globe.

Why should you join us? Because, if you are genuinely interested in trying to solve the last great mysteries of Mother Nature, there is nobody better than us with whom to do it.

Members get a four-issue subscription to our journal *Animals & Men*. Each issue contains nearly 100 pages packed with news, articles, letters, research papers, field reports, and even a gossip column! The magazine is Royal Octavo in format with a full colour cover. You also have access to one of the world's largest collections of resource material dealing with cryptozoology and allied disciplines, and people from the CFZ membership regularly take part in fieldwork and expeditions around the world.

The CFZ is managed by a three-man board of trustees, with a non-profit making trust registered with HM Government Stamp Office. The board of trustees is supported by a Permanent Directorate of full and part-time staff, and advised by a Consultancy Board of specialists - many of whom are world-renowned experts in their particular field. We have regional representatives across the UK, the USA, and many other parts of the world, and are affiliated with other organisations whose aims and protocols mirror our own.

You'll find that the people at the CFZ are friendly and approachable. We have a thriving forum on the website which is the hub of an ever-growing electronic community. You will soon find your feet. Many members of the CFZ Permanent Directorate started off as ordinary members, and now work full-time chasing monsters around the world.

Write to us, e-mail us, or telephone us. The list of future projects on the website is not exhaustive. If you have a good idea for an investigation, please tell us. We may well be able to help.

We are always looking for volunteers to join us. If you see a project that interests you, do not hesitate to get in touch with us. Under certain circumstances we can help provide funding for your trip. If you look on the future projects section of the website, you can see some of the projects that we have pencilled in for the next few years.

In 2003 and 2004 we sent three-man expeditions to Sumatra looking for Orang-Pendek - a semi-legendary bipedal ape. The same three went to Mongolia in 2005. All three members started off merely subscribers to the CFZ magazine. Next time it could be you!

We have no magic sources of income. All our funds come from donations, membership fees, and sales of our publications and merchandise. We are always looking for corporate sponsorship, and other sources of revenue. If you have any ideas for fund-raising please let us know.

However, unlike other cryptozoological organisations in the past, we do not live in an intellectual ivory tower. We are not afraid to get our hands dirty, and furthermore we are not one of those organisations where the membership have to raise money so that a privileged few can go on expensive foreign trips. Our research teams, both in the UK and abroad, consist of a mixture of experienced and inexperienced personnel. We are truly a community, and work on the premise that the benefits of CFZ membership are open to all.

Reports of our investigations are published on our website as soon as they are available. Preliminary reports are posted within days of the project finishing.

Each year we publish a 200 page yearbook containing research papers and expedition reports too long to be printed in the journal. We freely circulate our information to anybody who asks for it.

We have a thriving YouTube channel, CFZtv, which has well over two hundred self-made documentaries, lecture appearances, and episodes of our monthly webTV show. We have a daily online magazine, which has over a million hits each year.

Each year since 2000 we have held our annual convention - the Weird Weekend. It is three days of lectures, workshops, and excursions. But most importantly it is a chance for members of the CFZ to meet each other, and to talk with the members of the permanent directorate in a relaxed and informal setting and preferably with a pint of beer in one hand. Since 2006 - the Weird Weekend has been bigger and better and held on the third weekend in August in the idyllic rural location of Woolsery in North Devon.

Since relocating to North Devon in 2005 we have become ever more closely involved with other community organisations, and we hope that this trend will continue. We have also worked closely with Police Forces across the UK as consultants for animal mutilation cases, and we intend to forge closer links with the coastguard and other community services. We want to work closely with those who regularly travel into the Bristol Channel, so that if the recent trend of exotic animal visitors to our coastal waters continues, we can be out there as soon as possible.

Apart from having been the only Fortean Zoological organisation in the world to have consistently published material on all aspects of the subject for over a decade, we have achieved the following concrete results:

• Disproved the myth relating to the headless so-called sea-serpent carcass of Durgan beach in Cornwall 1975

• Disproved the story of the 1988 puma skull of

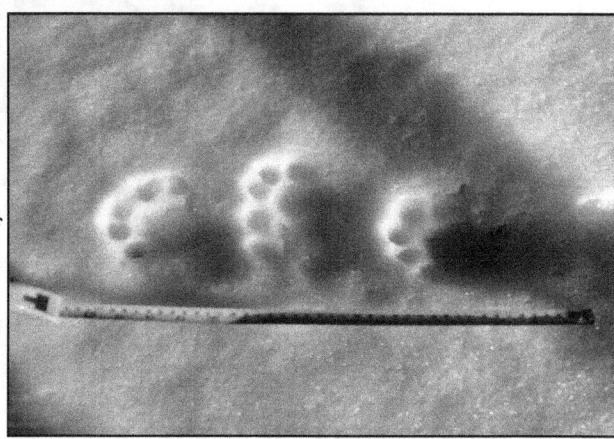

Lustleigh Cleave

- Carried out the only in-depth research ever into the mythos of the Cornish Owlman.
- Made the first records of a tropical species of lamprey
- Made the first records of a luminous cave gnat larva in Thailand
- Discovered a possible new species of British mammal - the beech marten
- In 1994-6 carried out the first archival fortean zoological survey of Hong Kong
- In the year 2000, CFZ theories were confirmed when a new species of lizard was added to the British List
- Identified the monster of Martin Mere in Lancashire as a giant wels catfish
- Expanded the known range of Armitage's skink in the Gambia by 80%
- Obtained photographic evidence of the remains of Europe's largest known pike
- Carried out the first ever in-depth study of the ninki-nanka
- Carried out the first attempt to breed Puerto Rican cave snails in captivity
- Were the first European explorers to visit the `lost valley` in Sumatra
- Published the first ever evidence for a new tribe of pygmies in Guyana
- Published the first evidence for a new species of caiman in Guyana
- Filmed unknown creatures

on a monster-haunted lake in Ireland for the first time
- Had a sighting of orang pendek in Sumatra in 2009
- Found leopard hair, subsequently identified by DNA analysis, from rural North Devon in 2010
- Brought back hairs which appear to be from an unknown primate in Sumatra
- Published some of the best evidence ever for the almasty in southern Russia

CFZ Expeditions and Investigations include:

- 1998 Puerto Rico, Florida, Mexico (Chupacabras)
- 1999 Nevada (Bigfoot)
- 2000 Thailand (Naga)
- 2002 Martin Mere (Giant catfish)
- 2002 Cleveland (Wallaby mutilation)

- 2003 Bolam Lake (BHM Reports)
- 2003 Sumatra (Orang Pendek)
- 2003 Texas (Bigfoot; giant snapping turtles)
- 2004 Sumatra (Orang Pendek; cigau, a sabre-toothed cat)
- 2004 Illinois (Black panthers; cicada swarm)
- 2004 Texas (Mystery blue dog)
- Loch Morar (Monster)
- 2004 Puerto Rico (Chupacabras; carnivorous cave snails)
- 2005 Belize (Affiliate expedition for hairy dwarfs)
- 2005 Loch Ness (Monster)
- 2005 Mongolia (Allghoi Khorkhoi aka Mongolian death worm)

- 2006 Gambia (Gambo - Gambian sea monster , Ninki Nanka and Armitage's skink
- 2006 Llangorse Lake (Giant pike, giant eels)
- 2006 Windermere (Giant eels)
- 2007 Coniston Water (Giant eels)
- 2007 Guyana (Giant anaconda, didi, water tiger)
- 2008 Russia (Almasty)
- 2009 Sumatra (Orang pendek)
- 2009 Republic of Ireland (Lake Monster)
- 2010 Texas (Blue Dogs)
- 2010 India (Mande Burung)
- 2011 Sumatra (Orang-pendek)

For details of current membership fees, current expeditions and investigations, and voluntary posts within the CFZ that need your help, please do not hesitate to contact us.

The Centre for Fortean Zoology,
Myrtle Cottage,
Woolfardisworthy,
Bideford, North Devon
EX39 5QR

Telephone 01237 431413
Fax+44 (0)7006-074-925
eMail info@cfz.org.uk

Websites:

www.cfz.org.uk
www.weirdweekend.org

THE WORLD'S WEIRDEST PUBLISHING COMPANY

HOW TO START A PUBLISHING EMPIRE

Unlike most mainstream publishers, we have a non-commercial remit, and our mission statement claims that "we publish books because they deserve to be published, not because we think that we can make money out of them". Our motto is the Latin Tag *Pro bona causa facimus* (we do it for good reason), a slogan taken from a children's book *The Case of the Silver Egg* by the late Desmond Skirrow.

WIKIPEDIA: "The first book published was in 1988. *Take this Brother may it Serve you Well* was a guide to Beatles bootlegs by Jonathan Downes. It sold quite well, but was hampered by very poor production values, being photocopied, and held together by a plastic clip binder. In 1988 A5 clip binders were hard to get hold of, so the publishers took A4 binders and cut them in half with a hacksaw. It now reaches surprisingly high prices second hand.

The production quality improved slightly over the years, and after 1999 all the books produced were ringbound with laminated colour covers. In 2004, however, they signed an agreement with Lightning Source, and all books are now produced perfect bound, with full colour covers."

Until 2010 all our books, the majority of which are/were on the subject of mystery animals and allied disciplines, were published by `CFZ Press`, the publishing arm of the Centre for Fortean Zoology (CFZ), and we urged our readers and followers to draw a discreet veil over the books that we published that were completely off topic to the CFZ.

However, in 2010 we decided that enough was enough and launched a second imprint, `Fortean Words` which aims to cover a wide range of non animal-related esoteric subjects. Other imprints will be launched as and when we feel like it, however the basic ethos of the company remains the same: Our job is to publish books and magazines that we feel are worth publishing, whether or not they are going to sell. Money is, after all - as my dear old Mama once told me - a rather vulgar subject, and she would be rolling in her grave if she thought that her eldest son was somehow in `trade`.

Luckily, so far our tastes have turned out not to be that rarified after all, and we have sold far more books than anyone ever thought that we would, so there is a moral in there somewhere…

Jon Downes,
Woolsery, North Devon
July 2010

CFZ PRESS

Other Books in Print

ORANG PENDEK: Sumatra's Forgotten Ape by Richard Freeman
THE MYSTERY ANIMALS OF THE BRITISH ISLES: London by Neil Arnold
CFZ EXPEDITION REPORT: India 2010 by Richard Freeman *et al*
The Cryptid Creatures of Florida by Scott Marlow
Dead of Night by Lee Walker
The Mystery Animals of the British Isles: The Northern Isles by Glen Vaudrey
THE MYSTERY ANIMALS OF THE BRTISH ISLES: Gloucestershire and Worcestershire by
Paul Williams
When Bigfoot Attacks by Michael Newton
Weird Waters – The Mystery Animals of Scandinavia: Lake and Sea Monsters by Lars Thomas
The Inhumanoids by Barton Nunnelly
Monstrum! A Wizard's Tale by Tony "Doc" Shiels
CFZ Yearbook 2011 edited by Jonathan Downes
Karl Shuker's Alien Zoo by Shuker, Dr Karl P.N
Tetrapod Zoology Book One by Naish, Dr Darren
The Mystery Animals of Ireland by Gary Cunningham and Ronan Coghlan
Monsters of Texas by Gerhard, Ken
The Great Yokai Encyclopaedia by Freeman, Richard
NEW HORIZONS: Animals & Men issues 16-20 Collected Editions Vol. 4
by Downes, Jonathan
A Daintree Diary -
Tales from Travels to the Daintree Rainforest in tropical north Queensland, Australia
by Portman, Carl
Strangely Strange but Oddly Normal by Roberts, Andy
Centre for Fortean Zoology Yearbook 2010 by Downes, Jonathan
Predator Deathmatch by Molloy, Nick
Star Steeds and other Dreams by Shuker, Karl
CHINA: A Yellow Peril? by Muirhead, Richard
Mystery Animals of the British Isles: The Western Isles by Vaudrey, Glen

Giant Snakes - Unravelling the coils of mystery by Newton, Michael

Mystery Animals of the British Isles: Kent by Arnold, Neil

Centre for Fortean Zoology Yearbook 2009 by Downes, Jonathan

CFZ EXPEDITION REPORT: Russia 2008 by Richard Freeman *et al*, Shuker, Karl (fwd)

Dinosaurs and other Prehistoric Animals on Stamps - A Worldwide catalogue by Shuker, Karl P. N

Dr Shuker's Casebook by Shuker, Karl P.N

The Island of Paradise - chupacabra UFO crash retrievals, and accelerated evolution on the island of Puerto Rico by Downes, Jonathan

The Mystery Animals of the British Isles: Northumberland and Tyneside by Hallowell, Michael J

Centre for Fortean Zoology Yearbook 1997 by Downes, Jonathan (Ed)

Centre for Fortean Zoology Yearbook 2002 by Downes, Jonathan (Ed)

Centre for Fortean Zoology Yearbook 2000/1 by Downes, Jonathan (Ed)

Centre for Fortean Zoology Yearbook 1998 by Downes, Jonathan (Ed)

Centre for Fortean Zoology Yearbook 2003 by Downes, Jonathan (Ed)

In the wake of Bernard Heuvelmans by Woodley, Michael A

CFZ EXPEDITION REPORT: Guyana 2007 by Richard Freeman *et al*, Shuker, Karl (fwd)

Centre for Fortean Zoology Yearbook 1999 by Downes, Jonathan (Ed)

Big Cats in Britain Yearbook 2008 by Fraser, Mark (Ed)

Centre for Fortean Zoology Yearbook 1996 by Downes, Jonathan (Ed)

THE CALL OF THE WILD - Animals & Men issues 11-15 Collected Editions Vol. 3 by Downes, Jonathan (ed)

Ethna's Journal by Downes, C N

Centre for Fortean Zoology Yearbook 2008 by Downes, J (Ed)

DARK DORSET -Calendar Custome by Newland, Robert J

Extraordinary Animals Revisited by Shuker, Karl

MAN-MONKEY - In Search of the British Bigfoot by Redfern, Nick

Dark Dorset Tales of Mystery, Wonder and Terror by Newland, Robert J and Mark North

Big Cats Loose in Britain by Matthews, Marcus

MONSTER! - The A-Z of Zooform Phenomena by Arnold, Neil

The Centre for Fortean Zoology 2004 Yearbook by Downes, Jonathan (Ed)

The Centre for Fortean Zoology 2007 Yearbook by Downes, Jonathan (Ed)

CAT FLAPS! Northern Mystery Cats by Roberts, Andy

Big Cats in Britain Yearbook 2007 by Fraser, Mark (Ed)

BIG BIRD! - Modern sightings of Flying Monsters by Gerhard, Ken

THE NUMBER OF THE BEAST - Animals & Men issues 6-10 Collected Editions Vol. 1 by Downes, Jonathan (Ed)

IN THE BEGINNING - Animals & Men issues 1-5 Collected Editions Vol. 1 by Downes, Jonathan

STRENGTH THROUGH KOI - They saved Hitler's Koi and other stories by Downes, Jonathan

The Smaller Mystery Carnivores of the Westcountry by Downes, Jonathan

CFZ EXPEDITION REPORT: Gambia 2006 by Richard Freeman *et al*, Shuker, Karl (fwd)

The Owlman and Others by Jonathan Downes

The Blackdown Mystery by Downes, Jonathan

Big Cats in Britain Yearbook 2006 by Fraser, Mark (Ed)
Fragrant Harbours - Distant Rivers by Downes, John T
Only Fools and Goatsuckers by Downes, Jonathan
Monster of the Mere by Jonathan Downes
Dragons:More than a Myth by Freeman, Richard Alan
Granfer's Bible Stories by Downes, John Tweddell
Monster Hunter by Downes, Jonathan

Fortean Words

The Centre for Fortean Zoology has for several years led the field in Fortean publishing. CFZ Press is the only publishing company specialising in books on monsters and mystery animals. CFZ Press has published more books on this subject than any other company in history and has attracted such well known authors as Andy Roberts, Nick Redfern, Michael Newton, Dr Karl Shuker, Neil Arnold, Dr Darren Naish, Jon Downes, Ken Gerhard and Richard Freeman.

Now CFZ Press are launching a new imprint. Fortean Words is a new line of books dealing with Fortean subjects other than cryptozoology, which is - after all - the subject the CFZ are best known for. Fortean Words is being launched with a spectacular multi-volume series called *Haunted Skies* which covers British UFO sightings between 1940 and 2010. Former policeman John Hanson and his long-suffering partner Dawn Holloway have compiled a peerless library of sighting reports, many that have not been made public before.

Other books include a look at the Berwyn Mountains UFO case by renowned Fortean Andy Roberts and a series of forthcoming books by transatlantic researcher Nick Redfern. CFZ Press are dedicated to maintaining the fine quality of their works with Fortean Words. New authors tackling new subjects will always be encouraged, and we hope that our books will continue to be as ground-breaking and popular as ever.

Haunted Skies Volume One 1940-1959 by John Hanson and Dawn Holloway
Haunted Skies Volume Two 1960-1965 by John Hanson and Dawn Holloway
Haunted Skies Volume Three 1965-1967 by John Hanson and Dawn Holloway
Haunted Skies Volume Four 1968-1971 by John Hanson and Dawn Holloway
Grave Concerns by Kai Roberts

Police and the Paranormal by Andy Owens
Dead of Night by Lee Walker
Space Girl Dead on Spaghetti Junction - an anthology by Nick Redfern
I Fort the Lore - an anthology by Paul Screeton
UFO Down - the Berwyn Mountains UFO Crash by Andy Roberts

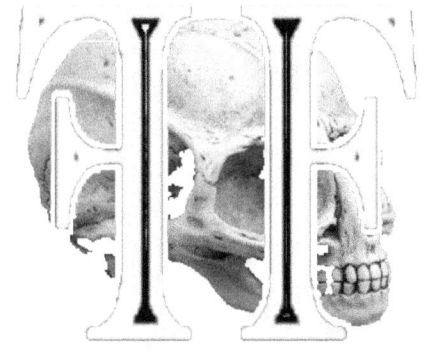

Fortean Fiction

J ust before Christmas 2011, we launched our third imprint, this time dedicated to - let's see if you guessed it from the title - fictional books with a Fortean or cryptozoological theme. We have published a few fictional books in the past, but now think that because of our rising reputation as publishers of quality Forteana, that a dedicated fiction imprint was the order of the day.

We launched with four titles:

Green Unpleasant Land by Richard Freeman
Left Behind by Harriet Wadham
Dark Ness by Tabitca Cope
Snap! By Steven Bredice